POWERLESS

POWERLESS
A Declan Mac Adventure

JEFF HYLAND

This novel and its contents are a work of fiction. References to actual individuals, job titles, historical events, or locations are used fictitiously. Names, characters, places, and incidents are a product of the author's imagination. Any resemblance to actual places, events, living or dead persons, businesses, governmental organizations, or locales is entirely coincidental.

Copyright © 2023 Jeff Hyland
All rights reserved.
ISBN-13: 9798854346139

Cover design by: Jerry Todd

Dedication

*For my family. Thank you for the encouragement
and advice along the way. I am blessed with a loving family.
Also, thank you to Dana for your guidance
and to the many friends who read this novel before publication.*

*To all of you, thank you for your insights and inspiration.
Without you during this process, I would have been* **Powerless**.

Chapter 1

London, United Kingdom

Every sense in his body was on high alert. His training and experience taught him to stay calm, but whoever created that concept was not being shot at.

Even if he lost his life, he absolutely must get the data on this flash drive to Langley. Still, he would much prefer delivering the flash drive while alive. His musings were cut short as another well-placed round cracked against the corner where he hid in the temporary refuge as pieces of stonework managed to spray his face.

Time to focus. These guys were obviously professionals and had no intention of a prolonged gunfight. He counted three of them in a close foot pursuit with one unwavering commitment – to kill him quickly. They were strategically maneuvering to cut off his lines of escape. He surveyed this dark and quaint street in London and wondered what awaited him as he formulated his plan. There were little more than arched stone doorways to hide from the insidious shooters who were tenaciously chasing him. His options were becoming more limited as the seconds passed — "Ticktock," the voice in his head continued to mutter. It had proven invaluable on multiple occasions as it clarified his murky spycraft world and guided him as an omniscient third party.

If he couldn't make it to his prearranged exfil Alpha or backup exfil Bravo, he at least needed to make it to MI6 at 85 Albert Embankment in Vauxhall. Given that he would have to sprint through a gauntlet of gunfire to either exfil location, he quickly dismissed that folly. He briefly considered swimming to MI6 via the River Thames but choked down that absurd thought. Even if he could swim like an Olympian, which he can't, they would quickly pick him off by their undoubted fourth man, a sniper perched on a nearby rooftop.

He needed to get to high ground quickly and gain the advantage to survive. Thanks to the age and charm of many southwestern London buildings, he spied several connected buildings with oversized downspouts going from street-level to roof gutters.

"Move or die," he grumbled, and with cat-like agility, he adroitly climbed the nearest downspout. The night was overcast, with a familiar London mist in the air that provided the camouflage he needed to ascend to his lookout safely.

While the roof was pitched with slippery tiles, he could still evaluate his battlefield. As expected, the three shooters on the ground were converging on his prior position. "Got you!" he thought to himself as he caught a massive break while hastily scanning the rooftops.

The sniper had neglected to cover his scope with an anti-reflective device, and the nearby streetlights presented an unmistakable glimmer revealing the shooter's position. Once he completed his battlefield assessment, he quickly pulled his head back, just in the nick of time. The sniper saw movement and took a wild but hopeful shot that narrowly missed its mark.

He could hear the sniper radio to his fellow shooters, "Target spotted on the roof of the southeast corner of your current positions."

It was time to make his move. He noticed the sniper was precariously standing on the gutter of his roof as he was vying for a better angle for a shot. While generally standing the test of time, those green-oxidized gutters had been notorious for requiring ongoing repair. He had a photographic memory that he drew upon to recall the sniper's perch. He crept around the bottom corner of the roof. He took out the gutter and downspout's supporting brackets with two successive shots.

The mayhem below was only starting. The sniper fell from the roof and landed unceremoniously with an abnormal thud. However, he had one stop on his way to the ground. Two other shooters were the unfortunate victims of his flailing body mass. Their deaths came instantly as the sniper crushed the two men below. Mac couldn't help but smile to himself as he quietly hummed the tune of The Weather Girls' 1982 hit single, "It's raining men, hallelujah. It's raining men...."

The last shooter was undeterred by his partners' unlucky turn of events and fired three rapid shots at the roof. While they all missed landing home, Mac knew the high ground was not always the best, and he was exposed. He scampered across rooftops as he envisioned being a chimney sweep in a beloved movie classic. Mac could not forget the ill-fated sniper's lesson and decided to escape via the street to evade the last shooter.

There were no doors or convenient elevators to assist in his descent, so he reverted to the downspout technique that suited him well several minutes earlier. After nearly losing his grip on the slick, aged metal, he gracefully landed and made a quick situational assessment. Not seeing the fourth shooter, he hurriedly strode down the street.

He reached up to his jawbone, and while lightly pressing on it to engage the microphone, he blandly stated, "This is Mac. Negative for Exfil Alpha and Bravo. Heading south on Vauxhall Walk towards MI6. No safe houses in the vicinity. One known shooter still in pursuit. The likelihood of avoiding contact is minimal. Suggestions?"

A woman's monotone voice responded in his ear, "Copy all, Mac. Working on it. With our thermal imaging, there are too many late-night walkers to ascertain bandits from the non-combatants."

Declan Mac had been in the situation before. It reminded him of his first few tours in the Middle East when he couldn't determine friend from foe. It meant you needed to keep all your senses on high alert and your head on a swivel, just as they pounded into you at "The Farm," the CIA's boot camp on steroids.

Mac's training taught him to sense something was amiss, and he slowed his walk.

"I'll bet you think you were pretty clever up on the roofs, killing my mates." The fourth shooter declared confidently from a hiding spot in the darkness around the corner. The light was just enough to allow a glow to emanate from his shiny and perfect teeth.

Mac froze in his tracks as the fourth shooter stepped out from the shadow. It wasn't the shooter's words that made him take pause. It was the Glock 17 pistol, favored by specific international special forces, pointed straight at him.

"Hand over the USB flash drive," the shooter said, showing his confidence in having the upper hand.

Trying to buy time as he was developing his plan, Mac played the terrified tourist and exclaimed in a shaky voice, "Holy shit! Is that a gun? Oh, God! Don't shoot! Look, mister, if you want my wallet, I'll give it to you. If you want a flash drive, I never carry those with me. I have no idea what you are talking about. I'm just out for a stroll. If you think I took something, you must be thinking about someone else."

The shooter was having nothing of it. With conviction, he marched over, pointed his weapon at center mass, and smiled, revealing those pearly white teeth. It was his first mistake and would prove costly.

A set of voices were shouting excitedly in the distance, with someone screaming orders to find their prey. Undoubtedly, the shouting was more shooters coming to finish the job. Unfortunately for the fourth shooter, he glanced ever so slightly toward the oncoming voices.

After years of developing his hand-to-hand combat skills and taking great pride in his tradecraft, Mac took advantage of the shooter's distraction. Mac twisted his body to the left while using his right hand as a club in an inward movement to knock the pistol toward the center of the shooter's body. A shot rang out, but its aim was harmless and more of a reaction to the blow.

Still stunned, the shooter tried to regain control and focused on his advantage with the pistol. That was his second mistake.

Mac took advantage of the momentum he gained and used his right hand to grab the shooter's gun hand, now flung across his torso. With the shooter focusing so much of his effort on the gun, it left many vulnerable body targets. Another shot rang out with another miss. Mac punched the shooter in the face with his left hand. Stunned, the shooter stumbled backward, and Mac lost control of the shooting hand. The shooter raised his gun, but Mac charged at him and managed to grab the shooter's wrists. The struggle continued for what seemed like forever while each opponent tried to gain leverage over the other. They found themselves holding opposite hands out wide, looking like awkward teenagers at their first dance while trying forcefully to lead each other to a forever-forgotten song.

Hearing the voices coming closer, Mac knew he needed to make efficient and quick movements to save his energy for what was to come. He used an aggressive twisting action to pry his right hand away from the shooter and, in one fluid movement, chopped the shooter's throat. Instinctively, the shooter relaxed the fight over the gun and grasped his injured throat with his other hand. That was the shooter's third and final mistake.

Mac simultaneously grabbed the shooter's jacket, dropped to a knee, and flipped the shooter over his shoulder using the shooter's body weight and momentum. The shooter looked like he was doing an aerial front roll, but as his feet flew over Mac's shoulder, his body would never make the entire flip. The shooter landed on his back and head on the wet brick street. The pavement knocked the air from the shooter's lungs, and he drifted on the edge of darkness from the head blow. That was all Mac needed. He grabbed the weapon with his right hand and threw a vicious blow with his left that landed square on the shooter's jaw.

The shooter went limp, and while he would be eating from a straw for the next several months, Mac spared his life due to a sense of fair play. He picked up the shooter's radio and hooked it on his belt while storing the gun at the base of his lower back, firmly held in place with his belt. Mac stood to his full 6'2" frame, flattened the wrinkles in his disheveled sports coat, and began walking again. With jet black, closely trimmed hair, piercing blue eyes, and rugged good looks, he easily could have been a movie star taking a brisk late evening walk. However, Mac knew this was life and death and anything but Tinseltown's outrageousness.

"Exfil instructions?" Mac said dispassionately in his comm as he strode down the street.

The same female voice replied in his ear, "On it. Fog compromised most options."

"Understood. Keep me advised."

Mac vigilantly focused on trying to hear any signs of the other goons. Unfortunately, they had gone radio silent. That meant anyone could be a shooter. He could not identify the difference between the innocents and the shooters.

Then Mac saw it. Two guys in the periphery of his vision were acting too casual for this late hour. The pair, coupled with the non-descript black van idling at the end of the block on an adjacent street, revealed a classic snatch-and-grab setup. Mac had nowhere to go. He had to do the unexpected.

Abruptly taking a right across the street, Mac headed directly toward the closest shooter. Given that the shooter was focused on not being noticed, hoping to slip right behind Mac as he passed, he was unprepared for Mac to walk up behind him. With Mac's lightning-quick movements, he grabbed the shooter's gun conspicuously tucked in a side holster and yanked on his jacket collar. The jerking forced him off balance while revealing the perfect soft spot. Mac rammed the butt of the revolver against the base of the shooter's skull. The shooter went limp at once.

Mac slowly laid the shooter down, keeping the sound at a minimum. In attempting to achieve the impossible and use the same move on his next victim, Mac snuck quietly behind the man. As he was about to execute his previously successful surprise attack, the shooter turned and whipped out a blade. This shooter wasn't just any knife wielder. He had a crazy look in his eyes and a grin to suggest he would enjoy this.

When you are in a knife fight without a knife, your best strategy is to run. Generally, you will lose something or everything if you stand and fight. Running wasn't an option. As Mac and the attacker began the slow, soft-touch foot movements, assessing each other's skill, Mac could tell this guy knew how to use his blade. Mac could only assume he would use slicing motions rather than a stab, aiming for vulnerable arteries to inflict maximum damage. After all, it was what Mac would do if he didn't find himself empty-handed.

Mac would have to wait for his counterattack opportunity. It would be ugly and painful, but there are no bloodless knife fights. Mac's jacket and the small protection it might afford him was the only saving grace.

As expected, the slashing began, and Mac was not winning any rounds in the fight. Mac tried a few ineffective kicks at his assailant, but they didn't land on anything critical. He gritted in pain and remembered all his training at the Farm using red magic markers instead of knives. If you are unarmed and fighting someone with a blade, you must first learn how to fight with a knife to know the attacker's weaknesses. Back then, everyone laughed at the number of red marker streaks across one another after a five-minute bout, but Mac wasn't laughing now.

After several minutes of taking the abuse, Mac noticed the knife-guy starting to reach more with each slice as his confidence gained ground. As the blade made another ineffective whip, Mac went into a close-quarters attack mode. He grabbed the knife-guy's hand. Mac pulled him fully sideways using the attacker's momentum, and the knife-guy was thrown off balance and trying to regain his stance. He came down on the knife-guy's shoulder blade with his elbow and heard a very satisfying snap. The weapon didn't drop, but the knife-guy went hurtling to the ground, and as he fell, he landed on his serrated knife as his useless right hand grasped it, rigidly pointing up.

Ignoring the blood on his forearm, Mac focused his attention on the black van at the end of the block with a forceful and determined walk.

"Two more bad guys down. I really could use some exfil alternatives before I do something stupid." Mac said into his microphone.

A deep male voice replied, "We wouldn't think anything less from you."

"Hmmm. Gunner, is that a compliment or a criticism?"

A new voice replied, "Brock here. Just do a Declan Mac. We all need another story to laugh about later. Don't worry about keeping track of the details. The team will embellish them over the first round of drinks that you are buying on the plane ride home."

Mac walked directly up to just behind the driver's window while slightly shielding himself from the side mirror view. He pulled the revolver from his waistband and rapped on the window with it, saying in a loud and stern voice through the slightly open window, "Hey buddy, this is the cops. You are parked illegally and need to move your car."

The driver's response was, "Yeah, sure, officer."

Mac could see the driver lean to the van's center console, undoubtedly feeling for his weapon to eliminate this nuisance in short order. When the driver returned with a silenced pistol in hand, Mac viciously smashed the glass window inward with his gun butt, which was quickly becoming more of a club than a gun. The driver instinctively shielded his face and closed his eyes to protect himself from the cascading barrage of glass. Mac seized that split-second moment and grabbed the driver by the shoulders, pulling him out through the window.

While Mac looked lean with an average build, it belied an uncommon strength and 210 pounds of muscle and bone structure. The driver was no match. As he tried to compose himself and respond to the surprise attack, Mac forcefully opened the van's door into the driver's face, which sent him sprawling unconscious on the sidewalk.

Mac took the driver's seat and put the van into drive. He quickly pulled out of the parking spot and finally began to enjoy the fresh London air as it filled the van through the broken window while he sped down the street. Mac gazed into the rear-view mirror and finger-combed his tousled hair to settle himself down for his hopeful exfil. He would never be able to live down the teasing from his team if he showed up disheveled or looked phased. He functioned best when he was under complete control during a crisis. Of course, part of being under control meant looking good on exfil and sounding cool and calm on the radio.

Mac said into the microphone, "Now proceeding in the same direction on Vauxhall Walk in a black van." He continued with a boyish smile, saying, "Have you guys finally decided to get into the game and find an alternative way out of this mess?"

"Affirmative, Mac. Continue on your current heading for exfil." The familiar, confident female voice responded.

"Negative." He had taken a quick look at the map detailing London streets several years ago and knew this was a road to nowhere with pedestrians everywhere. "If I do that, I will run out of road once I reach Vauxhall Pleasure Gardens."

She replied, "Do you trust me?"

"I like Ronald Reagan's operating motto, 'Trust but verify.'"

"Just keep driving. We'll see you in two mikes. Out."

Knowing and trusting your team members could make the difference between life and death in times like these. Mac's team each brought unique and complementary skills that jelled the group into a formidable force. Their talents made each of them invaluable. They had worked together for years and successfully overcame more impossible situations than he could count. They were professionals at the top of their game. While the public will never know their antics, the team was a legend behind the CIA's closed doors.

At that moment, Vauxhall Walk was a dead-end with half a dozen cement posts preventing drunken or otherwise lost drivers from absentmindedly driving into Vauxhall Pleasure Gardens. Mac slammed on his brakes. He knew he could never orchestrate the authorization to take his car into the Gardens. Vauxhall Pleasure Gardens was one of London's original "pleasure gardens" from the mid-17th to the mid-19th century. It was where both the elite and growing successful middle class came together to enjoy the newly evolving paid-for entertainment.

"I may not be paying an admission fee, but I certainly would enjoy partaking in the Gardens' yesteryear festivities. Its drinking, dancing, music, entertainment, and associated debauchery sound pretty good to me." Mac said to himself with a mischievous smile.

Known for well-maintained gardens of closely manicured scrubs and surrounding open grassy fields, the Gardens were a well-known gem in Kennington. However, Mac was not here to sightsee. He quickly padded through the wet grass and took refuge behind a tree. Feeling exposed and slightly miffed that he didn't control his steps, he went to his comms and said, "At the west end of the Gardens. What's the exfil plan and ETA?"

She replied, "Eyes south and listen."

Mac could hear the unmistakable chop of the helicopter's blades before he saw it in the misty sky. Out of nowhere, a sleek, jet-black Airbus Puma HC.Mk 2 helicopter shocked anyone in the vicinity and landed in the middle of the closest open field. The door slid open, and Mac saw his team waving to him to climb aboard. He could see the faint outline of the GAU-18 .50 caliber machine gun pointing out the gunner's window through the darkness. That machine gun could provide cover fire in the event hostiles were also enjoying the Gardens that evening. Based on his harrowing experience of getting this far, he expected a shooter to pop him at any second as he sprinted from his protective cover.

The shots never rang out. As Mac climbed onto the helicopter, he found his team's smiling and warm faces. "I never thought I would be so happy to see all your mugs. Thanks, team."

Valencia, the female voice that just helped save his life, said, "Don't mention it. You had us a little worried." The other three team members nodded in agreement.

Mac said, "I have one question. How the Hell did you get a helicopter to land in the Pleasure Gardens?"

Brock, Mac's second-in-command, said, "We had to pull a few strings and call in a few favors with the British government to pull it off. MI6 didn't need much persuasion with the intel in your pocket and our intention to share it with them."

Mac was Brock's commanding officer in their Special Ops unit in the U.S. Army. He immediately saw something special in Brock that was undeniable. His enthusiasm and confidence were contagious. He was a true warrior in every definition of the word. If you were in a firefight, Brock was the guy that you wanted with you. Mac pulled him into the CIA, and he has never regretted that decision. Brock rewarded Mac with his unwavering loyalty. They could complete each other's sentences and often did.

Mac sat back and closed his eyes. A wave of exhaustion came across him as the adrenaline stopped pumping, and he realized he had not truly slept for three long days. Before he dozed off to sleep, he replied to Brock, "Man, I love our allies, but I especially love those Brits right now."

Chapter 2

Reinhardt House, Bavaria
August 1752

Karl Reinhardt loved the smell of his father's cherry pipe tobacco in the workshop. Young Karl was 12 years old and envisioned becoming an inventor like his father, Ludwig. Karl deeply admired his father and was fascinated by his father's workshop. The workshop was huge and one of the town's most significant buildings. It was jammed full of bits of unusable machinery, tools to make machinery, and machinery to invent machinery. All the windows were high but provided adequate light, even with their grey, dusty coating. Karl loved going up to the partial third floor just to look out a window after rubbing it clean with his shirt sleeve.

He could not wait until all his friends from their Bavarian village learned about his father's genius inventions. Karl never told his father about his friends' snide comments as they teasingly labeled Ludwig a quack. He knew their cruel nicknames would kill his father with embarrassment. Karl felt trapped in their village, Rothenburg ob der Tauber. It had an ever-present reminder of his entrapment because it was surrounded by Medieval Walls from the 14th century, fortifying the town from attack.

Occasionally, Karl would sneak up to the walkways inside the fortress Wall. He would gaze at rows of half-timbered, half-stone classic houses with partially moss-covered red roofs and colorful flower boxes decorating windows. The village had virtually not changed since its settling, and he could even see cobblestone roads, spires reaching the sky, and holy church steeples. The view conjured pictures in his fanciful mind of Medieval knights on black stallions with silver metal coats of armor for themselves and their horses.

While Karl dreamed of a bigger life for himself, Ludwig had a world vision with a better experience for everyone. For years, Ludwig had capriciously pursued invention after invention with no real end goal in mind. Much to the chagrin of his more practical wife, Gertrude, Ludwig was a dreamer. He often held pictures in his mind of humankind harnessing all of earth's elements, from soaring on the wind to containing molten lava. This time was no different.

News about an American who had flown a kite in an electrical storm in June had traveled fast. Consistent with others in the village, Ludwig first thought this Franklin fellow was an idiot for getting soaked in the rain while risking certain death if lightning struck him. However, Ludwig's genius mind quickly realized the implications of Franklin's experiment. This experiment will change the world forever. Ludwig had a clear vision of a better tomorrow for the first time in his life. He immediately went to work on how to store and utilize this power from the sky.

Ludwig toiled relentlessly with every drop of energy and every neuron in his mind. He often drew daily designs and redesigns based on the failures of mock devices. Ludwig never viewed his failures as failures. His determined spirit was focused, and he knew each failure was getting him one step closer to success. Ludwig would describe his designs incessantly to young Karl to hone his theories. After hours of hearing his father's new multi-syllable engineering words, Karl began to understand his father. He could tell his father was fully engaged, and it was thrilling to see him so focused.

One challenge was that Ludwig could only evaluate his devices while flying a kite in a thunderstorm, just as Mr. Franklin did in America. As luck would have it, he enjoyed a stormy August with almost nightly thunderstorms. Ludwig flew so many kites that it was a miracle that no houses caught on fire. Replicating the experiment using a kite imitating Mr. Franklin's was simple. The challenge was to store the lightning in a device for later use. The devices continually exploded without saving electrical power.

Just as the pile of castaway devices was beginning to reach as high as Karl was tall, Ludwig screamed in excitement. At first, Ludwig simply admired his small 6-inch device, waiting for it to fail or somehow blow apart. Ludwig learned from his experiments that the device could be highly flammable and subject to explosion. However, this time it just sat there. Ludwig was astonished to confirm that his container was in perfect condition.

He slowly walked over to the device and picked it up. It was warm but not so hot that it would catch fire. He unfastened the metal band from the kite and wondered if the lightning was stored inside. Appreciating this critical step to success, he carefully set the device down. He reached for a small piece of scrap metal. He paused and said a short prayer, knowing that this could be the work of something much more important than a Bavarian inventor.

Ludwig set the small piece of scrap metal on the two power-releasing terminals affixed to the device's top. Instantaneously, he felt a searing shock go through his body, seemingly from top to bottom, as every nerve shuddered in pain. His mind also registered a bright flash of lightning from the scrap metal as it was in complete contact with the releasing terminals. He instinctively released the metal and stumbled backward with shaking hands.

"Karl, come in here now!" Ludwig excitedly called out for Karl to share his success.

Karl, playing just outside the workshop, heard his father's command. He had never heard his father use that tone and knew it must be something monumental. The anticipation of this moment showed in every bit of his body, and he screamed, "Papa, did this one work?"

As Karl ran into the workshop, stopping next to his father, Ludwig gave his son a big hug and replied, "It did! It did! It did! Let's name it together."

With his boyish dreams unfolding before him, he said, "How about naming it 'The Karl'"?

Ludwig smiled at his son's ownership of this invention. He knew it needed a more practical name that the world would appreciate. He patted his son's head and carefully replied, "I love that name, but maybe we should think about something that others would understand its purpose. I have been thinking about this. How about you choose between calling it the 'Benjamin' in honor of the original American kite flyer himself or the 'Storage' to recognize that it captures something?"

"Papa, you created it, not Mr. Franklin. Plus, the name needs to be more exciting than those names. Let's call it 'Blitzpeicher,' Lightning Storage!"

Ludwig thought about it for half a second and encouragingly replied, "Yes, I believe you have captured it. Blitzpeicher it is. Now I need a full-size machine and a demonstration to illustrate its importance to the world."

Wasting no time, Ludwig contacted the village's blacksmith, a long-time friend, to make the full-sized version of the Blitzpeicher. He described the six-meter diameter dimensions of his metal ball and the one-hundred-millimeter-thick walls. Ludwig also trusted his friend to create and attach the two rods that stored the lightning and partially protruded from the top of the Blitzpeicher. These rods consisted of a metal combination that was simple but simultaneously complex and effectively held the lighting until it was released through the top terminals.

The second most important part of the storage container was the fluid concoction that encased and cooled the rods. Before the final sealing of this massive cannonball, the fluid would be added as described by the blacksmith. The blacksmith attacked the project with the same enthusiasm that engulfed Ludwig. This fervor allowed Ludwig to begin focusing on his next critical task.

He and Karl were at the edge of the workshop as the blacksmith worked his magic. His vision was to find a toy that the Blitzpeicher would operate. Ludwig felt that Karl was the best suited to know the toys he and his friends would enjoy seeing come to life. However, Karl was distracted. The oppressive summer temperatures and the excessive heat from the blacksmith sucked the energy out of him. Ludwig began fanning Karl to cool him down.

Karl closed his eyes at the cooling breeze and said to his father, "Papa, I just wish I could be cooled like this all the time."

Ludwig stopped. Karl protested the loss of his cooling breeze. Ludwig said, "Son, you are a genius! We are going to have the Blitzpeicher operate a giant fan!" He hugged Karl and went to his drafting table.

Creating the first-ever working motor was less of a challenge than anyone could have imagined. Ludwig's working concept was to harness the lightning from one band and return it to the Blitzpeicher with the other to reuse it. While rudimentary, the motor spun the magnetized cylinder. Ludwig used a magnet to capture the lightning because otherwise, it would pass through the other materials without resulting movement.

Ludwig thought very little of the difficulties in designing his burgeoning invention. He had it created in a matter of hours by cobbling together spare parts in his workshop. He then attached the motor to his model-sized Blitzpeicher utilizing metal bands and watched the cylinder turn with vigor. Ludwig attached large fan blades to the cylinder with a series of pulleys. Unfortunately, when he reattached the motor to the model Blitzpeicher, it only ran for a minute before stopping. The Blitzpeicher spent through the last of its stored lightning. He desperately needed it full-sized.

As promised by the blacksmith, he created the enormous Blitzpeicher according to the agreed-upon specifications within a few weeks. It was magnificent. Ludwig had to admit that it did look like a massive cannonball. Thanks to the ongoing thunderstorms, Ludwig fully charged the Blitzpeicher with a thunderous crack of lightning that sent thousands of volts into the eight-ton ball in seconds.

The Blitzpeicher held steady and did not explode. He cautiously approached it and put his hand against its smooth outer layer. Like his small test device, the full-size Blitzpeicher was warm to the touch but not overly hot. He stretched his arms out and tried to squeeze its metal exterior like it was an obscenely overweight lover. He knew he would look silly if anyone came into the workshop, but he didn't care.

Ludwig grabbed a tall ladder and carefully attached long metal bands to the power-releasing terminals. Unlike his first attempt with the small test device, he carefully attached the bands one at a time while ensuring no inadvertent contact. He led the metal bands to the connectors on the fan's motor. Immediately, the fan blades began spinning as the lightning power source surged. He stared and marveled at the invention.

He knew what many of the townspeople were saying about him behind his back, as they considered him a fool who could not hold a real job to provide for his family. Yes, they lived in a lovely two-story classic, brown wood, tice-decorated house he inherited from his father along with a handsome sum of money. The inheritance allowed Ludwig to pursue his passion for inventions. Unfortunately, he continually drained their cash reserves, and the town knew it. At that moment, he decided he and Gertrude would quickly have a party for the village's elite as the first step to presenting this one-of-a-kind invention to the world.

The sweltering evening of the party could not have come quickly enough. How perfect a hot and humid night for the unveiling. Ludwig and Karl had carefully laid the metal connection bands from the workshop to the house across the alley earlier in the day. They also strategically placed the fan in the corner covered by sheathing for the unveiling at the exact right moment.

The village was abuzz with excitement to hear more about this lightning invention. Every invitation, even to the wealthy class, was accepted. This news was a welcomed reprieve from the continuing stories of the great migration to America of appreciable numbers of Germans and Bavarians. These families sailed across the ocean to settle in the American Thirteen Colonies in cities with names like Philadelphia and Dutch Fork. Many families and friends were separated and never heard from each other again.

Due to the excitement, Ludwig and Gertrude were besieged with requests for invitations to the unveiling. Unfortunately, the size of their entertainment parlor could only accommodate a limited number of people. That evening, Ludwig Reinhardt was the talk of the town, from the drunks in pubs to the village's elites sipping tea.

Karl was so proud of his father. He wanted to memorize everything about the Blitzpeicher so he could brag about it amongst his envious friends. Before the party, Karl snuck into the workshop and slipped his father's Blitzpeicher design drawings under his shirt. Karl knew he was not invited to his parent's party. Instead, he would take advantage of the evening and memorize every formula and design feature of the machine, making his father famous.

Ludwig and Gertrude were dressed in their Sunday best to greet their esteemed guests. After drinks were served and small talk had begun to lull, Ludwig knew it was time. As expected and desired, he could see the glow forming on the women and the sweat pouring off the creased foreheads of the rotund men as the heat built in the stuffy parlor.

Sensing the unveiling, Karl snuck to the top of the stairs with excitement. As Ludwig made a grand gesture with his arms, the crowd hushed in reverence to the pending revelation.

Ludwig proclaimed, "Thank you all for coming. Think if we could harness the power of the earth and skies. Envision our lives. Imagine the worldwide respect that Rothenburg ob der Tauber would garner."

At that pause, several of the power-hungry men gazed at each with confident head nods and sly smiles behind bushy mustaches. They selfishly pondered how they might personally gain from this newly attainable revelation.

Ludwig continued, "Tonight, I will show you how we can harness the power of lightning and use it for the world's greater good."

The same power-hungry men frowned at Ludwig's altruistic implication. Before having a chance to shout their objection, they quickly returned their attention to Ludwig as he strode to the corner with the fan.

Without other fanfare, Ludwig pulled the white sheathing away to expose the fan. He explained to the onlookers, "We no longer need to fear the power of our storms! I have invented a device to harness the explosive potential of lightning and use it for our benefit! Watch and enjoy as last week's storm now cools you off from the oppressive heat in this room!"

Several of the women giggled at the refreshing thought. Ludwig said a quick prayer for success under his breath and bent over to connect the fan's metal bands. Everyone felt the tension and excitement in the room. Ludwig heard the gasps in the room before he saw the fan blades moving. On command, the blades spun and simultaneously forced an overwhelming and refreshing breeze into the room.

Once their awe had cleared, the group broke into a glorious round of cheers and clapping. Gertrude broke down, crying with happiness. Ludwig could hardly stand up with a series of bone-crushing handshakes and slaps on the back with beefy and enthusiastic hands. For the first time in his life, he felt that other villagers truly treated him like an equal. The men politely allowed their wives to be the first to stand in front of the fan to cool themselves as they formed a line to get words in with Ludwig.

Amid the giggling and excitement, disaster struck. The fan blades stopped. Ludwig dashed over to the metal band connections, and everything seemed in order. Different scenarios flashed through his mind as he cursed himself for arrogantly having this party without adequately testing the Blitzpeicher for extended periods. How could he be so stupid?

He must get to his workshop. He began pushing his way through the crowd toward the front door.

Karl started to go downstairs, seeing his father beelining with the undoubted intent of salvaging the unveiling. Maybe he could help his father. But Karl stopped at the first stair. He knew he was not supposed to be part of the party and didn't want to embarrass his father further. He decided he should stay in his room until the crowd went home.

Ludwig burst into the workshop. Shocked, he stared into a thief's cold eyes and his six henchmen. After finding his composure from the shock, he marched right up to the bunch and exclaimed, "What are you doing in my private workshop? I must demand that you all leave at once. I have delicate machinery here, and I cannot accept you, daft buffoons, damaging my life's work. Now get out!"

The thief, a sleazy but gentlemanly dressed character, stepped forward. He smiled at the small man in front of him and said, "We intend on taking this oversized cannonball with us, and there is nothing you can do to stop us."

Ludwig looked at the Blitzpeicher and screamed, "That's outrageous! There's no way to move this eight-ton machine."

At that moment, Ludwig noticed why the fan had stopped working. One of these idiots must have clumsily disconnected the left metal band in their haste to steal it. They had absolutely no idea of the power held in the Blitzpeicher next to them.

In his flabbergasted state of mind, Ludwig made a fatal error. He grabbed a large wrench from the workshop bench and over-confidently ran directly at the thief with a warrior's scream. He took a mighty swing of the wrench. With the shock of this madman attacking, the thief was slow to react, and Ludwig landed a lucky blow on the side of the thief's head. He then swung around for the next attacker. Unfortunately, they were all bred from the same response gene and attacked him in unison. The strikes were relentless until one of the henchmen landed a death blow to the base of Ludwig's skull. Ludwig would never rise off his workshop floor.

The thief exclaimed to his henchmen that if the cannonball was immobile, they must open it so he could replicate it or at least sell the design to an unscrupulous investor. There was no way they could quickly open the cannonball's solid exterior metal. For such an event, the henchmen had brought a combination of oxidizing agents and combustible substances carried in a rough sack. The henchmen set it at the base of the cannonball and lit the fuse.

To describe what happened next, as the Blitzpeicher exploding, would not remotely give it justice. Once the fuse lit the rudimentary dynamite, a searing white light emanated from the innards of the Blitzpeicher. The resulting onslaught vaporized all living and dead souls within the confines of the workshop. Some say that the crack of the explosion was heard for miles in all directions outside the Medieval Wall. It destroyed everything in the workshop, the adjacent Medieval Wall, and the side of Reinhardt's house. Thankfully, no other villagers were injured except for a few damaged eardrums.

Stories of the incident were told, embellished upon, and retold by thousands of people in the area. Without facts, many a drunken pub patron concluded the village quack had blown himself and half the town up with one of his many ridiculous and worthless inventions. Village meetings were conducted, and villagers were instructed to refrain from dangerous science experiments unless they were a professional approved by the village's rulers. In their naive and myopic understanding of science and the workshop's events, no one knew Ludwig had created the first battery and first electric motor.

Young Karl was devastated. After the sparsely attended funeral, Karl stayed in his room for days, lost in the worst depression a child could endure. He decided to keep the fan as his only memento of his father. Karl was accustomed to being teased by his friends about his father. He thought his father would create something that would result in everyone giving their family the respect they deserved. However, more than anything else, Karl simply missed his dad. He felt the vacuum inside him ripping him apart. His world, while never perfect, was crumbling around him.

Creating his imaginary Medieval Wall around his room, Karl would hold the fan and daydream about all the excitement he and his father shared with the discovery. That was one of the best times of his life, and no one from the village could take that away from him. He knew the villagers were upset with his family, and he began worrying about his prized fan's safety and the Blitzpeicher drawings. He decided to store it in his room's best secret hiding place. For the Blitzpeicher drawing, he concealed it on a ledge deep inside the fan's housing where no prying eyes could find it.

In relatively short order, Rothenburg's Medieval Wall was repaired to its original 14th-century condition, where the blast had blown it apart. The Reinhardt's house was likewise fixed, but their pride was never restored. It was a dark time for the Reinhardt family. Unbeknownst to the villagers, this was also a dark time for humankind as it was the first time electric power had been stolen from the people.

Chapter 3

Declan Mac's House
Current Day

Out of habit, Mac made a quick assessment of the environment. He sensed movement from around the corner. The threat was undefined but very real. The sounds of quiet footsteps and clothes brushing against a fixed object, such as a wall, were undeniable.

He reached behind his back for the 9mm Glock secured by a concealed holster. The world slowed, and there was no time to second-guess his assessment. Mac crouched slightly, readying himself for the impending attack. He knew this was it. His only question was about the number of assailants and their method of assault.

From around the corner, the onslaught started. Unexpectedly, the attack came from low to the ground. The sneaky assailants shrieked with high-pitched voices. Mac's three young children came running around the corner of their house, screaming with excitement to see their daddy. The attackers consisted of two cute little girls in the lead and their well-loved, much younger little brother, doing his best to keep up from behind. Mac responded to the threat with a big bear tackle on the three of them as they squealed in mock terror to escape.

Mac snapped out of being a Field Operative. He rolled his eyes at himself. This process was the same routine every time he returned from an assignment. It was an occupational hazard to turn the CIA switch on and off. However, this was the life for many Operatives in America. Mac was hiding in plain sight.

Mac never understood why little kids always woke up so early every day. He told his fan club, "Hey guys, let's head into the house for breakfast. I'll bet Mommy will have something yummy for you."

As the three fought their way into the front door of Mac's well-kept, three-bedroom suburban house, Mac knew he was in his happy place.

The Macs lived in a quaint suburb of a thriving metropolis like Mayberry R.F.D. from *The Andy Griffith Show*. Most houses were adorned with American flags, and everyone seemed to know everyone else. Declan's wife, Mary, was perfect here. While she did not grow up in the community, you would have thought she was a descendant of its founding fathers. She was gorgeous outside, and Declan knew she was even more beautiful inside. She unselfishly shared her non-family time with their church, friends, and charitable organizations. Her life in Mayberry was perfect with her wonderful family, beautiful house, and thoughtful husband, who had a great job as a respectable business consultant.

Mary was not exactly sure what Declan did as a business consultant. She loved it when Declan had an in-town client who kept him sleeping in their bed at night. Of course, just like any successful consultant, Declan traveled on international trips that often extended for multiple weeks. While his traveling was hard on her and the kids, his time back home was magical. Mary and Declan frequently had a good laugh when he would arrive home from an international client, peppered with bandages on various parts of his body. He would just brush it off, and she would conclude that Declan must be much clumsier than his toned and athletic body would suggest.

Mac went upstairs for a quick shower. Thanks to his days in the Army, Mac always took a 'combat shower' that never lasted more than two minutes. Anything more than that was a waste of time and water. After drying off, he completed a quick physical assessment of the new damage to his body. The knife wounds on his forearms were healing nicely and required only a few stitches. He looked at the array of old knife and gunshot wounds on his torso and limbs, and he felt fortunate not to have any new life-threatening impairments.

Carefully applying fresh bandages to the knife wounds, he developed a story in his mind to explain to Mary how he got them. The instructors trained him at the Farm to use lies that included aspects of truth. However, the wounds from his CIA life were so outlandish that he avoided anything close to the truth. For Mary and the kids' safety, he could never allow them to know that he was a Senior Field Operative for the CIA. Mac took a moment to assess if he had ever heard of a CIA operative telling anyone what they did for a living, including their family. The answer was no. It wasn't just Declan having to live a double life; all Operatives hid in plain sight.

Declan found himself catching up on the morning news and emails while enjoying Mary's delicious breakfast. He looked up at her and was amazed at her beauty, even in this early morning. He hoped he would not receive one of the CIA texts alerting him about his next assignment anytime soon. His consulting firm was an actual functioning business practice with real clients and a front for the CIA to house clandestine assets.

The CIA was an early adopter of maintaining a respectful work-life balance. After returning from an assignment, Mac could generally expect to enjoy at least a week with his family. The Agency found that this balance was also crucial to maintaining the Operatives' secret cover with the outside world.

His reading was interrupted by Mary. She said, "Declan, this will be a busy week. We have something every afternoon with the kids and get-togethers every night with friends."

Declan half-heartedly replied as he looked up from his laptop, "That's fine, Hun."

"Declan, did you hear what I just said?" When Declan was home, she knew he preferred staying home and playing with the kids. She also knew he did not like to be interrupted at work. That concept always seemed silly to her. After all, he was a business consultant and not off saving the world from an inevitable demise.

"Yes, Hun. I'll be there."

"I know our schedule will be stressful for you, and I don't want you to schedule more business trips to escape home life.

I'm sure you are undoubtedly treated to all First-Class accommodations during your business life."

In Declan's mind, all he could think about was if she only knew his down-and-dirty reality. This home and their family were Declan's happy place. With a boyish grin, he said, "Well, I do miss my complimentary nighttime back rubs and constant five-star attention."

"Oh, I guess I did forget one little detail in the schedule. Our dinner tonight is just with the two of us. The kids have sleepovers, and we have reservations at your favorite restaurant."

Declan's boyish grin turned into a devilish smile as he mouthed to her, "What?" He then calmly said, "I think I can manage to rearrange my schedule to accommodate your needs."

An adrenaline rush of happiness surged through his body. As he started to do his goofy, self-created shimmy dance that he somehow assumed Mary thought was sexy, the kids walked into the room.

Declan froze from his dance and grabbed the kids by their waists. In an effortless move, he tossed them on his shoulders. The kids squealed with glee from their dad's roughhousing.

Turning to his wife, he gave her a wink and mouthed, "See you tonight."

* * *

While driving to his consulting office, he gleamed with joy as he reflected on the controlled chaos of his home. Even his house was perfect. It had those fake white shutters on the windows, and the front yard was enclosed with a damn short, white picket fence. He was not sure why they even had it. However, Mary had wanted it, and, as usual, he lost that battle. Declan loved every bit of his family and home, and he couldn't imagine his life without them. The CIA was right. The best way to have a work-life balance was to hide in plain sight.

Chapter 4

Mac's Business Consulting Office

Mac's workday was filled with follow-up calls to local clients needing advice on various matters. Most of his clients were successful with personal and professional accomplishments. However, just like any business owner, they didn't have anyone to discuss their most challenging business or personal matters.

Usually, the matters were about cash flow, financing, growing sales, or reducing expenses. While Mac was a CIA Field Operative, answering and advising on any of these matters was well within his wheelhouse. Mac was an outstanding business consultant, successfully advising several clients through crises or business challenges. These business skills were all part of his cover. Given his experience, he was fully capable of working at most major consulting shops around the globe. However, Mac preferred to save the world rather than consult with it.

He had a much more difficult time addressing the inevitable personal predicaments of some of the business owners. It was not that Mac didn't want to help. One of his innate skills was evaluating people and thoughtfully resolving touchy matters. His challenge was embedded in the ethical dilemma that can come with non-business issues. Mac would not allow himself to cross boundaries. He wasn't facing any dickhead's dramas or unscrupulous proposals today, at least not yet.

His day passed quickly, and by midafternoon, Mac was daydreaming about his upcoming dinner that night with Mary. It felt like it had been years since they were out with only each other. Mac couldn't remember when the two of them had been out since having kids. After their first child was born, Mac's friends told him to ensure he continued to develop his relationship with Mary. However, Mac's relationship with Mary was so strong that nothing could separate them. Their love for one another could not be better. Having or not having a parent's night out would not impact that. Still, tonight was going to be fun.

Mac's daydreaming was interrupted when his phone rang at a shockingly high-pitched volume. It was his newest client, Whispering Wind Industries. Mac had not yet met with Whispering Wind and had not been briefed about their needs. He was told they were an international company manufacturing long-lasting batteries and needed some strategic planning assistance. The CEO, Joe Whisp, was a rising star in business circles and had deep connections in the defense contracting world.

Joe Whisp introduced himself and welcomed Mac to their team. Whisp was an engaging guy who had the gift of gab. He explained that they were on the brink of significant growth and wanted a third party's view on strategically maximizing their newly found position in the marketplace.

Whisp said to Mac, "We need to get started right away. How about we kick this off with dinner at my club tonight?"

While Mac generally always tried to say yes to any client requests, he replied, "I'm sorry, Joe, but I already have plans."

Being the typical assertive and successful CEO, Whisp pushed back and said, "Declan, I need you now. Can you reschedule your plans?"

"No, sir." Feeling obligated to explain himself, Mac added, "Tonight is a long-overdue dinner date with my wife." If Whisp didn't like that explanation, then screw him.

"Well, you should have said that sooner! I have been married a few times myself. I wish I had taken some relationship-building time instead of just focusing on business. Hey, when are your reservations? Could we get together before then?"

"They are at 8:00 p.m., but I plan to be home by 5:00 p.m. to ensure everything is set. I must get the kids to their sleepover houses and take care of everything at home. You know how it is. Can we get together tomorrow at 10:00 a.m. for coffee instead?"

Whisp chuckled and said, "Declan, of course! I would rather have your undivided attention rather than have you thinking about your dinner date blowing up."

Mac thanked him for understanding and reassured him that Whispering Wind was a significant client of his firm. He also assured him he was up for the challenge. Once they agreed on the meeting time and place, they said pleasant but curt goodbyes. Mac stared at the phone as he reflected on this pushy new client and wondered if he had just upset the firm's most recent and most important client.

Chapter 5

Mac and Mary at Evening Dinner

The night was perfect. Mac and Mary were both wearing grown-up clothes, focusing solely on each other. Mac arrived home early from work so that they could push their reservation up by two hours. This effort only added to the excitement of the dinner as they considered having more waking hours at home alone for their long overdue "dessert." Too often, one or both fell asleep by 10 p.m. as they juggled their demanding schedules.

They were completely comfortable with the kids' sleepovers at a friend's house, and of course, Mac used the opportunity to act silly in front of the server. Mac had a way of using humor to lighten the situation without losing focus on the objective. His wit forced everyone to smile, kept everything in perspective, and reminded them everything would be okay.

Just before the after-dinner drinks, Mac's CIA-issued phone vibrated. Its unique vibration made him sit upright and instinctively feel for it in his pocket. He excused himself and walked to the restroom to check the message. The text was from the CIA's secure comms network. It was Brock.

Brock, who always kept communication concise, texted, "Compromised. Multiple attacks. You okay? Orders?"

"Whiskey Tango Foxtrot?" That was military-speak for What the Fuck. "All fine here. Team status? When were we hit?" Mac needed intel.

"It's bad, but no one was hurt. Within the last 15 minutes. Too much info. to text."

"Send the emergency directive to have everyone report to Langley ASAP. Also, have everyone text me their sitreps. I will take care of Langley's response."

Mac desperately needed the situational reports, otherwise known as sitreps. He was confident his team could make it safely to Langley since they had survived the initial attack. Someone else was in the restroom, so he dashed away and called Brock from a dark and unused corner of the restaurant.

Brock picked up on the first ring, and Mac jumped in with, "Brock, what the hell is going on?"

"They came after me, trying to make it look like a drive-by shooting while standing in my front yard. They couldn't shoot for shit. I think I hit two of the shooters while I was diving for cover. They attacked Valencia as if it were an everyday mugging while she was out for a run, but you know Valencia. With all her Black Belt ninja crap, she kicked the shit out of all three of them. She then had to hightail it out of there when the dudes' buddies drove up and started shooting."

Brock kept going and explained, "Gunner had it the easiest. He had just won another one of his WWE matches wearing that damn Devil mask and was walking out of the stadium through the participant's exit. He was approached by two guys who made the mistake of thinking they would have an easy taser target. He slammed both of their heads against the wall like the guys were rag dolls and kept walking. He thought they were just upset fans and dealt with them like a couple of gnats to crush with a hand slap. He didn't find out about the true threat until I reached him at his mother's house."

"Wait. You had to call Gunner at his mom's house?"

"Affirmative. You know that since Gunner's dad was murdered, he has been continually checking on his mom. He shuts out the world when he's with her."

"For being such a big guy, he's got this huge soft spot for his mom."

"He's a "momma's boy" for sure."

"Momma or not, he hasn't lost his eye on the ball when we're on an op."

"Copy that."

"Did they also attack Ryker?" Mac asked.

"Ryker, that crazy kid, was on the wrong side of town at a skate park. A couple of skater-looking punks started following him around the park. After a few minutes of the punks trying to keep up, he saw them both slip out handguns. The kid kept his cool and went flying off the backside lip of one of those barrel things. He dropped to his knees, hiding on the ground. When the punks flew off the lip behind him, he took them both out with a swing of his skateboard, catching them both in the head while they were mid-air. I am guessing that the next time, those punks will be wearing helmets. Either way, I am sure both punks will have new scars, compliments of Ryker. Ryker took off, not knowing who they were, and I pinged him on his trip halfway home."

"We were lucky this time, but they will come after us again if we sit idle. Next time, the attack will be more lethal." Mac stated.

"Agreed. Valencia grabbed the cell phones of the guys who attacked her. They look like burners, but maybe Ryker can unearth some leads."

"Excellent. I'll have to buy the whole team a beer. I guess I'll even have to buy you a beer, bud. We're going to battle. This is personal."

Mac then called his CIA boss, Rainey, to give her the sitrep. He said, "Rainey, this is Mac. We have a situation. Can we talk?"

Rainey was a pro from head to toe, and she said, "I'm ready. Go."

Mac could tell she was doing something else but knew his untimely interruption was necessary. While she sounded out of breath, she recovered quickly. Mac desperately wanted to know what he was interrupting but knew he would never receive the whole story.

Rainey was an enigma that was shrouded in twelve inches of hardened steel. Mac had done some back-channel research on her and could only uncover a few tidbits other than the official CIA-required background crap. She had a fearless and reckless streak, pursuing any activity at high speeds. Mac knew Rainey raced small, single-engine turbo-prop Formula 1 air racing planes. On the ground, she competed with a KTM dirt bike and skied in trees at death-defying speeds. He was sure the CIA Director didn't know about her passions, and if the Director did, he might consider chaining her to her desk.

Mac decided his questions could wait, filling Rainey in on the team's attack instead. She confirmed everyone's safety and told Mac to report directly to Langley. Mac knew the conversation was over and responded simply, "Roger that."

Once they hung up, Mac knew she would reach out to one of her cohorts at the FBI. Rainey knew how to get things done, and Mac admired her tenacity.

When Mac returned to the table, Mary read the concern and seriousness on his face. She asked, "What is it? Is there a problem with a client?"

He replied, "Mary, I'm afraid it's serious. I'm not sure about the details, but I think there's a time-sensitive problem at work. I'm sorry, but I need to get you home so I can address it personally at my office."

Mary, the consummate supportive wife, replied, "Of course, Dear. Do you want me to take a cab home by myself?"

Mac had already flipped his switch to CIA mode. However, that did not override his protectiveness of Mary. They both knew Mac had an irrational, often described as obsessive, need to shelter Mary and the kids from any harm. He could not turn it off, and Mary had to accept this quirk in his personality.

There was no way Mac would have her take a cab tonight, and he said, "That's not necessary. Let's just grab the check and get out of here. I'm sorry. Everything is going to be fine."

After Mac said his last sentence, he regretted it. He was just trying to give Mary comfort and assure her. Something in his core told him everything was all but fine.

Chapter 6

Mac and Mary's House

The drive back to Mac's house was quiet. Mac had all his senses working overtime. He asked himself, who could have attacked his team? Why wasn't he attacked? How did the attackers know the location of all these CIA operatives? After getting their asses handed to them on a platter, the attackers will be better prepared next time. His team certainly had dozens of dangerous enemies from the years of missions across the globe. They had foiled large and small attempts to shake up world power and damage democracy. Mac's thoughts immediately returned to their most recent missions, but he needed more information to determine the culprit.

Mac pulled into his driveway and parked in the garage. He was so focused that he did not stop to appreciate the comfort and safety of his own home. Mac went directly to their bedroom and closed the door. He opened a safe hidden within a secret compartment buried in their closet. No one, including Mary, could have found the safe thanks to the excellent CIA support teams' handiwork. Mac had four similar safes hidden in their house but wanted his go-bag out of the bedroom.

When he turned around, Mary was standing there with a confused look. "Declan Mac, what is that in our closet?"

Mac knew he was in trouble when he heard Mary use his full name. As he began to stutter out a response, he glimpsed at the undeniable red dot of a rifle laser sight painted on the left side of her white shirt. He did not have time to think. Mac dove at Mary, violently knocking her to the hardwood floor. At the same time, he heard a somewhat muted pop on the bedroom window. The bullet embedded itself harmlessly on the opposite wall on the same path where Mary had stood just a split second before.

Two more shots popped through the window in quick succession. These last two were close enough above Mac that the crack of the supersonic bullet whizzing by pulsed in his ears. He could not ascertain the caliber of the rifle from the three shots. He wasn't going to stick around long enough to determine if it was large enough to pierce through the brick siding of his house and leave them with no viable cover.

With a glance out the window, Mac saw two shooters approaching the house. He pulled Mary to a half-standing and half-leaning position.

Mac said in a quiet but clear voice, "Keep low and stay with me. I want your hand on my back at all times. I need to know that you are safe and with me while I am focusing on keeping us alive. We must go now. We cannot stay here."

Mary did her best to follow his directions. Mac could tell she was stuck somewhere between mindlessly following instructions and screaming in sheer terror. He knew he was their only chance of survival and needed to ensure her understandable fragile state would not derail his impromptu responses.

He threw the belt of his go-bag over his shoulder and pulled out a semi-automatic 9mm pistol. Even though he knew it was loaded by its weight, he still dropped the mag out, checking to ensure it was filled to capacity, and reseated it. He then flipped the safety off and pulled the slide back to ensure he had a round chambered with the hammer cocked.

Mac could not afford to miss any shots with their lives at stake, and the lower weight of the single-action trigger squeeze would be crucial to that first round. He would have loved to have given a gun to Mary so she could protect them from behind, but she had never even held one. In her state of high anxiety, it was just as likely that she would have accidentally shot him in the back. No, he would carry their weapons.

They successively went to each potential exit from their house, and Mac could see shooters converging on their position from all sides. The shooters took a couple of wild shots through the front window when Mac and Mary dashed past. Even if he could hold the shooters off long enough for the police to arrive, these pros would just mow the cops down. That was not acceptable. No egress would safely provide an exit on the street level. Mac had no choice, and he looked at Mary. She was a trouper, but she was terrified and could not process what was happening to them by looking at her wide eyes.

Mac smiled and said to her, "Sweetie, you are doing great and holding it together. These guys are about to enter the house, and we need to slip down into the basement before they find us. Okay?"

Mary could only respond with an aggressive head nod up and down. Just as they hit the basement stairs, Mac heard breaches from all four sides of the house. In the brief silence following the invasion, he made out the faint sound of an approaching helicopter. The bad was getting worse. He was sure the helo would pick up the shooters for their exfil, but he was concerned it might be carrying a bit more of a punch than would have been healthy for the two of them.

When Mac and Mary landed on the basement floor, the shooters had already begun a quick search. Mac could hear the shooters quickly working as they cleared room by room.

As Mac and Mary ran to the far side of the basement, Mac said, "I forgot to tell you we have a significant gopher problem. I was thinking about calling our local groundskeeper to get rid of them," Mac said, referring to his favorite golf movie, *Caddyshack*.

Mary finally got some words out and said, "What the hell did you say? Did you know there are men up there trying to kill us?"

"Yep. I noticed. Now, please step back while I look for the lever behind the TV."

Mary stared at him, dumbfounded. Mac noted he did not hear any more footsteps upstairs. That was not good, and Mac worked his fingers quicker on the secret lock. The lever dropped down with a loud clanking, and he pulled a five-foot section of the wall into their basement as it silently swung on its hidden hinges. As he did, a series of lights came on down a long tunnel that curved out of sight. Mary just stood there in shock. Mac grabbed her hand and said they had to go.

A series of concurrent events happened as they got about five feet into the tunnel. Fortunately, the first thing was that the basement wall closed behind them. The thick barrier saved their lives. The second thing was that Mac began pulling hard on Mary's hand to run down the corridor like they were kids rushing to the next ride in an amusement park.

The third thing was not as good. The helicopter had picked up all the shooters and, while hovering, turned toward their house. This team of killers was here to finish the job. Two AGM-114 Hellfire laser-guided air-to-surface missiles were released from their hardpoint. Their lovely suburban residence was immediately destroyed by successive explosions that should only have been heard on a battlefield. The house, filled with personal touches and loving memories, was a home, not just a dwelling. It was there one minute, and the next minute, it was flaming hot rubble with a skeleton frame.

Mac and Mary were thrown down from the explosion. The tunnel held its integrity and did not collapse.

Mac grabbed her face and gently turned her toward him. She looked fine, but he asked her, "Are you okay? Can you run?"

Mary choked out, "Yes. What just happened upstairs?"

Mac looked her directly in her eyes while enunciating each word separately to ensure she appreciated the seriousness of his directions and responded, "Just come with me."

He helped her up, and they continued their half-mile sprint until the end of the tunnel with a steel grate above them. That grate opened into the neighborhood park. After a quick 360-degree assessment and finding no danger, Mac unlocked the grate and climbed out with Mary in tow. He reached for his phone to dial Brock once the grate was locked.

Mac said in his calm radio voice, "My house was compromised and is destroyed. I need ASAP to…."

Brock cut him off and said, "Your kids are already on their way to Safehouse Walton. We heard about the chaos at your house and have a car headed your way to pick you up. The driver is using your phone to trace your location at the park. Are you or Mary hurt?"

Mac took several steps away and quietly commented, "Thanks, man. Mary is fine, and my only injury is to my ego. Now, I am even more pissed. I should have known they were coming after me, too. I walked the two of us right into their trap. To make matters worse, I am all out of stories to explain what just happened to Mary."

"Copy that. See you at the office shortly. Good hunting for that story. Out."

Mac hung up and turned to Mary.

Still shaking with shock, Mary could only muster one question for her husband, "Who are you?"

Chapter 7

Langley Situation Room

Mac's motley crew was shell-shocked and jacked up with anger as they debriefed their experiences from the attacks. No one had any answers. Everyone had differing opinions. There was one definite conclusion – they were under attack, and it was time to go on the offensive.

They were standing in the Langley Situational Room, debating their next move. The LSR had experienced countless world-changing strategy meetings, from the Cuban Missile Crisis to the 9/11 terrorist attacks. Its rich mahogany walls covered multiple layers of sound-dampening structures and electronic surveillance jamming devices. There were no windows. There was nothing in the room other than the expansive conference table, seats for several dozen, and a blank projection screen on the far wall. Once the door was closed, the sound seemed to evaporate into the air eerily. That also allowed for crystal-clear communication when someone was talking.

Rainey was a no-nonsense and hard-charging leader at times like these. She was a career CIA devotee and was married to her job. Rainey was gorgeous with her tall and slender figure, blonde hair, and piercing blue eyes. She caught the attention of every man when she walked into a room. Rainey could cut anyone in half with a stare from eyes that seemed to pierce right through you. Mac and his team's over-the-top successes drove much of Rainey's meteoric rise from CIA Analyst, and she unconditionally supported them in all their endeavors.

Rainey's style with people mirrored many successful leaders. Before developing a go-forward opinion, she inquired about the available information and culled the worthless details. The ability to do that took years and had been honed by trial and error.

She stopped the flurry of wild opinions flying across the room and focused on the team's youngest member, Ryker. She asked, "Ryker, what have you found on those burner phones?"

Ryker replied, "It's not what I found. It's what these idiots didn't even bother to hide. They were either greenies or way overconfident."

At that moment, Mac walked into the room. As usual, he was impeccably dressed in a dark suit, tastefully matching tie, and, of course, stylish brown oxford leather shoes.

Brock announced as his voice trailed off, "Speaking of way overconfident…."

That comment brought smiles to everyone's mouths except Mac's. Mac teasingly snarled back.

The team did not know or understand the extent of torment Mac was internalizing for his team and his family. Mac had a debilitating emotional challenge. He was a man who had stared down the worst in humankind. From his Army special ops days to his dicey CIA missions, life confronted him with emotionally charged situations. He effortlessly compartmentalized almost all those events that would have crippled most people. However, one experience has haunted him since its occurrence. It dictates a response that inevitably puts him in mortal danger repeatedly.

When he started with the CIA, Rainey assigned Mac to a team with four other highly skilled operatives. The team scored a few dozen very successful missions and had developed quite a name for themselves. Mac proved himself to be a capable and respected leader. It all came crashing down during an assignment in one of Central Asia's "stans" countries. The intel was all wrong. The team's intent was all right. Mac's voice in the back of his head was screaming at him to abort. He always trusted his intuition, except this time.

The succeeding calamitous chain of events resulted in the death of Mac's team members. Even though he was hit several times, Mac managed to survive. His physical wounds were deep, but his emotional wounds were even more profound. He had several visits from the CIA's shrink during his recovery period. She eventually released him to return to field operations but with a warning. She described to Mac her clinical diagnosis using a string of ten-syllable words that meant nothing to him. The shrink recognized she was not getting through to Mac. She told him in a motherly voice that he felt overly responsible for his team's death, and it had given him, in layman's terms, an "Overactive Protective Gene."

Facing and accepting his perceived failure was not his challenge. Everyone had failures. Mac's challenge was the guilt-ridden impact on him at his core. His Overactive Protective Gene made Mac always willing to accept personal, life-threatening risks to protect those around him. Superficially, that sounds like a strength. However, guilt created an unresolvable internal conflict. If he died protecting others at work with irrational actions taken at his peril, he left his family unprotected for the rest of their lives. He could not turn it off, and it defined him.

"Wow. Your little experience was crazy. How's your family?" Rainey asked. Everyone knew the importance of Mac's family to him and the importance of keeping his personal life separate from his CIA life. Rainey recruited Mac into the CIA out of a business consulting firm, and he was already married at the time. His situation made it easy to create the family-man persona outside the CIA.

Mac replied to Rainey, "Mary and the kids are fine at Safehouse Walton. I need to work on a cover story, but that is a problem for Future Mac."

Continuing to question him, Rainey asked, "How about you, Mac? Are you okay?"

Going back to his military days, Mac stood at attention with his eyes focused ahead, and he jokingly said in a loud voice, "Blown up, Ma'am!"

Everyone snickered with the *Stripes* movie reference, and Mac took his seat. That joke earned him a shoulder punch from Valencia and his returned mock pained look and childish exclamation of, "Ow!"

"Okay, Children. That's enough. Ryker, can you please continue?" Rainey used her best motherly voice to get the discussion back on track.

Ryker was slumped in his chair with his classic grunge fashion statement. Thanks to his brilliance, the CIA put up with his long, unkempt hair, tee shirts, baggy and torn blue jeans, and semi-fashionable gray and black DC Court Graffik skateboard shoes. His thrift-store, ill-fitted clothes covered an incredibly athletic physique with sinewy muscles and cat-like quickness. Ryker was always off at a skate park, surfing big waves at Dana Point, free climbing the nearest rock face, or base jumping from prohibited areas. His home time was filled with non-stop gaming on an array of computer equipment that rivaled the computing power of almost every company in America.

Ryker's brilliance was previously acknowledged with a full-ride scholarship to Cal Tech. Unfortunately, his disrespect for the establishment landed him in trouble several years ago while working on his Ph.D. For some reason, he found it entertaining to control all the cell phones in Russia simultaneously. He interrupted every call simultaneously using his best surfer dude slang with, "Surfs up, my dude! Let's ditch this 'craphole' country and hang ten at the Mav!" Ryker was talking about the Mavericks, otherwise known as the Mav in surfer shorthand, a dangerous big-wave surf spot in Northern California.

Many argued that Ryker's comment was much more memorable than Alexander Graham Bell's when he spoke the first words ever used on a telephone. Bell said, "Mr. Watson, come here. I want to see you."

Ryker became somewhat of an internet sensation after his hacking stunt. However, his fame was short-lived when the CIA caught him at the insistence of Russia's spy agency, the SVR RF. Rainey led the investigative team, and she gave Ryker three choices. One, he could be turned over to the SVR RF and spend the rest of his life in Siberia. Two, he could go into the Federal prison system for an extended stay. Third, he could use his skills as an employee of the CIA. Ryker chose well and accepted the CIA employment offer. He had been in Rainey's department and on Mac's team ever since.

"These yahoos were treating their burners like their everyday personal device," Ryker explained to the group. He did not need to clarify that a burner phone was a cheap prepaid phone with an untraceable phone number for temporary use.

Ryker continued, "Instead of making a call and destroying the phone as we do, they were making multiple daily calls on it."

Gunner said, "So what did they say, Techno-boy?"

Ryker smiled and said, "Well, that's the nicest thing you have ever said to me. I will take that as a compliment."

"Yeah, then earn it," Gunner retorted.

Gunner was tough but had a soft spot for the kid. He was all muscle developed from years of athletic competition rather than steroid use. At 6'4" and 260 pounds, he was a standout linebacker at his Ivy League school. Gunner surprisingly identified an innate ability to learn and retain languages effortlessly during college, a skill he regularly used on missions for the CIA. While the entire team was conversant in multiple languages, Gunner was the most fluent and generally took over the discussion when having command of an accent's nuances was necessary. He had planned to play pro football, but unfortunately, he blew out his knee and dashed his future athletic hopes.

After Gunner earned a degree in Foreign Affairs, the CIA heavily recruited him for his impressive combination of brain power, language aptitude, and athletic ability. He was a natural. Gunner loved perfecting his forestry survival skills and assisting intercity youth. The kids related to his accolades on the football field, African-American heritage, and concern for their success. They connected so well to Gunner that they would never have known he was raised in a wealthy family where his parents had successful careers. Gunner was close to his dad until his father's death, but everyone knows that Gunner's sensitive side came from his mom.

Ryker confidently replied, "As I was saying, these guys had several calls with a number registered at Whispering Wind Industries. I have not had enough time to dig into Whispering Wind Industries, but I will bet they are behind the attacks on us."

"Does anyone have thoughts on why and how Whispering Wind got hold of your addresses? Do I need to remind you that they are only available with top-level clearance?" Rainey responded.

Mac, who had been sitting quietly, letting his team talk through the background, said, "Wait. I have something on this. My consulting firm has been engaged by a high-growth business, Whispering Wind Industries. As I understand it, Whispering Wind reached out to my firm rather than any marketing approach we initiated. We thought it was unusual that Whispering Wind found our name and called us without any referring party. They even asked specifically for me. Before leaving my office, I did a little research on Whispering

Wind's financial filings. Just a few years ago, the company was literally at the brink of bankruptcy, and just like the Phoenix rising out of the fire, they pulled off this miraculous recovery with unbridled growth."

"That sounds like too much coincidence between the burners and your new client," Gunner replied as he was connecting the dots on the issues.

Mac continued, "Yes, and you all know I don't believe in coincidences. Here's another one for everyone to consider. Before I left my office today, I talked to Joe Whisp, the Whispering Wind Industries CEO. He asked way too many questions about the exact time Mary and I were going out for dinner tonight. Something did not seem right with his questions. It was almost as if he wanted to know when I would be home. I wrote it off as just another pushy CEO, but now I realize he was figuring out my exact itinerary."

Rainey asked, "How did he know your timing for the evening?"

"I told him we had an 8:00 p.m. dinner reservation, and therefore, he timed his attack for around 7:00 p.m., expecting us to be home still. Mary and I unexpectedly pushed our dinner up to 6:00 p.m., and we would have easily been there for a few hours."

Brock added, "That's where I come into the story. I called you about the attack on all of us and interrupted dinner. You cut it short and headed home early because of me. Sorry about that."

"Exactly. I blame you for the attack on the Mac homestead," Mac teasingly jabbed Brock.

Mac clarified, "We were home by around 7:00 p.m., just in time for the attack. With the inaccurate timeline I inadvertently gave Whisp, their attack on me would have been a complete bust if we had just stayed for drinks and dessert."

Rainey stated, "Okay, then it looks like we have a clear lead on who was behind the attack on the team. That still does not answer how Whisp acquired your personal information and addresses. It also does not answer why Whisp would do it in the first place."

Brock, who could not take the waiting any longer, suggested, "Screw this guy. Let's barge in there with guns hot and take out this little prick. I, for one, do not like being shot at."

Mac ignored Brock's call to arms and asked, "I wonder if Joe Whisp's name showed up anywhere on that flash drive we downloaded in London?"

Rainey reflected on the question and replied, "That flash drive contained an intricate web of people from all walks of life making money from an assortment of illegal activities based out of London. I am not sure how the flash drive ties into this. Shortly, MI6 will initiate a full investigation and blow apart the entire international crime ring. They asked me to tell you there are a couple of bottles of Dom Perignon waiting for you the next time you stop by."

"That is quite a thank you!" Valencia said.

Valencia was sophisticated and developed expensive tastes growing up in Manhattan and traveling worldwide with her parents. She preferred that others used her full name rather than shortening it to Val. Even further, showing her pure-bred Mexican heritage, Valencia pronounced her name with the Spanish pronunciation, replacing the "c" with a "th" sound. She was stunning with jet-black hair and a toned 5'2" physique, but her outward appearance hid an inward dichotomy. While lovely on the outside, she was very physically aggressive with multiple Black Belts in martial arts and universally accepted as one of the best snipers ever to walk American soil.

Mac noticed Rainey feverously working the keys on her secured computer networked via the CIA internal communication system. It was clear she wanted something from someone. When Rainey asked, she received it. Everyone in the room knew better than to interrupt Rainey when she was focused on a matter. Almost exclusively, her seemingly misplaced attention was likely to lead to an important insight into the discussion.

Rainey looked up and proclaimed, "We have it. Joe Whisp's name is all over the USB flash drive. The analysts in the basement are still unweaving the details. However, it appears that Whisp became heavily in debt to some unsavory characters a few years ago as he tried to save his company. They extorted him into performing several illegal and unethical business transactions. If the information on that drive were to become public, Whisp would be going to jail for a long time, and his company would be destroyed in the process."

Mac said, "That certainly looks like overwhelming motivation to have the team taken out and find out the flash drive's location. It's a good thing we had enough time to drop it off at Langley when we returned from the mission. Joe Whisp scheduled a meeting with me tomorrow at 10:00 a.m., but I am sure he does not expect me to show up, or at least, if I show up, I will have zip ties on my wrists. I think it is time we paid a visit to Mr. Joe Whisp at Whispering Wind Industries."

Chapter 8

Power Plant Conference Room, Rio de Janeiro, Brazil

The United States Secretary of Energy gazed out an expansive window overlooking Rio de Janeiro. Their conference room was spacious, but his attention was diverted to daydreaming about this spectacular city of Rio.

He had been to Rio a few times in the past. Situated on the Atlantic coast, Rio was probably best known for its beautiful sandy beaches that drew tourists worldwide. The backdrop of the beaches entailed impressive mountains and peaks blanketed by tropical forests. At the top of Corcovado Mountain was Christ the Redeemer, the most significant Art Deco statue globally, watching over the city with open arms.

Amid the Secretary's short reflection on Rio's beauty, the Rio Power Plant's Presidente walked into the conference room. The two gentlemen shook hands, and they turned toward the window.

The Secretary broke the brief silence and said, "You have a lovely city."

"Thank you, Mr. Secretary. It is an exciting place," the Presidente replied.

"Agreed. I would also say that your new power plant is exciting," the Secretary said.

While the Secretary would have enjoyed discussing Rio, he was not here for the city's beauty or culture. He was here to strike a deal for inexpensive energy for the U.S. for use in a catastrophic power event. The U.S. power grid's vulnerabilities were not lost on the Secretary, which could make this multi-billion-dollar investment worth every penny.

The Presidente said, "We believe we have accomplished a cutting-edge breakthrough. I hope we can strike a deal that helps both our facility and your country."

"I'm optimistic we will find common ground," the Secretary replied in an upbeat tone.

To confirm his understanding and set the tone for the expected negotiation, the Presidente asked, "May I ask why the U.S. is interested in our power facility?"

Based on well-known facts, the Secretary explained, "The U.S. has three major regional power grids. There are tens of thousands of electric transmission substations within the grids to deliver reliable electricity, like webwork throughout the country. However, not all substations are alike. Losing even a limited number of substations could prove catastrophic due to cascading power failures. Replacement of high-voltage transformers is also a major risk due to a vast majority of the transformers being provided by overseas manufacturers and each transformer being individually built to that location's unique specifications."

The Presidente asked with genuine curiosity, "The U.S. doesn't seem to have reliable power. Does that create a significant crisis for the country?"

"I would not classify it as a significant crisis. We have several fail-safe procedures in place. Risks to the U.S. power grid are well documented. Any potential shortfalls have been the subject of substantial discussions between Homeland Security, the Department of Defense, the Armed Services Committee, and the United States President. Each recognizes the inherent deficiencies and is taking actions to mitigate them, to the extent financially reasonable."

"In Brazil, we should be taking similar actions to protect our energy network. What type of responses has the U.S. implemented?"

The U.S. Secretary thoughtfully said, "That's a fair question and one that we should pursue jointly between each of our governments. For example, the U.S. was under continual cyberattacks from its enemies at one time but has created an effective system to detect and stop the infiltration. Every country should be concerned about other significant risks such as solar flares, electromagnetic pulses from nuclear explosions in the atmosphere, environmental catastrophes such as earthquakes, and coordinated terrorist attacks."

"Do you believe these are worldwide risks?"

"The threat to the U.S. power grid is the most unsettling part of my job. Most developed countries have grown comfortable with a standard of living that includes dependable and consistent availability of power."

The Presidente said, demonstrating his understanding of the repercussions of a mass lack of power, "I agree. The population does not appreciate the destruction of life as they know it in the event of an extended countrywide power outage. There would be no, or, in the best case, partial, electric lights, gasoline, drinking water, computers, internet, healthcare, cell phones, or mass food production. There would be a complete collapse of the country's financial system, throwing it into a massive recession."

The Secretary knew there was no secret why he made the trip to Rio. "Without the availability of basic life necessities such as food and water, millions would die, and the country impacted would be thrown back into the mid-1700s. It would be devastating. Even considering the cost of laying almost 5,000 miles of submarine power cables across the ocean from Rio to the U.S., this agreement with the Rio Power Plant has far-reaching implications. It is critical for our domestic security."

The Presidente of the Rio Power Plant said, "Mr. Secretary, this is an exciting event for our power-generating facility. We have worked for decades to develop this technology, and we believe we finally have it perfected. The investment from the United States will ensure we can supply power to all of Brazil and possibly other countries when our capacity increases."

"I have reviewed your conceptual framework, and it's impressive." The Secretary continued, "Could you explain the technology to this old engineer?"

"Of course. Of course. Over the last decade, much research has been conducted on seawater usage to generate electricity. Your media has been relentless in discussing the benefits of the ocean and the world's overabundant supply.

Keep in mind that it is clean energy because no fossil fuel remnants are being released into the environment. Unfortunately, American engineers have been stuck on repeat, continually pursuing an energy technology that costs more energy than it produces. Our engineers looked at the problem from a completely different angle and combined two technologies to achieve the breakthrough. This new technology gives us the opportunity for endless energy from ocean water."

The Secretary said with admiration, "As I have heard. The technology sounds truly amazing. Congratulations to you and your team on such a breakthrough."

The Presidente beamed with the compliment and felt confident he had already sold the Secretary just on his word that the technology worked and his artful presentation. He now has the Secretary eating out of hand and can ask for everything he needs and then some.

Knowing the loud voices associated with the environmentalists, the Secretary had to start asking the hard questions. With a stern look and concerned tone, he inquired, "Have you considered the impact on ocean wildlife or the release of sodium into the environment?"

Stumbling through the answer, the Presidente replied, "We are conducting environmental assessments on those issues now."

"Okay, I understand your process creates steam, and that steam is then used to create the energy. Will the excess steam have a meteorological impact due to the tremendous amounts of humidity being added to the atmosphere?"

With that question, the Presidente was uncomfortable with his response and decided to divert the meeting to his agenda.

"Mr. Secretary, I hate to break this question-and-answer session short, but we are on a tight schedule to have you speak with our Plant Manager. He's an excellent man who led the team that created the technology. It was his genius mind that created this feat. Our technology is clearly before its time."

The Presidente tapped on his phone, and the Plant Manager showed up on the large projection screen at the end of the conference room. He was standing in a control room that overlooked the plant. Under the expansive windows, there were hundreds of control panels with dozens of readout meters and lights. The Plant Manager was a short, overweight man who wore an oversized white lab coat to cover his girth. Atop his head was a white construction hat to complete his ensemble, and thick, black-rimmed glasses obscured his eyes.

The Presidente said to the Plant Manager, "Thank you for taking your valuable time to speak with us. Please let me introduce you to the United States Secretary of Energy. As you know, he is visiting our facility to discuss a potential investment from the U.S."

"It's a pleasure to meet you," the Secretary said.

"My pleasure as well, Mr. Secretary. What can I help you with?" The Plant Manager knew the Presidente's request was an order and not a request. He was not skilled at negotiations and conducting high-level discussions that did not directly entail his technology. All he wanted to do was bring clean energy to Brazil, and these administrative meetings were nothing more than a distraction.

The Presidente asked, "What's the status of going live at the facility?"

"Sir, we are hours away. We are going through our final checklists now."

"Excellent. Excellent. Could you please explain to this gentleman how your power plant will work? Please keep it as brief as possible."

The Plant Manager knew that comment meant for him not to share any of the valuable intellectual property with the other man in the room. He was happy to keep it more superficial, given that he did not have the week that would be necessary to describe the intricate technology and processes in detail.

The Plant Manager explained, "We are merging two technologies to create more energy than Brazil could ever use. The process combines seawater with nanotechnology that separates the salt from the water. As the nanobots perform their molecular separation, steam is created as the seawater is superheated without needing fossil fuels for heating. We take the super-heated water to turn steam turbines and create power. The nanobots then eat the salt so that there's no remaining residue. Does that make sense to you?"

"Well, conceptually, it makes complete sense. You describe your invention well. Once we sign our agreement, we will have many more questions. Also, you will have the full support and brainpower behind you from the U.S. Department of Energy."

At that comment, the Plant Manager bristled a little bit. The last thing he needed was outside energy engineers meddling in his technology. They would simply slow him down, and the world needed this technology. However, as instructed, he smiled and replied, "Your engineers would be most welcome at our facility."

"Terrific," while already knowing the answer but wanting to confirm, the Secretary asked, "Where is the power facility located, and are you secure?"

The Plant Manager replied, "The power plant is on an uncharted island two miles offshore. We utilize the entire island, and it's a perfect way to ensure there are no security breaches. We have ten well-equipped and highly trained special operations security guards on the island and an equal number on the shore dock. The dock provides the only service and delivery access to the island and is fully dedicated to the power facility. It's inaccessible to any unauthorized personnel. Additionally, we even have some unpleasant surprises on our dock if anyone breaches our restricted airspace without prior permission."

As the discussion continued, the Plant Manager and Presidente felt confident with their explanations and the impenetrable security protecting the power plant.

Down at the Rio dock, a different scene was unfolding.

Chapter 9

Rio Dock Servicing the Power Plant, Rio de Janeiro

Alberto, the young 24-year-old Brazilian special ops soldier, had just confirmed his all-clear for the umpteenth time today. His station was the FSAF SAMP/T antiaircraft weapon. Alberto was proud to be entrusted with this bad boy that could eliminate any airborne targets within 120 kilometers of the island. The ground-based SAMP/T is a theatre-level system designed to defend against hostile fighter aircraft, cruise missiles, short-range ballistic missiles, and crewless aerial vehicles. The state-of-the-art weapon could fire eight Astor 30 interceptor-guided missiles in succession at enemy targets with a simple push of two buttons concurrently on his command-and-control keyboard. The radar was equally as impressive as the Astor 30 missiles and was the defense system's backbone. He would sometimes lovingly caress the big antiaircraft weapon as his imaginary first girlfriend if he were ever lucky enough to meet her.

Alberto also had a Russian-made SA-24 "Grinch" MANPADS next to him to complete the Rio dock's formidable air defense of the island. The Grinch was a man-portable air defense system that fired a surface-to-air missile against low-flying aircraft from a shoulder-fire position. The MANPADS was their backup defense if the antiaircraft weapon was unsuccessful. Like any prepared spec ops team, these soldiers had primary and secondary plans with the firepower to prove it.

While Alberto was assigned to operate the ground-to-air defenses, he was well-trained and combat-ready, just like the other guards assigned to this station. They were all Brazilian spec ops and capable of defending the island against any ground or air assault. The soldiers on the island were equally prepared and focused on defending against a water assault, given the dock's daunting air defense capabilities.

Like a sea monster sneaking up from the depths of the ocean to quietly sink an unsuspecting ship, two black-clad mercenaries-for-hire slowly rose from the water. They quickly hid behind an old pier sunken into the sand. Both men were adorned with camouflage face paint. After removing swim gear and dry suits, they performed quick weapons and comms checks. While their rifles were designed for Special Forces use in water conditions, they still removed the barrel's obligatory condom. The condom protected the end of their weapons from filling with water, and they drained their barrels to ensure no jamming or blockage. Their firearms were fitted with silencers, allowing them to operate stealthily. Of course, each carried a military-style knife that was sometimes a preferred weapon of choice to remain undetected. The lead mercenary pointed to the lookout tower, signaled the junior teammate with a few brief hand gestures, and the two silently split for their assigned tasks.

The first critical kills were the two soldiers in the watchtower as the junior mercenary made a quick dash to cover behind some seaweeds. He could feel the sharp seaweed cut his exposed skin but ignored it as he knew his life and mission depended upon it. Crawling to his desired shooting spot was trickier. The watchtower soldiers continually moved around their perch with keen eyes surveying the area. Patience was critical for this shot. If one of the soldiers went down before he could shoot the other soldier, the survivor could alert the ground troops. The soldiers would slaughter the mercenaries.

While a shot was well within his typical range from this distance, the mercenary was not carrying his beloved Accuracy International AX308 sniper rifle. This disadvantage meant he was sacrificing some precision. He also had to factor in the onshore breeze. He noticed the soldiers smiling and making comments as they passed each other. Within five minutes of patiently waiting and staring down the scope attached to the barrel of his rifle, the soldiers gave him his opportunity.

The two soldiers stopped and faced each other. The closest one had his back to the mercenary. The opposite soldier seemed to pull something out of his pocket and handed it to the nearest soldier. It was a cigarette. He put the cigarette in his mouth and cupped his hands around the flame from the lighter shared by the other soldier.

The rifle recoiled against the mercenary's shoulder with no more than a spiff sound. He saw the blood splatter as the bullet penetrated the base of the first soldier's neck and the face of the second soldier. Both dropped immediately without a sound. The mercenary clicked his comms twice to alert his partner that he should proceed with phase 2 of their operation.

Phase 2 was no less ruthless. The next soldier scanned his field of view as the mercenary slipped behind him. With one hand covering the soldier's surprised mouth, he jammed his blade deep into the soldier's throat. The soldier had no fight as the mercenary quietly laid him down on the pavement. Unable to reach the following two soldiers before detection, he took advantage of the element of surprise by firing two suppressed rifle shots in quick succession. The rounds found their marks a moment later, and the two bodies silently fell limp. The mercenary hurried to drag the corpses out of sight, obscuring the bodies in foliage and kicking sand over the remaining blood spots to eliminate any evidence of the events that had just occurred.

The next group of soldiers was indiscriminately taken out in succession. Their devious foes eliminated each unsuspecting man without even affording them the chance to fight. The ruthless attack was executed without emotion. It was almost as if the mercenaries were simply taking a casual Sunday stroll for a cup of the rich and full-bodied Brazilian coffee.

The last two soldiers were problematic because they were visible to one another. The mercenaries split the responsibilities and agreed upon a coordinated attack. Once in position, with a double click on their comms, their plan went into action. One of the mercenaries aimed his weapon at Alberto, standing on an idling skiff. In the next five minutes, Alberto had intended to motorboat to his partner on the island, who would trade with him and take the next shift with the surface-to-air antiaircraft weapon. The final soldier stood and focused on the antiaircraft weapon's radar, waiting until Alberto's relief showed.

The primary antiaircraft weapon operators took four-hour shifts to stay fresh and alleviate the fatigue of continually staring at the screen. Neither he nor Alberto had noticed the carnage that had taken place around them. The mercenary began to move into an attack position to use his knife. He tactically needed to ensure the soldier on the boat didn't make it to the island and return with reinforcements, especially for that damn deadly antiaircraft weapon.

Just as the mercenary took the shot, a choppy wave struck Alberto's skiff. The unexpected wave spared Alberto from certain death. The bullet went wide and shattered the boat's windshield. Alberto noticed the black-clad assailant and dropped to the deck while raising his weapon. He knew he needed to warn his fellow soldier manning the radar as bullets ricocheted all around him. Alberto took a chance and glanced towards the Rio dock and watchtower. There were no other soldiers other than his friend on the radar.

While hiding from gunfire as he lay on the boat deck, Alberto used a rescue pole and raised the two tied-down lines off the dock cleats. He needed to depart quickly to get reinforcements from the island once he warned his friend. Alberto used another wave's crash to rise to a kneeling firing position and braced his rifle on the boat's side. His aim was accurate. He caught the mercenary in the throat and flipped him backward off his feet.

Alberto could not see any other infiltrators, but he was too far from his friend to yell and warn of the attack. He reached for the walkie-talkie on his belt and, upon finding nothing there, cursed himself for leaving it on the dock during the shift change. Alberto knew that his friend must be alerted, and this time, he needed to stand to achieve the proper angle as he turned his weapon toward the man who was one of his best buddies. Alberto was hopeful for calm water to assist in his aim. He squeezed the trigger, and the shot found its mark. Next to his comrade, the metal water container exploded in a splash of flying water with a bullet hole in its center.

The soldier jumped with surprise at the noise and splash of water on his face. He quickly glanced around while he cursed in reaction. He saw Alberto pointing his gun at him and then pointing at a black-clad intruder sprinting toward him. The mercenary took a play out of Alberto's book and dropped his right knee to assume his preferred shooting position. He considered Alberto an imminent threat and aimed at him. The bullet found its mark, hitting Alberto in the abdomen. As Alberto collapsed, he fell on both the steering wheel and throttle, shooting the boat skirting out to the water stuck in a perpetual circle pattern at high speed.

The final soldier was slow to react in his shock. The mercenary turned his weapon to the guard and killed him with a single shot. He turned toward the antiaircraft gun, emptied his magazine into the electronics, and heard a satisfying hiss with the big gun's shooting platform, dropping like the head of a disappointed child. The mercenary then sprinted to his partner, who lay dead with massive blood loss soaked up by the sand. He knew he could not leave any evidence of their presence behind and heaved his partner over his shoulder as he shuffled to their dive gear.

With his dive gear reacquired, the mercenary waded into the water, pulling his dead partner with him. In a deadpan voice, he said to a no-name person on the other end of the line, "Mission Clear Sky complete. One KIA. In water and returning."

"Copy that," came the response.

Reversing his stealth technique to breach the Rio dock area, the mercenary slowly dropped into the water and swam to a yacht where the mission had started. It was anchored three miles offshore to take the mercenaries to safety quietly. Strangely enough, the luxury yacht's engine and electrical components were all covered in Faraday cages and containers.

Chapter 10

Power Plant Island, Rio de Janeiro

A relatively low-flying Saab JAS 39 "Gripen" military jet was screaming toward the island. Without the antiaircraft weapon threat, the pilot could focus on the precision release of his fire-and-forget payload. Using his cockpit's wide-angled Heads-Up Display that provided mission and weapons information visible above the jet's forward panel, the pilot could maintain full mission awareness, allowing him to release his under-wing package at a precise moment. He fired his weapon with a trigger flip. The pilot then exited from the payload detonation radius by putting his Gripen into full afterburner and hard-right turn. This move pushed his aircraft to its maximum performance capacity of Mach 2 while pulling 9 Gs.

The payload was not a bomb intended to flatten the power plant. Instead, it was a device programmed to release an electromagnetic pulse with just enough attack area to cover the island and close vicinity.

The Secretary continued his discussion with the Plant Manager on the power plant conference room's big screen. The Secretary asked the Plant Manager, "Do you feel your technology is reliable?"

The Plant Manager replied confidently, "Sir, except for a natural disaster or an attack, this plant is unequivocally...." The Plant Manager's picture and the audio went completely dead.

The Presidente laughed and said, "That certainly was an awkward and inconvenient time for our video system to go down!" He dropped his gaze to his phone and began tapping, but he could not get in touch with anyone. He then tried the landline and cursed as it sounded like their lines were dead. As the minutes passed, the Presidente frantically tried contacting the island with unsuccessful texts, calls, and video conferencing.

The Secretary strained as he looked out the conference room window toward the Rio dock and the island. He could still see the island, but something stood out to him as unusual. There was a small skiff doing fast circles just off the Rio dock. He picked up a pair of binoculars sitting on a credenza and confirmed his fear. He could see a soldier lying on the controls of the skiff as it did continual circles. He grabbed the Presidente and said, "We need to get down there ASAP!"

As the Presidente drove, he unsuccessfully tried to contact the soldiers guarding the Rio dock. Their car screeched to a halt at the dock entrance that they found unguarded. They sprinted to the waterfront and found one fatally wounded soldier in front of the antiaircraft weapon. While neither man could be considered an agile spring chicken, they jumped onto the remaining skiff tied to the dock, released the mooring line, and rocketed to the circling boat. As they pulled aside the speeding, out-of-control skiff, they used a hook to snag it and tie it off. The Secretary reached over to the skiff's throttle and managed to shut down the circling boat's propeller. Alberto fell off the throttle and landed on the boat deck.

The Secretary climbed over to the attached skiff and checked for a pulse. Surprisingly, the man was still alive. He said, "We have to get him to a hospital immediately. It looks like he has lost a fair amount of blood. Let's get him back to the Rio dock and on dry land."

"Agreed. I will call an ambulance on the way there while you try to stop the bleeding."

"Why would someone attack your Rio dock and not the power plant?"

The Presidente replied apprehensively, "I have no idea, but I am concerned we cannot raise anyone on the island."

After pulling Alberto onto the dock, the EMTs arrived with impressive quickness. They said that while Alberto had lost excessive blood, his vitals were stable, and he had a good chance of a full recovery. They would know more after the surgery. With that quick triage, the EMTs whisked Alberto to the ER.

The Secretary and Presidente proceeded back to the skiff and headed to the island. When they arrived, the soldiers guarding the island were in crisis mode, assuming they were all victims of a coordinated attack. They explained they heard a large crack directly above them, and then all their communications and vehicles went dead.

When entering the facility, the Secretary noticed one glaring concern. The soldier was pointing his weapon directly at them. The Presidente jumped with curt demands, "I am the Presidente of this company. Put your weapon down. We are not a threat. We are taking the elevator to the command center."

The soldier pointed his weapon to the ceiling and replied, "Sir, excuse me. I did not recognize you, and we are on high alert. My apologies, but you will not be taking the elevator to the command center."

"We most certainly will be taking the elevator. Now move out of the way before I fire you."

"It's not a matter of choice. The elevators are not operational. Sir, in fact, nothing is properly functioning. Everything electronic physically appears okay on the surface, but it is worthless. The stairs are your only option and are just around the corner."

They saw total pandemonium when they opened the door at the top of the stairs. Every person was focused on something and screaming out information. On the other side of the room, they found the Plant Manager. He said, "I am sorry, but I do not know what is happening. The technology was working fine for one minute, and then the entire facility went dark. I cannot explain it."

Assessing the situation, the Secretary shared his gloomy perspective. "I think I can tell you what happened. You were attacked with an EMP. That's the only answer that makes any sense."

The Secretary pulled his phone out of his pocket and dialed his most trusted CIA senior contact, Rainey.

Rainey picked up on the first ring and asked, "Hello, Mr. Secretary. What can I do for you?"

"I have just witnessed a potential terrorist attack at the new Rio power plant. My best guess is that it was some sort of EMP."

"Not that I doubt you, but how do you know that? Is there a way to confirm it?"

"I am standing in the Control Center of the Rio power plant as we speak and am witnessing the fallout of it myself. The only definitive evidence I have is that every piece of electronics is useless. They might as well be boat anchors. I have not been briefed on any other technology with this destructive energy source other than an EMP. The power plant is on an island just off the coast of Rio, and it appears no other electronics were fried other than on the island. That suggests someone must have targeted an EMP directly over this island. I need your best team on this immediately."

"Tell me more about the situation so I know what my team is walking into."

"I'm here to secure a critical backup energy source for the U.S. My trip is covered under a veil of secrecy to ensure no one else gets the idea before us. However, the facility went dark before their new power plant went online. If it were an intentional attack, it could have resulted from the U.S.'s interest in the plant, or it could have been from some other insidious initiative. I am not sure what happened here, but it's clearly a threat to national security. If it were an attack, the culprits could just as easily attack the U.S. At a minimum, the event here eliminates our ability to secure a high-priority backstop energy source for the country." The Secretary deeply understood the critical nature of his responsibilities and the U.S.'s dependence on a reliable power grid.

"I agree with your risk assessment. Do you think it was a solar event or possibly even nuclear?" Rainey already knew the team best suited for this mission. Before boarding the CIA plane, she needed to brief them on all available intel.

The Secretary explained, "As you know, an EMP can occur from an energy surge released during a solar flare or human-made event such as a nuclear explosion. However, I do not believe the Rio EMP was a nuclear explosion. There has been no suggestion of a nuclear detonation. I did not see a mushroom cloud, a blinding flash, or any other indication related to a high-altitude event. Also, we track the buildup of the sun's solar flares, and none have been identified. Therefore, the EMP must have come from some other event."

"Do you have any other theories on the method used to release the EMP?" Rainey asked.

"The impact on the earth will depend on its release altitude and strength. Given that it appears the only area negatively impacted was the Rio power plant island, it suggests the EMP was detonated at a relatively low altitude and above the island." The Secretary had quickly and accurately deduced the method of attack.

Rainey continued to dig and asked, "Have we finalized our technological advances allowing us to run postmortem tests on equipment potentially victim to an EMP? I have heard about some good advancements made in the research and development area within the Department of Energy."

"We are making progress, but we are not there yet. Consider that every electronic device contains circuits intended to accommodate a certain amount of current. An

EMP emits immense energy through an electrical circuit, frying it and rendering it useless. I mean all electronic devices from power plants to computers to even cell phones. Other than from the fallout of a nuclear explosion, we have not found a reliable detection tool that can unwind the melted mess."

"Shit," Rainey exclaimed as the gravity of the matter sunk in, with the only means of determining the cause was to have boots on the ground. She continued, "I'm glad you called. I'll get the team together as soon as you and I hang up."

The Secretary said with desperation, "Thanks. As you can imagine, it would be devastating if there was such an attack on U.S. soil. It would lead to mass starvation, millions of deaths, and widespread anarchy. The only protection from an EMP is keeping your electronic components in what is called a Faraday cage that blocks the current. Get your team here now before the next attack potentially hits U.S. soil. If we don't shut this threat down now, we risk being thrown back to a technological era of the 1700s."

"I am on it, sir."

As soon as she hung up, she sent a group text to Mac's team to ensure they assembled at Langley for their new mission briefing. Rainey's job afforded her the unpleasant knowledge of knowing when a country or the entire world was facing a meltdown. When the crisis was the greatest, and everything was on the line, she always turned to the same man.

Chapter 11

Whispering Wind Industries

Mac received Rainey's text as he was standing in front of the first-floor reception desk of Whispering Wind Industries. He needed to take the hour and finish the meeting with Whisp before losing this opportunity forever.

He could not help but notice the over-the-top security in the building. He counted twelve security cameras in the lobby and outside entrance, ensuring video coverage of every imaginable angle. Glancing at the security guards' deadpan eyes, Mac could tell they all had seen combat and death. They all had "the look." The shoulders in their suit jackets measured at least 50 inches, and by the looks of it, their muscles were large enough that any flexing would risk tearing a seam.

While not outwardly visible, thanks to their suit jacket and slacks, Mac noticed each guard had at least three concealed weapons. They all carried Uzi submachine guns inside their jackets, a handgun in an ankle holster, and a spring-ejection knife hidden by their shirtsleeve. Undoubtedly, they had other tricks that Mac could not quickly identify as he walked by them. These guys were ready to repel an incursion from a small army.

The receptionist announced to Joe Whisp that Mac had arrived for their 10 a.m. appointment.

Mac could overhear Whisp replying, "Who?"

"His name is Declan Mac, sir."

Unable to hide his surprise, Whisp responded with a high voice, "That's impossible. How can that be possible?"

Whisp had just received the text report from the shooters stating that the CIA team had survived the attack. However, the communication also said Mac had died in his home's explosion, and the USB flash drive was destroyed.

Unsuccessfully trying to shield his mouth and the phone's mouthpiece from Mac, the receptionist said in a hushed tone, "Sir, it most definitely is possible. I have already confirmed his identification and credentials. I have Declan Mac standing in front of me."

Trying to gain some level of composure, Whisp replied, "Yes. Yes. Of course. Mr. Mac is my 10 o'clock appointment. Please send him up."

As Whisp hung up the phone, he had a panicked look and texted his shooter's commander, "Mac survived the explosion and is here in my office visiting me! Is it possible that the damn flash drive was also not destroyed? You have no idea of the consequences of your complete mission failure. I know it was a long shot that we could destroy the flash drive before it was delivered to the CIA, but I thought you could have at least killed the CIA jerk who stole it and his team. I should never have trusted you, and now I must fix your fiasco. Double my security detail once I finish this meeting with Mac."

The only response back was, "Mac's house destroyed, but status of flash drive unknown. Security enhancement acknowledged."

* * *

Two guards that rival the size of Gunner escorted Mac onto the elevator. After pushing the "PH" button that undoubtedly stood for "Penthouse" thirty floors above them, the guards both stood behind each of Mac's shoulders. He could see their reflection in the polished elevator siding and noted that they stood in the preferred quick-action style of personal security forces. Their feet were shoulder width apart and partially staggered to maintain balance with their hands held at the ready in front of their bodies. Mac, uncomfortable with their advantage, was thankful for the mirror-like walls that allowed him to maintain eyes on both with alternating glances.

Mac was surprised the guards did not push him through the opened elevator doors. Instead, they politely waited for him to step off the elevator. The guards then rode back down without a word.

Mac walked towards the figure standing at the far end of the room. He depressed his comms to inform Ryker, "At Checkpoint Adams."

Ryker said back in Mac's ear, "Confirmed. Tap me when Checkpoint Eisenhower complete."

Sitting in a van in the building's lower parking level, Ryker and the rest of the team pretended to be from a delivery service. If the gate guard had paid closer attention, he would have seen rows of computer screens and monitoring equipment covered by tarps. Fortunately, the guard was not interested in the frozen food drop-off on the lower level and did not even glance at the van's cargo.

Mac could see Whisp on the opposite side of the room. Whisp was impeccably dressed, consistent with the expectations of a high-powered CEO. He was slender with prominent, bushy eyebrows that seemed to define his face. His nervousness was apparent as his eyes constantly darted around the room, and his hands flittered in perpetual movement. It was clear to Mac that Whisp was freaking out, almost to the breaking point. Mac could see Whisp confidently controlling a Boardroom or charming a sales prospect in a less stressful situation.

As Mac self-assuredly strode up to Whisp, he stared him in the eyes. He introduced himself, using his best business consultant's voice, "I'm Declan Mac. You must be Joe Whisp. I am sorry we could not meet last night, and I appreciate your understanding to delay our meeting until today. Your office is beautiful." Sometimes, using pleasantries was the best way to put someone at ease, even if they tried to kill you the night before.

Still obviously unnerved, Whisp replied, "Thank you, Declan. I suppose success does have some privileges. How was your dinner last night? It was with your wife, correct?"

"It was lovely. We ended up with an early reservation at my favorite restaurant." Mac continued staring at him. Through his training, he could calm himself to take advantage of all his senses. His heart rate slowed. Even still, he could not get out of his head that this man ordered the attack on his team and almost killed Mary.

"That's great. Having an earlier-than-expected dinner is always nice because it gives more time for everything afterward."

"So true. The evening went out with a bang," Mac replied. His witty choice of words was not an accident. He could not get last night's chain of events out of his mind and wanted to see if he could stir a response from Whisp.

Whisp slightly grimaced. There was a stifling elephant in the room. He continued with the intended game and inquired, "I know you just returned from an international trip. You probably have not had a single minute to yourself with the demands of your office and home."

"You would be surprised how much time one can squeak out when necessary. A business consultant's life is jammed with moving from task to task, both personal and professional. Speaking of which, how were you able to transition from a highly leveraged entity on the brink of bankruptcy to this incredibly successful entity today? The turnaround seems almost too good to be true."

Shifting gears easily to his comfort zone, Whisp presented his company's transformation like a presentation to a Wall Street investor. "It is true that we previously struggled in the automotive battery manufacturing industry. Our fundamental problem was that we could not afford the research and development investment necessary to remain competitive. We had allowed our equipment and processes to become antiquated and inefficient."

"That sounds similar to many companies that are struggling in a low-margin industry."

"Yes, and our customers were demanding a longer battery life at a lower cost. Further, most automotive manufacturers have announced the transition to electric vehicles. We were in a poor strategic and financial position."

"At that time, the new investor fortuitously enters your life, right?"

"The investor was a gift that was laid on our lap. He came out of nowhere and completely reversed our fortunes."

"Who is the investor?" Mac was hopeful but doubted Whisp would make the mistake of disclosing the name.

"I have a lock-tight Confidentiality Agreement precluding me from sharing anything about the investor. I am sorry about that, but I am sure you understand. His name should have no bearing on the consulting services we need from you."

"Understood." Mac used that one word to convey his understanding of the other side's position but did not necessarily agree with it.

"All I can tell you is that I am sure you would know the investor's name if I was at liberty to tell you. Be assured he has been and will continue to be a very credible source of capital for my business."

"That is certainly a wonderful turn of events for the business. Is this mystery investor just providing capital? Hopefully, he is bringing other benefits to the table." asked Mac.

Whisp replied, "He has this genius engineer who works for him who is unbelievable. While I have some incredible IT folks who can break into virtually every IT system globally, this engineer is even better. He is helping take me to the next level."

While on a roll, Whisp bragged with a confident smile, "I mean, I can get my hands on anything I want from any server anywhere. These guys are crazy good and sit just on the other side of the wall beside me. I want to keep that skill set close. There's no competitor in the world I don't know everything about."

At that moment, Mac felt confident Whisp was responsible for hacking into the CIA system and identifying his team's whereabouts and top-secret cover lives. Mac could not understand how Whisp could break into the U.S. government's Secret Internet Protocol Router Network, otherwise known as SIPRNet. It contained all top secret and classified information in a closed network. Whisp's IT department must have found some initial access point like any good hacker. It would be helpful to know Whisp's access point to stop future breaches.

Mac knew he had a significant advantage in identifying information during this discussion – Whisp's ego had no bounds. Mac asked himself if Whisp realized he had just admitted to conducting corporate espionage and breaking dozens of federal laws. Narcissists are dangerous and can share incriminating details about themselves because their mouth has no governor. They feel as if the world revolves around them and that they are above the law.

To keep Whisp talking, Mac asked, "That sounds like an incredible asset that gives you a powerful strategic advantage. The skills in your IT department will help make our consulting project much more far-reaching. What did the investor's genius engineer do for you?"

"I am not sure how he came up with the idea. It's straightforward, and yet it's complex enough to be patented.

Given adequate time, I'm confident I could have designed it myself. Unfortunately, I need to run this company."

Feeding Whisp's ego, Mac replied, "I am sure your skills are only limited by the hours in the day."

Whisp smiled at the compliment and decided to capitalize on the discussion. He said, "Look, I am not a modest man, but at least I speak the truth. Most people I meet are schmucks and shower me with accolades because they want me to help them, given that I'm a powerful man. I can tell that you are not a schmuck. You are a successful guy who can see a great opportunity when presented to you. Whispering Wind is a great opportunity for you."

"Joe, if you are suggesting that I join your company, I am flattered. Of course, you understand that I am gainfully employed, right?"

"Sure, I know your current employment status. However, speaking hypothetically, would it be interesting if someone doubled or quadrupled your salary?"

Mac decided to play along with this charade and asked, "You don't even know what I make as a consultant. It seems like an overly substantial increase."

"I pay my people very well and require total loyalty. With that level of compensation, I would expect the delivery of even something a little extra."

"Extra?"

"Oh, I'm sure it's nothing for you to acquire. We will discuss those details once we finalize a salary and significant incentive compensation program."

Playing the part of a person intrigued by the discussion, Mac leaned slightly closer to Whisp but knew he had to push back rather than appear too eager. He said, "Joe, what actually happened when the company was in such a big crisis and then turned itself around? It seems that I need to understand the past to see your vision for the future."

Joe squinted his eyes and nodded at Mac. He hesitated and said, "Okay, I will let you get under the tent a little. That will help you with the framework to understand this amazing opportunity and my leadership skills. A few years ago, we were in a bad way with old technology and declining revenue. Unfortunately, I had a momentary lapse of judgment and accepted rescue money from a group of foreign sharks. They had me by the balls once I took the money to save Whispering Wind. The rest I am going to say is confidential and just between you and me, right? Are you okay if we talk in conceptual terms so I can deny it if it ever comes up in any other conversation?"

"Certainly, Joe. Whatever you say."

"If a desperate company accepted cash from some bad guys, I would expect they would slowly pull the legitimate business into their illegal empire. First, it was probably small, like hand-delivering a package for them. That would irritate a high-powered CEO, but it would be a small price to pay relative to the influx of cash. When other cash and transactions began flowing through the company, its accountant might refer to it as an international money-laundering hub."

Joe looked down and appeared like he recalled a problematic memory. He said, "The CEO should have known foreign sharks wouldn't stop there. You can imagine the extent to which bad guys could push the CEO. Not that it mattered what happened to any collateral damage, but they did not understand that the CEO had a company to run and could not be bothered with such petty time-wasting matters. Out of nowhere, a new investor came along and bought the sharks out."

Mac replied, "I am still confused. You got yourself mixed up with some unsavory characters, but why would the new investor be interested in Whispering Wind? I would think he would avoid anything that appeared illegal."

"I didn't say Whispering Wind was involved. We were just talking in generalities. However, if there were problems with a current investor, I would certainly share those with a potential new investor. I shared the company's depths with the investor and the resulting implications of the sharks' control over the situation. I fully expected the new investor to walk. To my surprise, the investor seemed pleased to hear about these problems and became even more interested in the company. The investor must have seen something in me that allowed him to conclude that this was a winning investment. After we closed, money kept flowing in. The investor's admiration and confidence in me and my business acumen must have grown by the day."

Utilizing an authoritative schoolteacher voice, Whisp stated, "I realize you are not an engineer. However, I think you need to understand the new battery technology we have developed."

Mac felt the new battery technology could provide insights into Whisp's motives. He structured his response to capitalize on the oversized ego of the man in front of him and replied, "Thank you, Joe. Please keep in mind that since this technology is not my area of expertise, the technical terminology may not be clear. I am sure you have forgotten more about batteries than I will ever know."

Whisp simply nodded. Looking as professorial and visionary as possible without talking over the head of Mac, Whisp stated, "The battery manufacturing plant is in Thailand and is a state-of-the-art facility. This battery is like no other the world has seen. It lasts for an almost limitless period on a single charge, thereby making all current automotive batteries worthless."

"That could change the world."

"Yes. Think about it. Every vehicle has an alternator to charge the antiquated-technologically enabled battery and power all the engine's electrical systems. With my battery, we eliminated the alternator, simplifying all electrical delivery for the vehicle. The major complaint of electric cars is the limited distance they can travel on a single charge. Now consider that my battery may need recharging every few months or longer. The internal combustion engine in vehicles will eventually become a thing of the past."

Continuing with his dissertation, Whisp said, "The power of this battery is not lost on the Department of Defense, or as we in the inner circle call it, the DOD."

Mac thought to himself that Whisp's desire to be admired was driving him to make sophomoric comments. Whisp had no idea of his audience. He wanted to impress upon Mac that he was somehow within the nucleus of the DOD. Whisp had no idea that Mac not only knew what it represented but that he was previously a DOD employee. When blowhards like this start on a roll, it is usually best if you let them talk themselves into trouble. Mac sat back and let Whisp spew out critical details of his operation.

Whisp continued, "With only a prototype battery, the DOD contracted with us to deliver on a deal worth millions of dollars of sales. It was a total pain in the ass getting through the bureaucratic red tape for a security clearance. However, we are such an important strategic partner that those yahoos gave me a top-secret clearance level."

Mac again recognized a crucial insight that Whisp's IT group could backdoor into the CIA via the DOD by capitalizing on Whisp's clearance. The CIA may never know how Whisp secured the confidential information on his team. However, it was worth having Ryker investigate the concept once they had access to the Whispering Wind IT system.

Whisp persisted with his tutorial, saying, "The first battery was invented in 1800 by Alessandro Volta, an Italian physicist. This genius created the ability to derive electricity from an ongoing delivery source."

"How does this relate to your new battery," Mac asked.

"In some respects, they are similar. Currently, vehicle batteries deliver electricity via two electrodes, one positive and one negative. The electrodes are where the electricity either goes into or out, which is all the typical person understands. The internal parts are surrounded by battery acid and encased in heavy plastic to hold everything together. My new battery utilizes electrodes, but that is where the similarity ends. From the metal composites used in the electrolyte fluid, my battery is, technologically speaking, lightyears ahead of the current, antiquated batteries."

The desktop computer pinged with an incoming email for Whisp. He turned to it and excused himself for a moment to respond to the email. Whisp was one of those impulsive people who could not resist immediately responding to emails or texts. Like many executives, Whisp generally kept his cell phone on the desk within reach in front of him if he received a time-critical communication that necessitated a response.

Mac took advantage of the distraction and stood up, walking to the windows and pretending to gaze at the view. He casually slipped his hand into his pocket and pulled out a listening device. This listening device was a next-generation technological marvel that looked just like a piece of clear tape. The small circle was only an eighth of an inch in diameter and virtually undetectable. It had an effective range of ten miles and could eavesdrop on both sides of a cell phone conversation. As Mac walked past the desk, his hand brushed across the top of Whisp's cell phone, and he applied the invisible listening device. Mac continued to the window and quietly said into his microphone, "Go Checkpoint Eisenhower."

"Checkpoint Eisenhower confirmed," Ryker said and turned toward his computer screen in the back of the van as he easily accessed Whisp's cell phone.

Mac waited at the window until Whisp informed him they could restart their conversation.

"Sorry for that interruption. Can we get back to our discussion? I'm swamped, as you can tell. We need your consulting assistance to establish a worldwide distribution network. I am afraid we will receive stonewalling from the existing battery establishment. You know how big business can eat us, little guys, for lunch," Whisp stated.

Mac was ready to end the meeting. He knew Whisp was offering him a bullshit consulting project that had no purpose. He said, "Look, I need to complete detailed competitive analyses to determine the most effective strategic distribution structures that will ensure efficient, profitable sales."

"That is what I am looking for."

"Okay. We have our project scope set. I have to get back to the office and will follow up with you tomorrow."

"That timing works for me. We need to get to work," said Whisp.

Mac knew that Whisp had no intention of engaging in a consulting project. He fully expected Whispering Wind Industries to present him with a financially lucrative employment package to buy off his allegiance.

Both stood up and shook hands. Whisp reached down for his phone to call the guards to escort Mac out. Mac said, "I have had three Venti cups of coffee this morning and need to lose some of it. Do you mind if I use your restroom?"

"Of course not. The bathroom is just around the corner and down the hallway."

Chapter 12

Whispering Wind Industries Restroom

Mac turned to the hallway, and Whisp made an escort request call to his guards. While Mac was walking down the hallway out of sight, he slid a tiny two-pronged device into an electric wall outlet. This device, created by Ryker, could access all company data. Ryker called it a Data Drawdown Device.

With the team, Ryker's invention was more affectionately known as a Triple D. A quirk of the system was that a second Triple D must be inserted into a non-adjacent electric outlet. Ryker warned everyone that the Triple D had not been field-tested and, while a remote possibility, it could be detected by the Whispering Wind IT firewall. Therefore, once it completes the download, Mac must immediately retrieve the Triple Ds and exit.

Mac went into the multi-stall bathroom and inserted the second Triple D into one of the power outlets. He then said into his microphone, "Go, Checkpoint Clinton."

Ryker said, "Checkpoint, Clinton. On it." He went to work with his fingers flying over the keyboard as he worked on downloading data.

After about a minute, Mac questioned with a one-word question, "Sitrep?"

"Working on it."

As if on cue, there was a knock at the door from the two security guards. "Sir, we are ready to escort you downstairs."

"Out in just a minute," Mac replied.

Mac then said to Ryker, "Sitrep?"

"Working on it."

Mac knew he could not pull out the Triple D without Ryker completing his download. Unfortunately, the guards were becoming impatient and knocked again.

Mac said out loud, "Just about done."

Time was running out. The guards were not going to be pushed off anymore. Mac had his hand right next to the Triple D, ready to pull it out, and said in his microphone, "Ryker, I need to exfil now. Times up."

The guards' suspicions were growing to the point that they did not care if they broke social norms. They knocked loudly and forcefully burst into the restroom.

Mac was casually leaning over the sink, washing his hands. He smiled at the guards and said, "Personal hygiene is important to me. I'm sorry this took so long."

After drying his hands on a towel, Mac walked ahead of the guards out of the restroom. Three-quarters of the way down the hallway, Mac turned around to the guards, explaining, "I am sorry, fellas. I left my cell phone in the restroom. It will just take a second to grab it."

Before waiting for a response, Mac strode quickly into the restroom. Knowing he had no more delay tactics, he pulled the Triple D out of the electric outlet and slipped it into his pocket. The restroom door flew open, slamming on the connecting wall with the two suspicious guards barging in, expecting to catch Mac in some threatening act.

With an innocent smile, Mac reached into his pocket and pulled out his cell phone, showing the guards as he rocked it back and forth. "Got it. Sorry again, gents."

Walking down the hallway, Mac could barely make out the remaining Triple D in the electric outlet. His mind was racing on how to retrieve it inconspicuously. He considered stopping in front of it to tie his shoe, but there was no way that stunt would work with these guards. They were way too serious-minded and hyper-focused on his movements. Mac also considered tripping in front of it, but there was no way he could reach the Triple D. He would have to leave it and glance down as he walked past it.

The ride down the elevator and exit onto the street in front of the building was uneventful. To alert the team for the pick-up, Mac said in his comms, "Checkpoint Roosevelt."

"Leaving now," Brock said, who was sitting behind the wheel of their vehicle. Brock did not need to hear more than that call sign to know that it was the time to exfil time and get the hell out of Dodge. He threw the van into reverse, and the tires squealed until they found good traction.

"I could not retrieve the second Triple D without detection," Mac said to Ryker.

"That is a huge problem. We have an even larger problem with only one of the Triple Ds connected."

"Define a larger problem."

"Worst case scenario, the single Triple D, powered by a hyper energy pack, could overload all the electrical circuits on the floor," said Ryker.

"Okay, so they blow a few fuses," Mac said as he tried to appreciate the magnitude of the issue.

"It's a little worse than that," Ryker replied with a pained look on his face based on the results of his lab testing of the Triple D.

"What do you mean a little worse?"

Chapter 13

CIA Van Outside of Whispering Wind Industries Office

The Whispering Wind Industries penthouse floor exploded in a fiery ball that blew out all the windows and incinerated the entire floor. The explosion was so ferocious that no one on the floor had time to register what had happened to them. All souls were lost, including the IT department and Joe Whisp.

Shards of glass and slivers of metal were raining down on Mac. He instinctively covered his head and crouched as he ran away from the onslaught. The team's van screeched to a stop, and the side sliding door flew open. Mac dove in the back while Brock accelerated away before the door was closed. Mac turned to Ryker and just raised his eyebrows. He did not need words to express his thoughts.

"Oops." Ryker simply said.

"Oops? What just happened?" Mac replied.

"I was concerned something like that could happen. My guess is Whispering Wind's fail-safe firewall shut down its system once it detected the Triple D breach. The Triple D went into hyper-load as it tried to push its way back into their system. The more it tried, the hotter it became, and the hotter the electrical system surged on the floor. The Triple D runs on a unique power supply with the same explosive properties as your favorite Big Bang, C4. You end up with a big boom with that amount of heat generation."

Ryker pursed his lips together and forced out his cheeks while bringing his fingertips together. Theatrically, he simultaneously let out the air in his mouth and pulled his hands away from each other while spreading his fingers like an enormous explosion.

Mac closed his eyes and shook his head like a disappointed parent. Asking the question that the whole team wanted to know, "Did you get anything off their system before the boom?"

"Unfortunately, no. The Triple Ds download is a simple algorithm resulting in either a binary yes or no outcome. I might pull a few bits of stored data from the tiny memory included in the one recovered Triple D, but it will not be a lot. I was seconds away from having a full download, but someone did not wait until I gave them the go-ahead. Instead, he pulled one of the Triple Ds out of the electrical socket."

"Well, that someone was pretty damn close to getting his cover blown by a couple of goons because your Triple Ds were taking so long to do their job. Even worse, your little toys almost got me blown up," Mac said with a smirk.

"Okay. Okay." Ryker said with a smile, "I guess not all the kinks have been worked out. But it was still a productive field test that identified an itty-bitty weakness in the prototype." Ryker's attempt to downplay the explosion that incinerated an entire floor of the building earned him a groan in unison from everyone in the van.

In trying to gain some acknowledgment of the Triple D's success, Ryker added, "Look on the bright side. At least most of those people with the knowledge of our cover identities, including the Whispering Wind IT department, are no longer around to further blow our covers outside the CIA."

"The way I see it, kid, you just blew your shot at a great job with a cool IT department," Gunner said to Ryker. Everyone burst into laughter.

"The way I see it, I just created the perfect job opportunity. With no one left in IT, I don't have any competition and can write my customized job description. I would love not having a boss." Ryker turned to Mac with a devious smile.

"I should be so lucky!" Mac countered, and everyone snickered. Mac, craving any information Ryker learned during the short visit, asked, "Do you have anything at all for us?"

"As a matter of fact, yes. Before the little accident, Whisp made a call to a guy named Blackwood. I will play it back for everyone." Ryker punched a series of keys on his laptop and flipped a couple of switches on the panel. The van was filled with the voice of the recently deceased Joe Whisp.

"Blackwood, we have a problem."

"Tell me." The response apparently came from someone named Blackwood.

Whisp said, "My elimination of the CIA team was unsuccessful."

"That's not good. I told you to simultaneously take the team out and recover or destroy the flash drive. How many did you terminate?"

There was a pause before Whisp answered, "None of them."

"None of them!" Blackwood, sounding like he was in full irritation mode, screamed, "You had the element of surprise. You had strength in numbers with overwhelmingly greater firepower. You are all idiots! Did you at least retrieve or destroy the flash drive that incriminates you for everything from theft to murder?"

"This team is filled with superhumans. The next time I send in hit squads for them, it will be ferocious and without discrimination. I'm not sure of the status of the flash drive."

"Whatever. Just don't get caught and compromise all my plans. Any other good news, Whisp?"

"Well, there is one more thing. The lead on the CIA kept his meeting with me this morning and just left," Whisp responded.

"Just left? You are more stupid than I thought. Why is the CIA working on a situation domestically instead of the FBI? Why would you not just detain him and torture him until he gave up the location of the flash drive."

Whisp confidently replied, "I have a better plan. He was here under the pretense of his cover job as a business consultant. He loved me, and I do not think he's suspicious of me. Otherwise, why in the world would he come here? I had him almost asking me for a Whispering Wind job because he was so impressed with me. Today, I set the hook, and tomorrow, I'm going to reel him in. The business world is so easy and predictable. I'm going to make him a job offer tomorrow that's so generous that there's no way he will stay in his ridiculous government career. The incentive portion of his compensation will be tied to retrieving the flash drive for me. He will say yes, but if he declines, I will send in the next hit team with double the number of guys."

"Whisp, if you do not take care of this within the next two days, I will cut off your balls and put them in a jar at the front of my collection. Now wrap up that worthless distraction in the next 48 hours and come here to...."

At the break in the replay, Ryker added, "Well, I guess the call was cut off when the line went dead."

The team broke out in a chuckle when Mac clarified, "Everything and everyone on that floor went dead."

Chapter 14

Rio de Janeiro

After their flight to Rio de Janeiro, Mac's team went to the U.S. Embassy. The CIA operations officer greeted them. Fortunately, he was eager to help and knew a great deal about the new power plant that was close to going live. The operations officer had been read into the file once the U.S. Secretary of Energy expressed an interest in expanding the U.S.'s interest in the new power plant.

The U.S.'s relationship with Brazil had its foundation based on similar democratic values, resulting in an important alliance with the U.S. The Brazilian U.S. Embassy was in a multi-story, white, modern building protected by a contingent of U.S. Marines. However, after the potential EMP terrorist attack, there was nowhere in the world the team felt safe.

The operations officer explained, "The Brazilian government has done a remarkable job of keeping the power plant incident out of the local papers, but that won't last long. There are rumors already starting to spread. I understand nine of the ten guards were killed. Those are local guys. The word will spread like wildfire once the families are informed. If you are planning some quiet snooping on behalf of the U.S., I strongly suggest you accomplish it today."

"Could you take Gunner and me to the Rio power plant office? I would like the rest of the team to stay here and dig into records to determine if they can find any connection between other leads we are following." Mac decided to divide and conquer to cover all the bases in the least amount of time.

"That's no problem at all. Your team can work in our conference room. We have plenty of reports and analyses for them. The power plant office is several kilometers away from here, so we should take my car. I will drop you off and return to help the team with their research."

After the quick ride to the power plant office, Mac and Gunner stood across from the Presidente, still exhibiting a complete state of shock. He was a shadow of the man full of bravado when he met with the United States Secretary of Energy. The Presidente was so stressed about the situation that he looked like he could have had "the gripper" heart attack at any moment. Trained to evaluate people within seconds, Mac could tell the Presidente's blood pressure must have been out of the roof.

The Presidente said to Mac and Gunner in a defensive tone, "I believe the Secretary correctly identified the cause of the plant shutdown as an EMP. I swear to you that the technology was working. There's no way I would have taken any U.S. money without a proven technology. Gentlemen, I assure you, we do not do business that way."

Mac replied, "Sir, we do not believe it was a failure of your new technology. We believe you were targeted exactly because of your new technology."

"Targeted? We were not even operational yet. Could this have resulted from some rogue militant group looking to make a point?"

"At this juncture, we are not ruling anything out. Are you confident it was some form of an EMP?" Mac asked, getting right to the heart of the matter.

Without hesitation, the Presidente said, "Absolutely confident. Someone attacked our dock soldiers and eliminated our antiaircraft weapon. The power plant is on a self-contained island, just as well guarded, but there was no physical attack. After the dock was neutralized, there was a low-level explosion above the island."

"Was there damage to the island as a result of the explosion?"

"There was no physical damage, but that leads to the most important point. Every electronic component became immediately inoperable. Every circuit was fried at once. There's nothing known that could cause immediate failure of everything electronic other than an EMP. Of course, a solar flare could lead to the same result." While still shaken up, the Presidente was confident in his conclusions.

"It was not a solar flare. First, we would have seen a solar flare from our monitoring stations well before landing anywhere on the Earth. Second, no solar flare took out all your dock soldiers with bullets and knives. That's an impossible coincidence. The Secretary is completely convinced you experienced a terrorist attack utilizing an EMP."

"I agree with you. I just do not know why. We have not had any direct or indirect threats on the facility."

"Maybe someone viewed you as a competitive threat and decided to take out your facility before you became an alternative option for inexpensive, green-friendly power."

"I must admit I don't trust some of my competitors. They freely throw around their political clout to ensure they shut down threats to their organizations. We are…"

The Presidente paused as tears started welling up in his eyes. "Let me correct that. We were certainly a threat simply based on our ability to produce inexpensive energy at a limitless level. However, I can't imagine any of our current competitors stooping so low as to destroy our new plant."

"Maybe it was a new competitor." Mac knew the Presidente was in a fragile state of mind and probably not much use to finding the culprits who attacked them. Mac continued, "I think we probably have as much information as possible from here. Can you have someone drop us off at the Rio dock so we can go to the island?"

"Of course. There's an automobile waiting for you at our front entrance that can drop you off anywhere. I am not sure you will learn much from the island. We will try and rebuild from scratch, but it will take us three to four years. I'm ruined. Everything is lost."

With that, the Presidente dropped his head into his hands and began uncontrollably sobbing.

Chapter 15

Rio Power Plant, Rio de Janeiro

After being dropped off at the Rio dock entrance and being waved past security thanks to the Presidente's advance call, Mac and Gunner walked through the area of the aftereffects of the attack. They noticed several soldiers and workers addressing a variety of necessities. If they had not known about the carnage and devastation, it could have been any busy dock worldwide. Upon reaching the antiaircraft weapon, Mac and Gunner found a couple of workers repairing where it had been riddled with bullet holes.

Gunner asked the two workers, "Do you know when the next skiff is running to the island?"

One worker replied, "It should be within five minutes. They have been continuously running all day."

"What's the deal with this weapon?"

"The antiaircraft weapon? We cannot fix it without a laundry list of replacement parts."

Gunner could not help feeling like they were being watched. "How long until the weapon is operational?"

"It will probably take three months. However, it does not matter. As I understand it, the island is completely shut down, and it will take years to start back up again. We will have a state-of-the-art weapon with nothing to protect."

"Good luck with that. Please excuse us. I see the skiff is almost here," Gunner said.

Mac and Gunner approached the pier, and Gunner sensed something slightly different about Mac. The feeling was making Gunner's neck tingle.

After they took their seats at the back of the skiff, Gunner whispered to Mac, "Did something feel weird to you on the dock?"

"Yes. I couldn't put my finger on it. Did you see anything?"

"No, but I felt it too."

"Well, once we disembark back on the dock, we will need to keep our heads on a swivel," Mac said.

"Roger that," Gunner replied.

Before long, they found themselves walking into the now-defunct power plant complex. It was an expansive building that was open in the center and filled with massive containers on stilts, a large pool of water, and a series of fans that laid still and quiet. There were workers dressed in white coats and hard hats everywhere. To add to the confusion, they were scrambling about like ants. Mac and Gunner dressed in their obligatory visitor's coat and hard hat. They marched up a four-story set of stairs to a walkway encircling the facility. At the opposite end of the walkway was a large jet-black office with huge windows overlooking the entire operation.

Once inside the office, they were greeted by the Plant Manager.

"Nice to meet both of you. The Presidente told me you were arriving," the Plant Manager said in perfect English.

Mac replied, "Thank you for having us. We will be brief because we know you are working around the clock."

"Thank you. What can I do for you?"

"We would like to tour the plant and hear what happened directly from you."

"Spending much time in our Control Center is useless. Simply put, we had a complete meltdown of all our circuitry."

"Does anything work?"

"No. Every single electrical component is fried. The only thing that works is this." He handed Mac a well-used and tanned stick with numbers on it. "I have carried that with me since I was in college."

Mac did not need to examine the stick to know it was a slide ruler that dated back to the early 1600s.

Gunner asked, "With no power to the plant, how can we see anything in here?"

"As you can see, we have no windows in here, so it was pitch black after the attack happened. We have boated in dozens of large portable battery-powered lights to at least see what we are doing. Several of my men are also working on restoring electricity here from an underground cable. Just getting electricity functioning in the plant will be a Herculean task. Every bit of incoming electricity was attached to a circuit, and all those circuits are fried."

Mac replied, "You said attack. Why do you think you were attacked?"

The Plant Manager responded, "It's quite simple. A few years ago, I was part of a technical research team that studied the effects of EMPs on circuitry. This mess is the classic result of an EMP. There's no doubt in my mind based on the way the circuits burned and melted. I have seen this previously from the research. Follow me, and I can show you."

As they toured the facility, the Plant Manager demonstrated the damage to components and equipment.

"What are these large containers on stilts?" inquired Mac.

"They contain the nanobots that are the foundation of our technology," the Plant Manager said.

"Were they damaged?"

"It is too early to tell. Certainly, the componentry that operates the containers housing the nanobots was destroyed. The exact mixture releasing the nanobots was based upon a highly engineered process. While we can recreate the approximate formula, each container's formula was tweaked repeatedly over the last year."

"What about the turbines that are in front of us?" Gunner asked.

"There was so much destroyed in the operating mechanisms, it will be more efficient to buy completely new turbines," the downtrodden Plant Manager responded.

"It sounds to me like the EMP was devastating to your facility. How quickly will you be back in operation?" Mac questioned.

"It's going to take years to get us back up and running," the Plant Manager said.

"I am sorry to hear that. I know you were very close to going live. Look, we do not want to keep you from your job. Thank you for taking the time with us, and good luck," Mac replied with deep sincerity.

The three shook hands, and Mack and Gunner made the trek back to the skiff.

Chapter 16

Rio Dock, Rio de Janeiro

Gunner broke the silence as they were once again in the back seats of the skiff and said, "It seems like there's no doubt the power plant was attacked with an EMP. Based upon someone taking the antiaircraft weapon out, I'd also say the attack had to come from the air."

"I agree. Plus, it was a hell of a shot from an airplane to drop the EMP device directly above the island," Mac replied.

"You mean a hell of a lucky shot. That pilot must have known he had all the time in the world to drop his payload."

The skiff landed at the Rio pier, and the two walked to the onshore dock. The dock looked the same as they had left it. There were workers feverously trying to repair the damage, cranes jutting into the sky, the security tower setting off in the distance, and an assortment of mechanical equipment ready for shipment to the island. The voice in the back of Mac's head was screaming at him again. Mac felt like he was being watched.

Out of nowhere, bullets began peppering all around them. Mack and Gunner hit the deck, crawling behind their cover, and the dockworkers and soldiers did the same. Gunner took a glance over the equipment protecting their hiding spot. His risk-taking move was welcomed with a barrage of gunfire.

Gunner said, "I think there are three on the far side behind those stacks of crates and two on the ledge about forty feet up. Unfortunately, we're pinned down, and there's no way we can get a shot at them. However, the soldiers' vantage points around us do not give them an angle to aim. We're stuck here until they pick us off one by one."

"That's not exactly true, and you can prove it." Mac grinned with a wink of his eye.

Gunner did not like the sound of that and replied, "Oh boy, here we go with another one of your crazy schemes. Let's hear it."

"The plan is simple. We need to get you to higher ground. You are a better shot than me, and we need those skills."

They were both expert marksmen. Mac felt staying in harm's way with minimal cover was riskier than making a break for the crane. He decided to have Gunner take the less dangerous job of being the sniper. It was Mac's Overactive Protective Gene going into high alert again.

Gunner nodded and pulled out from his coat pocket an assortment of pieces that would mean nothing to an ordinary person. Gunner was not the average Joe. He efficiently snapped pieces together like Tinker Toys to produce a modified Ruger SR-556 Takedown AR-15 rifle. Gunner's favorite modification on this weapon was a NightForce NXS sniper scope with an extremely powerful 25X magnification, allowing accurate shots at well over 1,000 yards. Gunner treated it with care because it cost almost as much as the Ruger rifle.

Mac was popping up regularly, returning fire without expecting to hit any of the shooters. His sole purpose was to keep them honest and not storm their position. Mac said, "I will give you cover fire. You need to climb up that large crane over there to give yourself a full field of fire."

"I see. *The Art of War*?"

"Let's just call it 'The Art of the Only Way We Get the Hell Out of This Alive.' Seriously, Gunner, if I don't make it out alive from this less-than-desirable cover spot, you need to E&E."

Gunner certainly did not need to be reminded that E&E, in military speak, means Evasion and Escape.

Mac continued, "We need the team to know what happened here so they can respond."

"Mac, I know why you are saying that, but we are in this together. Good or bad, we are both all-in to see this through to the end," Gunner knew they were outnumbered and in a tough spot.

"We certainly have been in worse spots than this." No other words were necessary from Mac.

Head nodding to each other, Mac and Gunner acknowledged the danger in front of them but with the comfort of knowing they had one another's backs. Mac simply said in quick spurts with a pause between each word, "On three. One. Two. Three!"

At three, Mac popped up and continued with a barrage of gunfire at the shooter's crates. When his mag ran dry, he smoothly seated a new full magazine, pulled the slide back, and started firing again. There was virtually no pause in the cover fire, and the shooters kept their heads down. Mac could not drop, using his cover, because he could not let the shooters get a bead on Gunner.

Gunner arrived at the shipyard crane base, somewhat surprised he didn't take a bullet from the shooters. Mac's cover fire worked. He flipped his assembled Ruger rifle over his shoulder and began climbing.

As he looked below, he could see the firefight unfolding. The shooters were not going to wait much longer. They began lobbing grenades at the hiding positions of their targets. Most of the grenade explosions were around their primary mark, Mac. Fortunately, Mac's cover did its job and kept the shrapnel at bay.

Arriving at his desired position, Gunner calmly pulled out his rifle. He was steady and comfortable. As he gazed through his sniper scope, all he could say on his comms was, "Shit."

Mac clicked back with, "Gunner, I don't like the sound of that. Talk to me."

"The shot is a no-go. Wrong angle."

"No problem. I have another idea."

"Great. Now it's a Double Declan Mac."

"Think of the bright side. You will have another great story to tell. Did you bring your international Longshoreman union card?" Mac said while the constant onslaught of bullets redefined his hiding space.

"Every once in a while, you make me think about applying for a position in a different profession. I'm in. Go ahead." After Mac briefly explained his backup plan, Gunner said, "On it."

Gunner climbed into the crane's cockpit and briefly familiarized himself with the crane operations. From Gunner's perspective, the controls were not that complex. Of course, that assumed he was not responsible for moving large containers and placing them in exact positions without treating them like bowling pins. If he didn't have to function with a crane operator's skill, what could go wrong?

The shooters kept getting closer with their grenades exploding danger-close. Mac wondered how many grenades a few guys could carry. Mac said on his comms, "Any time, Gunner. It's getting a little dicey down here."

"I don't know, Mac. I am getting the hang of this. I'll bet longshoremen make more than we do on our government salary."

"Make your move. You can practice later."

"I have a container lifted and am beginning to swing the container around toward the shooter's ledge hideout. That should give me enough of an angle and provide the cover I need to start returning fire at them," Gunner replied.

Gunner's lack of experience with the crane became quickly apparent. Like most things in his life, his reaction to moving the large metal container was way too aggressive. Instead of slowly moving it, he viciously swung it like a pendulum toward the shooters. It was not attached using the strength necessary to hold that level of torque. The lines snapped, flying like a rectangular bowling ball at the shooters' positions. Unfortunately for the shooters, they were the bowling pins.

Before the shooters could respond, the container did its damage. It landed on the fringe of the upper ledge, ripping open and spilling most of its stored inventory spraying. The container's final fate and resting place were to adhere to the principles of gravity. It slipped off the ridge and fell on top of the bowling pins below. The three shooters were crushed by its immense weight when it landed with a thunderous crack, slamming to the ground. There would be no more grenades thrown by those shooters.

At least initially, the final two shooters remaining on the ledge seemed to fare okay. The container missed them, but it still had some pin action left in it. The inventory that spilled across the ledge was barrels of crude oil. It was more appropriate to call it slippery oil. The fourth shooter slipped everywhere, hoping for some handhold to avoid sliding off the slanted ledge. The fifth shooter was nowhere to be seen and must have been washed away by the crude oil.

Mac saw that the fourth shooter was fighting for his life. He needed him to find out who sent this kill team to the Rio dock and provide insights on the previous attack and EMP release. Mac jumped up and sprinted to the ladder leading to the ledge holding the fourth shooter. He flew up the ladder, taking two rungs at a time. Jumping off the ladder, Mac began to slide and almost fell. After catching and righting himself, he carefully but quickly shuffled to the fourth shooter. He could see the terror in the shooter's eyes while dangling over the side of the ledge and holding on for dear life with his fingertips.

Mac said, "Hold on, man!" He fell to the ledge's surface and grabbed the wrists of the shooter.

"Please. Please help me. Don't let me fall!" the shooter screamed back.

"Who sent you?"

"Yes, I will tell you. Just pull me up!"

POWERLESS

As Mac tried to grab lower on the shooter's arms, a shadow descended over them. It was a sunny day, and, at first, Mac could not register what caused the shadow.

He turned his head to see the fifth shooter standing next to him with a handgun pointed at his forehead.

"Interesting. How the hell did you survive this slippery mess and make it here without falling?

This was it. After years of being a CIA operative, he finally looked death in the eyes. This cluster wasn't Mac's expectation of his final seconds. He was covered in the slippery oil and couldn't help but stare at the shooter's smile. It was a smile only a mother could love. He was missing several front teeth with a blood-soaked mouth from a likely nasty fall. With the shooter's bright, rosy complexion, Mac could not help but think he probably had devil horns hidden under his mop of dark hair.

Trying to ignore the sinister devil above him, Mac attempted one last-ditch effort and said, "If you kill me, I will drop your friend to his death."

The shooter only shrugged and stretched his arm out straight toward Mac as he looked down the barrel. With the shooter's callous response, there was no honor amongst this crew.

Mac accepted his fate and took a breath, waiting for the shot.

Unexpectantly, the man's sternum in front of him blasted open with a splat of flying bone and blood. Mac half anticipated an alien head popping out of the hole in his chest like in a science fiction horror film. The shooter did not shoot. He dropped open his mouth, and his eyes became as wide as saucers. The shooter only partially registered that he had just received a death shot, traveling from his back and exploding out the front of his chest. His legs crumpled underneath him. He dropped to the deck and rolled off the edge.

Mac followed the likely path of the round and saw Gunner standing on the crane's metal crossbars. He had his sniper rifle pointed in Mac's direction and waved his beefy hand. Mac only had time to return a half-upward head nod to Gunner for saving his life.

Being so distracted by the fifth shooter, Mac almost forgot about the other shooter dangling precariously over the edge. He turned to him, but it was too late. The shooter's grip was too far gone. Mac could no longer hold him, and the shooter began to fall. As if the shooter was hoping Mac had an undisclosed plan to save him if he traded information, the shooter yelled out, "Blackwood...." Before he could get more words out, he fell to his death into a broken mess below.

* * *

On their car ride back to the others at the CIA office within the Rio embassy, Mac called Brock.

Brock asked, "Did you learn anything new at the Rio dock or power plant island?"

"Negative. Confirmed our suspicions about the EMP. Gunner and I ran into five more shooters at the dock to ensure we did not make any more inquiries."

"You guys, okay?"

"Both filthy, but we are fine. It did not turn out so well for the shooters. Gunner played a wicked game of bowling with them."

"Were you able to question any of them?"

"All we were able to pick up was from one of the shooters who said the same name we heard on the recording, Blackwood."

Brock teased Mac by asking, "There were five guys, and you only got one word out of them? I thought you were more skilled than that."

Smiling at Gunner sitting beside him, Mac replied, "We were close with one of the shooters, but he slipped through my fingers."

Chapter 17

CIA Jet

Aboard the CIA jet heading back to Langley, the team struggled with the next steps. They had more questions than answers.

Valencia stated to no one in particular, "We found no actionable intel from the power plant offices. Employees filed no grievances, and no threat or ransom letters were received."

Brock responded, "We did find one piece of good information. All the test results and internal memos we read confirmed that the Rio power plant technology functioned properly before the EMP fried it. They were ready to go live."

Gunner contributed his perspective by adding, "We now have reasonable confirmation an EMP took out that power plant. It does not seem like an inside job, and the Plant Manager is taking it personally and damn frustrated."

Ryker, sitting in his preferred seat because it had no windows that caused glare on his computer screen, added, "I have nothing so far also. I will switch my search engines to see if I can find any usable data on the one Triple D Mac pulled out of Whispering Wind. If the connection stopped at exactly the right time, the Triple D might have a tiny amount embedded."

Mack walked into the main cabin looking dapper after his shower and fresh clothes. As usual, he was in complete physical and mental control of himself, even after coming within a thin hair away from getting killed a few hours ago. Mac added to the conversation by reminding everyone, "Do not forget that the last shooter said the word Blackwood."

The main cabin with the team was void of helpful data points. Mac encouraged them to brainstorm out loud and share even seemingly crazy ideas with each other. They all knew the only rule was that no one could ridicule another team member for any concept, as unrealistic as it might sound. Ridiculing ideas stifled creativity by ensuring wacky ideas would never bubble to the surface the next time. Mac found that the wackiest and boldest ideas out of left field often led to previously not considered solutions.

Ryker yelled out over the other voices, "Hold on, everyone! I think I scored some intel on the recovered Triple D. We all know where Whispering Wind has their manufacturing facility, right?"

In unison, they all responded with head nods, wondering where Ryker was heading with his findings.

Ryker triumphantly said, "Thailand. It confirms what we already learned from Mac's visit."

"That's not new intel. Did you learn anything else?" Mac asked.

"Whispering Wind's Thailand plant was one step away from a full liquidation before Whisp took the money from the gangsters. From what Whisp documented in cover-his-ass emails to his personal files, he said they were the worst kind of gangsters and into everything bad. After taking the gangsters' money, Whisp felt he had no option but to become part of their criminal empire. Then an investor came along like a white knight and retired the gangster's debt."

"I think we should rename the company and call it the 'Phoenix' because they rose out of ashes." Mac clarified.

After speculation about other potential Whisp motivations, Ryker jumped back into the discussion with additional information. "I have one last germane data point from the Triple D. Whispering Wind just completed enclosing their manufacturing facility in a Faraday Cage."

A few of the team responded with quizzical looks.

Brock responded with, "A far away, what?"

Ryker corrected him. "A Faraday Cage. A Faraday cage, or shield, blocks electromagnetic fields that can be caused by highly charged events such as solar flares, lightning strikes, or, in our case, EMPs. It was named after its inventor, Michael Faraday, in 1836. A Faraday cage works by covering or enclosing electronics with a mesh of conductive material that's grounded all around the cage. For Faraday shields, it's a continuous covering enclosing the electronics. They are used in a variety of situations for sensitive equipment. You can even buy Faraday shields in the form of a pouch on the internet if you want to protect your precious cell phone."

Bringing it back to their specific situation, Ryker continued, "It had to be incredibly expensive to enclose an entire plant in a Faraday cage. I cannot fathom why someone would enclose a plant like that unless they were a sci-fi freak worried about doomsday scenarios."

Valencia noted, "That's one heck of a coincidence. Whispering Wind Industries battery facility installing a Faraday cage and an EMP attack in Rio. The only unusual issue is they are in different parts of the world."

Mac jumped in and said, "Brock, tell the pilot to reroute. Langley can wait. We are heading to Thailand."

Chapter 18

Whispering Wind Battery Manufacturing Plant, Thailand

Mac and Valencia headed for the front gate after parking their rental car in the Whispering Wind battery manufacturing plant's parking garage.

As they walked up to the simple front entrance, Mac said, "This mushroom dome does not look like any plant I have ever seen."

Valencia added, "I am not even sure what I am looking at."

Mac added, "This almost looks like one of those biospheres people stay in to simulate the moon or some other self-contained environment. You can barely see through the metal mesh that covers the entire plant. This lattice is a Faraday cage, just as Ryker explained it."

"If they refuse to see us, we can easily break into this wire contraption. It does not look like there's any security."

Valencia pushed on a keypad button to announce themselves, like entering some New York multi-apartment brownstone.

"Immediately step back, look into the video camera on your left, and display your credentials," a voice from a speaker barked at them.

They both responded as directed. Mac would not allow this bullying treatment and said, "My name is Declan Mac, and this is my associate. Joe Whisp engaged our consulting firm from the corporate office to ensure the plant operates efficiently. We are here to identify excess costs to eliminate. We have been traveling for quite some time and would like to speak with the Plant Manager now."

Mac knew there was no way for the guard or the Plant Manager to confirm his story. There was no one in the States to call. However, he had met with Joe Whisp, and therefore, it was partially honest. Also, it never hurts to knock people back on their heels. His tactic was to make it sound like Mac and Valencia had the power to fire whomever they wanted in the name of efficiency. People reacted to that role the same way worldwide. It was met with a mixture of overt helpfulness while silently being terrified they could be on the termination list. These consultants were dangerous and needed to be treated with kid gloves.

The gate lock buzzed open, and this time, with no hint of threatening superiority, the guard said, "Please step inside the gate and stop for the next security check."

The following security check was thorough. The first thing Mac noticed was that the guards were visibly armed. Each wore green combat clothing, a black beret, and black combat boots. Their weapon of choice was an AK-47, the Russian-made assault rifle preferred by many militaries and militant groups. Mac could not tell if they were carrying other weapons, but it was unnecessary. Mac could see snipers from the plant's rooftop scoping him and Valencia. Mac was glad neither of them carried any weapons during the pat-down and inspection of their bags.

While never comfortable, field operatives often had to go into potentially hostile situations with no outright weapons. With their covers as business consultants, it would be out of place if they were packing a concealed weapon of any sort. Given the unforeseen risk with fifteen visible AK-47s and the menacing sniper rifles pointed in their direction, it was safer for them not to carry handguns. Mac was not concerned with his lack of firepower. The typical office has no less than 25 items available for lethal weapons in close hand-to-hand combat. Mac has used them all at different times in his career.

Mac and Valencia were led into the Plant Manager's office. There were no family pictures around, suggesting he was single or did not want anyone at the plant to know he had a family. He was short, fit, and had dark hair. Mac noticed his eyes had a confused and panicked look. It was clear the guard forewarned him at the gate that these consultants from corporate were in Thailand to fire people and could terminate anyone at will.

After shaking hands, everyone sat down. Mac and Valencia didn't say a word. This strategy was to add to the tension in the room.

The Plant Manager broke the silence and asked, "Welcome to Whispering Wind Industries' Thailand plant. We were not informed of your consulting agreement. How was your trip here?"

Consistent with the ruse, Mac responded with, "Tiring and long. We had better justify the travel cost and effort to get here. Most plants we see have some level of inherent inefficiency. Don't worry. We will quickly identify the excess costs to eliminate. Usually, it's as simple as firing several people or changing management to someone more cooperative."

The Plant Manager looked to be in an almost outright panic attack. In a weak but gallant effort to redirect the discussion, he replied, "Yes, I am sure you had a very long trip. I am here to help you with anything you need. I have been at this facility for a very long time, and I am sure I can provide anything critical for your analyses. We run a very efficient operation here, and our production is running at full capacity."

"Really? How do you know you are running efficiently? Do you have efficiency reports that compare your productivity to other battery operators?" Mac easily slid into the business consultant role and began asking typical consulting questions.

"Well, no. But when you walk into the plant, you can see for yourself my people work at a breakneck pace."

"I am sure everyone works fast. Our concern is that everyone is working smart. Do you have an ERP system?"

"I'm not sure I have ever heard of that term."

"An Enterprise Resource Planning system is an integrated management tool that coordinates real-time business processes. Once fully installed, it provides critical managerial information for the efficient operation of a business."

"No. We have been so busy the last two years with the new technology and cranking out products that we have not had time. Before that, we did not have the money. We never bothered looking into an ERP system for our operation." The

Plant Manager's weaknesses in running the facility began to scream at Mac.

Valencia asked, "It sure looks like you have cranked up your security for a simple battery manufacturing plant. This facility is guarded like a nuclear power plant. Can we take costs out of there?"

"I don't have anything to do with the security. Those guys report directly to corporate headquarters and are not included in my financial statements."

Assuming the Plant Manager was not lying about the security expense's location, Mac and Valencia knew it was a dead-end and not worth pursuing further. They needed to keep the heat up on the Plant Manager, knowing that stress causes people to be more likely to slip secrets.

Mac looked at him with disappointment. He said, intentionally using Whisp's first name, "Joe is quite concerned you are falling behind, and costs are getting out of control."

Valencia took a slight but calculated risk, saying, "With the huge expenditure for the Faraday cage that encases your facility, how do you justify the cost?"

Not realizing that he was confirming Valencia's question regarding the authenticity of the Faraday cage, the Plant Manager replied, "The Faraday cage was not even my idea. Putting a Faraday cage around this plant seems stupid, and I told Mr. Whisp that in no uncertain terms. I cannot imagine why we would ever even benefit from a Faraday cage."

That was it. The Faraday cage was confirmed. To give the Plant Manager a little win before he completely broke down into a chocolate mess, Mac said, "We completely agree with you. The Faraday cage is overkill. There's no way you will ever have a return on investment for that capital expenditure."

Nonchalantly, Mac asked out of nowhere, "Hey, did you deal with Blackwood on that?"

Chapter 19

Whispering Wind Battery Manufacturing Plant, Thailand

The Plant Manager frowned at the mention of Blackwood's name and rocked his head back and forth. He replied, "No. Mr. Whisp instructed me to build it directly. I have never heard of this guy, Blackwood. Who's he?"

Mac said, "No one. He must be from a different client. Since you do not have any ERP reports, we will have to analyze your operations the old-fashioned way. It will take some time, but we will have answers at the end of the analysis. When can you start providing us with production and expense reports?"

"Immediately."

"I understand you are manufacturing a new battery design here. Tell me more," Mac also wanted to confirm the evolution of their product.

"Yes. About two years ago, Mr. Whisp sent us designs for a new and next-generation battery. We didn't even know that Whispering Wind had an R&D department. Thank goodness they secretly did. I think we were losing money on every battery we sold."

"Have you sold any of your redesigned batteries yet?" Valencia asked.

"No. Mr. Whisp thinks there will be a huge initial demand, and he wants inventory to the rafters before an announcement of the technological breakthrough."

Mac replied, "Understood. Joe mentioned that to me, too."

The Plant Manager offered, "Let me show you to our conference room. I will have my assistant bring the reports to you shortly. This afternoon, I would be happy to give you a plant tour. That will give you the necessary context for your questions and a better perspective on our operations."

"That works well for us. We need to complete several analyses in a short time," Valencia noted.

After being directed to the conference room with obligatory directions to the coffee pot and restroom, Mac and Valencia found themselves alone.

"It does not sound like the Plant Manager knows anything about the mystery investor. How do we get that information if the guy running this joint does not even know him?" Valencia quietly said to Mac.

Mac replied, "I need time alone in his office. We cannot take the chance that he would simply leave us here by ourselves tonight. Even if he left us alone, I bet one of those guards would be stationed right outside our door."

"Ok. I can take care of the Plant Manager for a short period while you're doing recon. I'll have him give me a plant tour."

Mac said, "Copy that. Make sure to give me a heads up when you are returning so that I'm not caught in the wrong place at the wrong time."

Valencia walked into the Plant Manager's office. He seemed pleased to see her. Mac could not hear the two of them, but he could see their banter and laughter.

"Do you run this entire plant by yourself?" Valencia asked the Plant Manager. The question was phrased to help establish a welcoming relationship and feed his ego.

The Plant Manager said proudly, "Yes, I run this entire plant, but I have assistants providing me information so that I can make the important decisions."

Valencia replied, "You mentioned a plant tour when we first arrived. I would like to start my work with it because it gives me a better perspective of the business flows. Could you take me on that tour now?"

Chapter 20

Whispering Wind Battery Manufacturing Plant, Thailand

Mac gave Valencia and the Plant Manager a few minutes to leave the office area for the tour. After scanning the hallway, he slipped into the Plant Manager's office. Unlike the movies, Mac rarely found good intel hidden in a secret safe. The first place he looked was on top of the desk. His photographic memory was an incredible asset at times like this. Mac could recall every piece of paper and its location on the desk with a short, focused stare.

The Plant Manager was not a very neat fellow. Papers were strewn across every corner, including a series of directives from headquarters, production staffing plans, and plant financial statements. Mac returned each document to the same place he found it. He did this as a precaution because the Plant Manager could be someone messy on the surface but knew where every disorganized piece of paper was located. He changed his attention to the laptop connected to an oversized screen.

The laptop was password protected. Mac inserted a memory stick into the USB port. It was loaded with communication software tied directly into Ryker's machine. Mac sent a simple text to Ryker, saying, "Access required."

"Copy. Communication in process and looking for a solution." Ryker texted Mac.

After a few minutes with no apparent progress, Mac texted back, "Status?"

"Sophisticated protection on the machine. Working on it," Ryker texted.

Mac was accustomed to having Ryker jump past any computer password protection or firewall software and roll right into the machine's files and other data. Mac called it the "Jump and Roll." For once, Ryker's "Jump and Roll" was not working.

Getting impatient, Mac teased Ryker with a text saying, "I'm changing the name for this to 'Crawl and Fall' unless you can open this machine quickly."

Just after sending the text, the Plant Manager's computer opened with a caricature of a smiling Ryker and a bubble comment saying, "You're welcome for the Jump and Roll."

Mac grinned. He knew Ryker had come through for the team again. As Mac began rifling through emails, he noticed four boxes on the side of the screen. Each box was a live video feed from a different camera location, including the conference room, the hallway leading into the office area, the plant floor, and the entrance.

After reading one long but useless email, Mac saw movement on the screen in the hallway. A guard was walking directly toward the Plant Manager's office. Mac considered his options, which included taking the guard out. However, he passed on that option because he did not know how to explain it if the guard did not return to his post after completing his rounds. Mac also looked under the desk. Based on the guard's thorough pat-down at the front entrance, he suspected the guard would do a complete inspection of the office. Instead, Mac opted to hide in the Plant Manager's closet. The guard was about to reach the edge of the office windows.

Mac was lucky and had enough space between the shelving and the closet door to stand. Seeing the guard through the gap created between the edges of the closet's double doors was an added benefit. The guard, dressed in his full military fatigues and carrying his rifle, walked past the office door. Mac thought, "Oh, thank God."

However, the guard stopped a few paces past the office. He put his hands defiantly on his hips, looked up to an imaginary sky, and blew air out of his mouth. He said out loud to no one, "I know, I know. Rounds must be thorough. Closely check everywhere that someone could be hiding! This is ridiculous. No one could get past our front security detail without permission." In a dejected manner, he turned on his heels and walked directly into the Plant Manager's office.

The first place the guard looked was behind the door. He appeared surprised to see that the Plant Manager's suit jacket was not there. The room's only furniture was the Plant Manager's desk, an oval working table, and eight chairs. No one could hide behind the table and chairs, so he walked behind the desk and looked down. The floor was empty.

The guard stared at the Plant Manager's desk with a frown. He talked out loud to himself again and said, "I could do your job. You probably make in a month what I make in a year. Someday, you will work for me."

There was only one more place to inspect: the closet. The guard decided to take a quick peek into the closet and continue his rounds. He turned and opened the double doors with a look of trepidation on his face.

All he saw in the dark closet were the same white shelves that were always there. Talking to his imaginary friend, he said, "Now you have me all jumpy. Stop that. You will make me look like an idiot in front of the others. This building is the most secure facility in Thailand." He took a deep breath and let it out as he shook his head and threw closed the closet's double doors.

Mac was not a magician. He had not learned how to make himself disappear, even if occasionally, the skill could have proven very useful. However, going undetected in certain situations was a critical espionage skill. Seeing the guard start his inspection by looking behind the door, Mac knew there was no way the guard would pass on looking in the closet. His only option was to climb up the walls quietly by pushing his feet against one sidewall and his hands against the opposite sidewall. Facing downward, he alternatively moved his hands and feet toward the ceiling.

By the time the guard had opened the closet door, Mac's arms and legs were shaking from the exertion, but luckily, he had not started sweating. The drops would have easily given his hiding spot away by showering the guard once he stuck his head inside the closet.

Mac paused in his spider-like position for another minute until he was sure the guard was long gone. He dropped to the floor, landing on his feet in a cat-like move. He returned to the Plant Manager's computer with a renewed sense of purpose. It did not take long for Mac to find his first lead. While the emails did not reveal the investor's identity, one described a hand messenger dispatched from the investor for the plant's regular status report. The hand messenger was due to arrive today. Mac stored the email in his photographic memory. The investor must not trust anything electronic, including telephones.

Still focused on reading emails, Mac almost missed new movement in the hallway video feed on the computer screen. This was not good. Mac did not have adequate time to make it up to his spider's perch in the closet. He saw two people walking down the hallway, a guard with another man in tow. Mac had no other choice but to drop to the floor and hide behind the desk. He craved having his pistol.

The guard escorted the hand messenger into the Plant Manager's office. They each took a seat in the chairs in front of the desk. The hand messenger had been to this office before and made himself at home by grabbing a couple of pieces of candy from a candy dish.

The hand messenger said to the guard, "This guy is never in his office when I show up."

The guard responded defensively, "Our Plant Manager is a very busy man. He does not have time to sit around waiting for you to show up at some unannounced time."

"Whatever. It's still really irritating. You know I must hand-deliver the status reports to the investor within a compact window. Last time, I was about five minutes late, and

I honestly thought he would have his big henchman kill me on the spot. They can easily replace me with a different messenger. So, you will have to excuse me if I seem a little anxious to receive the package and be on my way."

Not sounding a bit worried at all, the guard said, "If that's what you say. Why don't we have you wait in your usual office? There's no one assigned to that office, and it's empty."

"That is fine, but you must take me past that free coffee machine with those little pods. I desperately need some caffeine, and the price is always right."

The two men walked out of the room and down the hallway. It was too risky for Mac to stay in the Plant Manager's office much longer, but he needed additional intel. He still did not have the investor's name and sat back in the chair to search for intel documents on the computer. His phone vibrated with a text in his pocket, and he pulled it out. It was from Valencia. She had run out of time using her feminine influence and charm. Undoubtedly, the Plant Manager concluded he still had a plant to run, and this distracting extracurricular activity must be postponed to an evening discussion. Valencia's text read, "Exfil now. On our way."

Mac was still waiting for the search to complete. There were a ton of files on the network, slowing down the search results. Mac had enjoyed his last two hiding spots but did not treasure the idea of pushing his luck. He knew the search was almost complete. While sitting there, he formulated a plan in his head.

The Plant Manager was confidently striding along with Valencia. As they walked past his office, Valencia glanced over with relief to see it was empty. They turned directly into the conference room, and Mac was fixated on his laptop screen.

"Mr. Mac, you certainly must enjoy traveling with such an intelligent associate," the Plant Manager said.

"Of course. Valencia is one of our brightest and most efficient consultants. She always knows how to turn a major distraction into the foundation of our plan," replied Mac.

"I can certainly see that conclusion from any sane person," the Plant Manager said. Turning to Valencia with a self-assured grin, the Plant Manager said, "It was a pleasure spending time with you, and I look forward to continuing our discussion."

"You are much too kind. Thank you for the tour. It was what we needed to be successful at your facility," Valencia replied.

The Plant Manager nodded at Mac and turned out of the conference room.

Once out of earshot, Mac said, "Your timing couldn't have been any better. Did you learn anything useful during your tour?"

"There was nothing out of the ordinary. The Plant Manager limited his editorial comments, and I saw nothing strange in the plant. It looks like a legitimate battery manufacturing facility."

"The plant may be legit, but there is something strange with corporate reporting. There's a hand messenger down the hall that will be delivering a package to the investor. The messenger is regularly here and looks too comfortable to have his antenna up. I have a half-baked plan."

Chapter 21

Whispering Wind Parking Garage, Thailand

After collecting their things from the conference room, Mac and Valencia left for the Plant Manager's office.

Mac said to the Plant Manager, "You have been very helpful today. Your assistant delivered the reports we need for our analyses. Unfortunately, we are both running out of battery, pun intended."

The three of them all smiled at the weak attempt at humor. Mac continued, "With our jet lag, we are going to head to our hotel and get a good night's sleep so that we are ready to start early tomorrow."

The Plant Manager, looking disappointed, said, "Of course. I was hoping we could arrange to have dinner together tonight, but we can wait until tomorrow night if you wish."

With that, they said their goodbyes, left via the front gate, and took the outside elevator down to the below-ground parking garage.

"Are you sure this messenger guy has a rental car?" Valencia said.

"No. However, a rental car is the fastest way to the airport, and I know this guy has a short turnaround time. He played it cool in the office, but I think he was crapping his pants because he had to wait for the package he was supposed to hand-carry to the investor. We need a discussion with this guy. We are on the only floor of the parking garage that allows guest parking. If he has a rental car, it's parked on this floor."

Valencia tried radioing the plan to the team, but there was no signal. There was no signal for Mac as well. The problem must be that the garage had no cell phone service. They would have to update the team on the plan once they were no longer subterranean.

Almost on cue, the hand messenger exited the parking garage elevator and strode to his rental car. He was carrying a thick and sealed manilla envelope with purportedly the documents he was charged to deliver. Mac and Valencia jumped out of their car and jogged over to the hand messenger. As Mac expected, the hand messenger was so focused on leaving that he did not notice any movement around him. At the bumper of his car, he was surprised as Mac and Valencia slipped behind his shoulders. In shock, he screamed out, "Hey!"

Mac pulled a syringe out of his suit jacket pocket in a practiced and coordinated movement that looked like a writing pen and thrust the needle into the hand messenger's neck. Mac pushed the plunger down to the stop and withdrew the needle. Just as it left the messenger's skin, his legs crumpled beneath him while Mac and Valencia caught him under his armpits. His chin dropped to his chest, and his body was a wet rag. The CIA had tools at its disposal that were exceptionally effective.

The research and development department completed a variety of initiatives that were critical in field operations. Syringes that look like simple writing pens but contain various drug concoctions resulted from one initiative. The hand messenger would wake up in about four hours with no recollection of the recent events.

After picking up the hand messenger's package, Mac and Valencia dragged him toward their car. The hand messenger's feet slid behind him, and there was no fight from the manhandling. Mac popped the trunk, and they dropped his upper body into the compartment. As they were flipping his legs up, a guard saw them. Whether the guard was alerted by the hand messenger's inadvertent yell or just making his rounds for security checks, he appropriately assessed the unusual situation.

"Stop at once! Security!" the guard yelled.

Not wanting to wait around for the guard to question them regarding an apparent kidnapping, Mac and Valencia finished flipping the hand messenger's legs into the trunk and slammed it shut. The guard covered about half of the ground to the car before Mac could back their car out of the parking spot.

The guard screamed on his radio to alert the other guards of the kidnapping. He ran the short distance back to a security car parked in an assigned spot and threw the car into reverse. The chase was on.

The rental car struggled with Mac's sharp turning and screeching tires, which were not made for aggressive driving. Frequently on the 360-degree corners, Mac inadvertently slammed the rental car into the ill-fated parked autos around the corner. Those autos provided a convenient side bumper as he determined the most effective angles to orchestrate the narrow garage at maximum speed.

Valencia opened the glovebox and felt for one of her favorite toys. Her hand found the handle of her polymer-framed 9mm SIG Sauer P320 pistol. With its 17-round capacity, the P320 felt like an extension of her arm. She racked the slide back and put one in the pipe.

Mac said, "Every time I hear you do that, it reinforces the comforting concept of locked and loaded."

With an almost gleeful grin, Valencia looked at Mac and said, "I never leave home without it." She added, "We have four flights to go up, and that security car is gaining fast on us."

Mac calmly said, "Copy that. Suggestions?"

"How about let's start with getting a rental car that handles better than this cheap piece of shit?"

"What? Do you know the daily cost of premium rentals? However, I'm concerned we didn't take out the full vehicle damage insurance." Both Mac and Valencia smiled and knew they were in their element.

Chapter 22

Thailand Streets

Mac and Valencia took another corner too quickly, resulting in being violently thrown to the side by another version of Mac's bumper cars. The sudden stop of their forward momentum allowed the guard the necessary time to aim and fire his weapon at the rental car. The rear glass exploded, but no significant mechanical components were hit. Mac slammed the accelerator to the floor, and the underpowered little engine showed it was still peppy.

With two floors to go, the back windshield was peppered with automatic fire. Valencia was returning fire but had the disadvantage of being thrown around in the skidding car's dash for safety. The guard held his gun outside his window with one hand and effectively drove with the other hand. He was blanketing Mac and Valencia's car with bullets, and their best bet to stay alive was continuing to move.

The rental car was not made for this handling. The tires were its main challenge because they were not wide enough for Mac's demands on them. They were made for fuel efficiency, not a Formula One auto race.

Mac caught a break. The guard had emptied his mag and pulled his weapon onto his lap to reload with another mag. This relieved Mac from the onslaught of lead tagging their car with an assortment of dings and thuds. Mac yelled to Valencia, "We'll be at the exit once I make this last corner. I think we're finally clear of this death trap,"

Mac and Valencia made the corner and faced the welcoming daylight from the garage exit. Unfortunately, their luck was not going to hold out. Two guards anticipated this outcome and stepped out to block the exit lane with their guns pointed at Mac and Valencia's car. The guards began to empty their magazines at the oncoming vehicle. Valencia did not need any instructions on her next steps and acted without hesitation. She hung out her window and dropped both guards with two double taps from her SIG Sauer. She then calmly slipped back into her seat.

The rental car went airborne as it escaped the parking garage ramp exit that was steeply angled upwards. When the vehicle no longer touched the pavement, it became eerily silent. The only sound was the engine revving. For a second, they seemed to float in mid-air. Unfortunately, the car didn't have wings, and gravity did a number on them.

Like all good things that must come to an end, so did their flight. The car landed hard, with Mac trying to gain control as it slid from side to side. Fortunately, traffic was light around the plant, allowing Mac to focus on steering in a straight line.

Valencia took advantage of being free of the communications black hole and pinged the team to give them a sitrep. "We are outside the manufacturing facility and mobile. Plan changed. Need immediate exfil."

Brock's voice came on in both their ears, "Copy that. Likely water extract. Additional sitrep?"

"Confirmed Faraday cage and new battery design. Our cover is blown. We have a passenger that might be able to lead us to the mystery investor."

"Copy that. You were always good at making friends. We commandeered a flat-backed pleasure boat on the Chao Phraya River. We are fueled up and docked on the south side of Bangkok. Given that the Chao Phraya runs through Bangkok, it gives us perfect cover for a quiet exit."

Valencia had a different take on their planned water cruise. "You what? The Chao Phraya. Negative. We need air exfil. Our vehicle is shot up and slower than the pursuers who are hot on our tail. A southern pickup location requires driving through congested parts of Bangkok." She quickly ejected the mag in her pistol and checked for the remaining rounds. She added, "Plus, I am almost out of ammo. Other options?"

"Negative. Airspace is temporarily shut down over Bangkok due to some construction at the airport. This exfil is the best alternative. We did not anticipate a rapid exfil and planned to use this yacht as our command post."

"On our way to your coordinates. Out." Valencia hung up and said, "Shit. We're fucked."

Mac was weaving in and out of traffic as it began to build while approaching Bangkok. Bangkok was like any other major city, with heavy traffic in the best case and complete stop-and-go traffic jams during the day's worst times.

Valencia asked Mac, "What's your plan with the traffic?"

Mac replied while focusing on driving, "It's not the traffic that concerns me. I am worried about the potential deaths of pedestrians, motorcyclists, bicyclists, and Tuk-tuks filling the streets and sidewalks. They could get mowed down. My biggest concern is those ubiquitous Tuk-tuks that drive so aggressively, thinking that cars and trucks will always avoid them."

Looking in the half of his rearview mirror that was not shot apart with bullets, Mac did not like what he saw. He said to Valencia, "We have five tails on our six, and they're closing fast. They must have brought their fleet of bad-guy cars. I think they want their hand messenger back."

The five guard cars followed like snakes slithering around the traffic on the path created by Mac. Mac knew he would have to make some split-second decisions that could make the difference between life and death.

An overly confident guard hung out the passenger side window, firing crazy shots from the front guard car. The unpredictability of those shots made them dangerous, especially for those unsuspecting souls in Bangkok.

Bangkok is a thriving metropolis and the Thai capital known for its food and shopping. The problem was that there were food vendors and street shopping everywhere. It was a wonderful place to go incognito and lose a tail as a pedestrian. Unfortunately, there were currently six 3,000-pound, potential killing machines rocketing toward those unlucky enough to be in their path. Mac had to avoid the city's busiest parts, or the death toll would be huge.

Mac needed to slow the five pursing cars, so he headed for the Victory Monument roundabout. He knew the guards would tire of circling in the roundabout and eventually stop. Their likely plan would be to stop on turnoff streets to allow an easy shot at Mac and Valencia as they drove past. The first circle around went as expected, and the guards followed quickly behind them. Halfway into the second circle, Mac saw the lead guard car talking on his handheld microphone from the car radio, just like in police cars. Mac deduced that the next trip around was when they were setting their trap.

Once out of Mac's vision, all five cars slowed and pulled off with guns, ready for a shooting gallery. However, Mac was planning for that. He exited just opposite the guards before the guards had the chance to rip Mac and Valencia apart with bullets like Bonnie and Clyde's final stand. It took several helpful seconds for the guards to realize Mac was not taking another circle of the monument.

When they realized their failed strategy, the guards gunned their engines in unison to get back into the chase. In their frustration, none of them checked for circling traffic. The fifth car was crushed by a 16-foot box truck driving in the outside lane. The car's front corner panel took most of the impact as the entire vehicle was thrown to the side while the massive truck barely veered off its course. The guard's engine began to hiss and spit out steam. He tried to restart his car in a useless attempt, but fortuitously for Mac and Valencia, he was out of the chase.

The four remaining guard cars were rocketing down the road to catch up. Mac could see them approaching quickly. He told Valencia, "I am going to slow up and let the lead guard catch up."

Valencia screamed back, "Did you say that you are going to slow up?"

Mac said it again and quickly explained the complete plan.

Valencia simply nodded and responded, "Let's do this."

Just like the steering wheel was on the right side in Thailand, you also drove on the left side of the road. Mac slowed up, allowed the left lane next to them to be clear for the guard, and ensured no other cars or pedestrians were nearby. Their timing was critical.

As the lead pursuer pulled alongside Mac's car on the passenger side, he smiled with the expectation of an easy kill. Valencia smiled back. The guard shrugged his shoulders and pulled his pistol from his lap, pointing it directly at Valencia. At that exact moment, Mac jerked his steering wheel to the left, aiming at the guard's car. The weight of Mac's car forced the guard to veer off into the parking lane on the side.

Unfortunately for the guard, a semi-trailer was sitting with its rear doors open and ramps leading up into its storage area. Without slowing, he flew up the ramp into the back of the trailer. Upon abruptly crashing inside the trailer, the car burst into flames, and the resulting explosion lifted the trailer's rear wheels a foot off the ground.

There was no time for a celebration. Mac and Valencia were driving past the famous Erawan Shrine that provides an ornate structure holding the bright gold statute of a sitting Phra Phrom, the Hindu god of creation. Unsuspecting worshippers were encircling the Erawan Shrine with their hands together in prayer. This spot was dangerous for the guards' bullets to pepper Mac and Valencia's car. Mac had been driving flawlessly until now, but his luck ran out.

While swerving around a slower junky car in front of him, Mac chose the wrong lane and found himself behind an even slower junkier car. It was inevitable. Like the constant lane-changers in rush hour, Mac and Valencia were boxed in, eventually finding themselves stuck behind a slower car.

The lead pursuer took advantage of the tactical mistake and accelerated past Mac. Once Mac reversed his mistake, he saw the guards' likely strategy. After all, it was what he would do. Mac concluded that the lead guard would maneuver in front of Mac and Valencia's car, and the guards behind them would close the trap. Mac would be forced to slow to a stop, and Mac and Valencia would be executed where they sat.

Mac saw his chance. He accelerated, forcing their car just past the back-left bumper of the guard's car. Mac learned his next move during his CIA "Farm" training. He violently jerked his steering wheel to the left, striking the guard's rear quarter panel. The inertia of the impact caused the guard's car to begin sliding sideways, with its tail end quickly moving forward.

The screeching tires could only hold the pavement for so long, and the guard overcorrected for his sideways-moving vehicle. At the excessive speed they were traveling, the front side of the guard's car lifted off the road as it began to flip over, thanks to pushing force from the front of Mac's car. The guard's car continued to flip while airborne, just like a pool diver executing a spinning blur of movement for a perfect dive. Mac instinctively ducked, but his roof was untouched by the airborne guard's car. Unfortunately for the guard behind Mac, gravity caused the airborne vehicle to land on the trailing pursuer. The guards were all killed simultaneously in a ball of fire.

The fifth guard skillfully skirted around the two smashed guard cars in front of him. He accelerated, quickly gaining on Mac and Valencia. Mac saw the guard approaching in his rearview mirror and shared his last plan with Valencia. Valencia checked the magazine in her P320 pistol and realized only two bullets were left. She was going to need to make them count.

As Mac slowed, he drew the guard car close to their passenger side. Mac hoped the guard would pull up next to them, allowing Valencia the kill shot. However, this guard would not make the same mistakes as his associates. He pulled his weapon outside his window and carefully aimed at Mac to take out the driver.

Valencia made a tactical change of plans. She popped half out her window facing towards their rear with her P320 pointed at the guard. She fired her two remaining bullets in quick succession, but she only needed one of them. They hit the guard center mass, and he went flying backward in his seat before he could even pull his trigger. The newly driverless car slid off the road and rammed the concrete fencing protecting one of the many Bangkok canals. The car continued its momentum and flipped end over end into the water, fortunately hitting no one.

Valencia crawled back into the car.

Mac said to her, "Nice shot. You had better put on your seatbelt. Traffic today is a killer."

"Oh, please. There you go again with those Mac jokes," Valencia said while rolling her eyes at the comment. They both exchanged a glance and had to smile at each other. They knew each was a critical component of the team's success, and neither could have survived the chase without the other one.

Mac pulled off the main road and went down an access road to the dock. The team had the yacht backed into a docking slip, with its open aft looking way too inviting. He drove off the edge, settling at the aft of the boat. Everyone stared in amazement at an idling car filling the open rear.

The car was bullet-riddled and barely running. When Mac turned off the key, the vehicle made a painful chugging sound and took its last breath. The yacht was weighed down by the car, but its massive engines pulled the boat away from the dock.

Mac said to the team, "Thanks for the boat cruise. Our new advisor is resting comfortably in the trunk. Could someone please pull him out and question him when he wakes up so we can finally learn the name of the mystery investor?"

Chapter 23

The Democratic Republic of the Congo, Power Plant Unveiling
Ten Years Ago

Forest Blackwood was standing on a tall stage, feeling like a king speaking to his people. He knew he was not a king, but having hundreds and hundreds of people gazing up at him made him feel adored. Blackwood had never received this type of reception before, and it was a little embarrassing for him. He was an altruistic and shy man in his late 30s. Forest had always lived in the shadow of his wealthy family. The purpose of the speech was to announce the availability of dependable power to this impoverished country.

Forest was tall with handsome features. His slender frame and good looks were consistent with his aristocratic heritage. Frustrating those chartered with managing his estate, Forest had a generous heart. At age ten, he lost his parents and tried to live his life consistent with his vision of their expectations. Through his years of persistence, Forest pursued engineering in school and earned his Ph.D., thereby bestowing the title "Doctor." Forest wore a custom-made dark wool suit with a white cotton shirt and a red silk tie for this occasion. While this selection did not fit Africa's oppressive heat and humidity, it was consistent with his comfort zone.

The event, covered by all the major news outlets globally, was the unveiling of a new-generation power plant providing inexpensive electricity to the Democratic Republic of the Congo, formerly known as Zaire, until 1997. Not to be confused with its neighbor, the Republic of Congo, which has a significantly higher GDP, the Democratic Republic of the Congo was a country in need of many essential life services for the impoverished population. Electricity could pave the way for a better life.

Forest wasted no time once the applause stopped to address the crowd in a prepared speech. "I want to thank the government of the Democratic Republic of the Congo for allowing me to speak with you today and for allowing us to provide inexpensive and reliable electricity to the Congo." He paused to accept the applause and waited until it slowed.

"Central Africa, especially the Democratic Republic of the Congo, will enjoy long-lasting benefits from our electricity. Without this electricity for those impoverished, there is no light in the evenings, no cooling for homes, no dependable health care, no regular drinking water, and no ability to keep food safe for consumption. All these life necessities are desperately needed. We are pleased and honored to be selected as your provider." There was additional applause from the crowd, and Forest stopped and nodded to them with a smile.

Forest motioned for Zag to step up on the stage. "Let me introduce you to the genius engineer who worked with me to invent this geothermal power plant. This is Zag." The crowd clapped for Zag, but not as strongly as they did for Forest due to the crowd's lack of appreciation for the remarkable technological breakthrough.

Zag fancied himself a genius scientist. He was a short, heavy man with grey hair perpetually disheveled and fashioned like Albert Einstein. He rarely changed his clothes or white lab coat because he viewed it as a waste of time. He believed any technology was fair game for him to use and frequently reverse-engineered many designs to claim his own. This lack of moral compass made Zag the perfect partner with Forest. While Forest knew Zag was stealing technology, he chose to ignore the theft and consider it a price to pay for the broader goal.

To educate the reporters in the crowd, Forest explained, "Geothermal power harnesses the heat in the earth to generate electricity. We have inserted a large conduction pipe deep towards the earth's core that carries the never-ending supply of the planet's heat safely to the surface. We are not producing fluorocarbons released into the atmosphere like a coal-fired plant because we use geothermal power. We simply use that heat to produce a continual source of clean energy. Our plant does not even take up your land because I have built it about a kilometer offshore."

For the grand finale, he said, "Oh yes, there's one more thing. We are providing our electricity for free to impoverished areas! You heard me correctly. Impoverished areas will receive free electricity!" With that, the crowd went wild with applause and admiration for the man creating a better world. Forest modestly accepted the roar of applause, bowing as if he had just given a Broadway performance.

Forest held up an oversized lever to simulate the power plant going live and pushed the lever up. As he would someday soon regret, he pronounced, "It would be evil not to give power to these people!" Forest smiled with the lever in the up position, posing for the endless stream of camera people and the ever-important photo op. Those pictures with Forest and his infamous proclamation were distributed worldwide in a matter of hours. The crowd erupted in more applause and cheering. Forest waved to the adoring fans and stepped off the stage with Zag.

At the bottom of the steps, Forest said to Zag, "Confirm for me one more time. Are you confident in this new technology? The people are counting on us."

Zag replied, "As sure as we can be. The power plant's basic functioning is taken, umm borrowed, from four designs invented in other countries. I took what I thought was the best of each design. We utilized several shortcuts to deliver the project on time, and I did not expect to fix those shortcuts. My biggest concern is the thickness of the thermal core and the strength of the thermal core's sheathing. We had to cut back on both of those, thereby weakening it and subjecting it to torque. However, based on my calculations, I am hopeful it is adequate for our needs."

"As long as it lasts for a little while, I think that is fine. We are just proving a concept that will hopefully work long enough to receive worldwide acceptance. I cannot tell you how exciting it was to have everyone applaud me."

"Forest, you need to focus on these potential problems. I'm sure you loved the clapping, but please hear me out. My second concern is that we did not have the time to install adequate step-down units that would shut down the system in the event of a power surge. Therefore, if we have a power surge, it would be sent in seconds to all those using our electricity."

"I don't want to hurt anyone. You know these are details which I cannot concern myself. The details are for you. I'm focused on the big picture. Is the plant working as it should?" Forest asked.

"Hey, the plant is working just as I told you it would, right? Simply based on that, it's clear that the other four geothermal energy design engineering teams were just adding features to save their asses in doomsday scenarios. Those wimps were just not willing to stand up and take a chance. After all, what could go wrong?" Zag continued.

Forest had always known about Zag's concerns but decided to overlook them to ensure a timely unveiling of the power plant. Shortcuts were a way of business, and this business venture looked incredibly successful. It was well worth the risks.

The photo op and speech were very effective in achieving their intended purpose. News outlets and internet sources were abuzz about the new geothermal power plant. They loved the tagline that it would be "evil" not to give its power to the people of the Democratic Republic of the Congo. The ensuing weeks and months were a constant flood of this previously recluse billionaire. Forest's picture was found on every known business and social magazine cover.

Businesspeople were equally excited about capitalizing on Forest's geothermal power technology. Forest began receiving unsolicited offers from several aggressive investment bankers who wanted to take his business public and provide him with a multi-billion-dollar payout. The private equity firms and multinational enterprises in the energy space were not going to be outdone. They made unsolicited offers to Forest that would have dramatically added to his massive inherited estate. However, Forest was committed to his strategic direction, and he stubbornly refused all the deals that would allow him to cash out of the business partially or fully.

Forest also had a limited number of critics. However, he smoothly addressed each of their concerns and assuaged the rabble-rousers and naysayers. Forest habitually agreed to take all interviews. Occasionally, the interviewer was combative and tried to trick Forest into a slip-up.

In one interview, Forest was asked, "Everything that creates energy either pollutes our atmosphere or has great risks. Where does your technology fit into that continuum?"

"You are basing your question on your myopic understanding of the historical technology used to generate energy. Mine is a new technology. Nothing is released into the environment. For that matter, the heat comes from the environment, and we are just harnessing it," Forest calmly replied.

"But won't geothermal energy cause the earth to heat up on the surface? We already have a major problem with the heating of the earth and the resulting melting of the polar ice caps," the combative interviewer asked.

"My geothermal energy is different from what has been done in the past. While traditional geothermal energy entails boring holes into the earth's surface to a depth of approximately 300 feet to capture escaping steam, my technology is a complete paradigm shift. We drill down 2,000 kilometers into a mantle layer where the temperature is approximately 5,000 degrees Fahrenheit. We then insert a thermal core that routes the heat up, converting it to energy. I can tell from your questions that your background research is on the old generation of geothermal power. You are comparing a horse-drawn carriage to today's racecar," Forest haughtily commented as his irritation began rising.

"Okay, but what happens if the heat escapes?" the interviewer continued to press with his questions.

Forest rebuked the direction of the questions by responding almost as if he were talking to a child. He said, "Young man, we have many sophisticated safety procedures to ensure no heat escapes. Providing safe energy to the people of the Democratic Republic of the Congo is much too important to take any risks."

The interviewer ended the discussion in a snide and, by now, overused phrase, "Oh yes, I forgot. I believe I heard someone say, 'It would be evil not to give power to these people."

Chapter 24

Blackwood Castle, United Kingdom
Nine Years and Six Months Ago, Six Months After the Opening of Congo Power Plant

Forest was turning into a shrewd businessman. He certainly knew the value he created with the geothermal power plant and the positive changes for Africa. After six months of dependable energy delivery, he felt confident with the technology.

The world had quickly rallied behind Forest. Countries donated wiring, fixtures, lightbulbs, appliances, air-conditioners, televisions, phones, computers, and internet service. The world wanted to provide the Democratic Republic of the Congo with every convenience offered in today's modern society. It was a significant feel-good moment for the world as the donated items arrived in droves on tanker ships from countries worldwide. Thousands of jobs were created to install infrastructure and appliances. There was a euphoria experienced in the Congo like never before experienced. People were even considering moving into the Congo rather than the historic migration away from it.

In an overstuffed leather chair in the study at Blackwood Castle in the United Kingdom, Forest was basking in his surroundings. The castle was a lovely estate dating back over 500 years and had all the classic attributes of a stately stone structure deserving of a castle description. Most of its massive 120 rooms had not been used for centuries, but each was impeccably maintained.

The castle sat on thirty acres of plush grounds and green grass fields that stretched as far as the eye could see. The exceptionally tall walls were connected in the corners by cylinders and angled bastions. Hundreds of years ago, they functioned as a lookout if an invading army stormed the castle.

The stone exterior was interconnected with the living quarters. The walls of the living quarters were adorned with artifacts and artworks from the masters. The wall nooks were filled with coats of armor and a variety of weapons from another era. Between each room were vaulted stone archways, reaching up to exceptionally high ceilings. Of course, throughout the castle were the obligatory deep stone fireplaces used to heat rooms at one point in time. Each piece of priceless period furniture was carefully placed in its exact resting spot and never moved. Blackwood Castle reeked of old money and elitism.

Sipping a fine brandy, Forest stared at the ceiling when Zag walked into the room.

Zag asked his boss, "What's on your mind?"

"I'm just envisioning the full implementation of my plan. Using your geothermal energy plant design and my vision and money, I think we are ready to move to the next stage." Forest replied.

"Agreed. I am comfortable with the buildout of a new plant. Maybe we could start small and construct a plant in the Solomon Islands. With their small population of about 650,000, we could provide all their power needs as we do in the Congo. We could locate the plant in the Coral Sea or the Pacific Ocean." Zag stated.

"My dear Zag, you are not thinking big enough." Forest began spinning an oversized globe of the world. "History books reward those bold enough to think beyond societal limitations. We should erect three more ocean-based power plants, just like Africa, to control the energy supply to North and South America." Forest stated.

"Have you considered where we will locate the plants?"

"Of course. We will control North America's western half by placing a power plant outside Seattle, Washington. The eastern half of North America will be provided by a power plant a few miles outside Acadia National Park, Maine. Finally, we will own South America with our third new power plant outside Arica, Chile, close to Southern Peru. Once we produce all the Americas' electricity, we will have expansion opportunities in Europe and Africa. Eventually, Russia will be receptive, even with its excessive levels of natural resources."

Zag replied with enthusiasm, "I love it. We can build the plants. We will make a fortune."

"No. You are still missing the point. We will give most of the power away for free and only capture enough profit to cover our investment."

"That is ridiculous! If we charge just a few pennies less than what it costs from their existing coal and nuclear power plants, countries will still flock to us because of our green footprint. Will we jack up the price when they tear down their old, pollution-spewing facilities, and they no longer have a choice!" The veins in Zag's neck were bulging, and his face was reddening.

"No! That would be greedy. We are not doing this to enrich our pockets. Our only objective is to help society and the world." Forest could not believe Zag's insubordination after all these years, including his substantial financial support. Forest allowed him to pursue his passion for creating technological inventions. All Forest asked in return was to support his philanthropic vision of a better world.

Zag looked like he was about to explode and stormed off, saying, "This is complete bullshit. We can create a monopoly and make billions of euros for ourselves."

Forest took a deep breath and let Zag leave to cool down. In a day or so, Forest would follow up with Zag and have an adult conversation about the topic while smoothing out any hurt feelings.

While Forest proved himself a shrewd businessman, he lacked the desire to turn his shrewdness into lining his pockets with money. He enjoyed the last six months of accolades. Several important people in politics and the press were talking about awarding him the Nobel Peace Prize. He could not believe it, but most said he was a shoo-in. He would be remembered forever. Zag was completely missing the broader vision. Forest did not need more money to live, and he loved the idea of being considered in history as a societal benefactor.

However, as many have said, "Fate is a cruel mistress."

Minutes later, an earthquake struck off Africa's coast, registered as a massive 9.0 magnitude event. Many people were knocked to the ground, and buildings fell upon their cracked foundations. Within 20 minutes, the first tsunami hit land at 60 to 80 kilometers per hour, washing tens of thousands of coastal residents out to sea. For hours afterward, additional tsunamis ravaged the already crippled beach villages resulting in several more deaths.

With all this devastation caused by the earthquake, the worst was caused by the geothermal power plant. Zag's intentional shortcuts in the manufacturing of the plant were the culprit. Had the plant been manufactured according to the specs identified by qualified engineers, the plant could have easily survived with little or no damage. However, the power plant's initial damage was from the torque on the thermal rod that snapped, causing a massive surge in heat into the plant.

The colossal heat resulted in an almost nuclear explosion-level blast that sent millions of volts of electricity into all the newly installed components and wiring. The lack of any surge protection installed at the power plant was the primary culprit for the next event of the chain reaction. It was estimated that over a million people lost their lives due to electrocution from touching metal connected to the power surge. After the initial electrical spike, several electrocuted people continued smoldering, giving off a disgusting stench.

Forest was informed about the earthquake within 30 minutes but could not get in touch with anyone. No calls were going in or out. He was forced to watch the television's live coverage like everyone else, experiencing the devastation in solitude. The reporters began to accumulate the estimated death count. He was in shock, and every minute seemed to last an hour.

For Forest, the earth just stood still. It took several hours for Forest to hear about some of the deaths caused by his power plant, and tears began running down his face. At first, he could not determine the power plant's status because everyone was focused on the land. Eventually, a helicopter was sent to the power generating facility. Several people swore that they saw what was described as a bright yellow and orange mushroom cloud in the sky. As the helicopter flew over the power plant's previous location, there was only water.

It took a week for anyone to learn that the water temperature had significantly risen due to the thermal core still emitting unbridled heat from the earth. After a month, a submarine's torpedo finally exploded the damaged underwater components into a million pieces. The vacuum created by the hole was filled to ensure no further heat was released. Unfortunately, the ecological damage was done. All aquatic wildlife died within several hundred miles of the power plant.

After the power plant explosion, the loss of life and economic devastation to the African coastal countries and the Congo were overwhelming. All the significant strides and jobs created by the newly provided electricity to the region were eliminated. Millions of people continued to perish as the weeks progressed, and droves of people were forced to migrate away to neighboring countries where life-saving services were available.

Forest became an immediate target as the press realized more deaths were caused by his geothermal power plant than by the earthquake and tsunami. The media, who once adored him, turned on him like hyenas surrounding a wounded gazelle. The unforgiving online, soulless, and faceless social media took over where mainstream media let up slightly. Every blog, post, and video pushed the cruelty bar higher. Forest became the butt of every late-night talk show host's monologue as they justified the callousness of their jokes for the sake of a punchline and better ratings. He was even called before the U.K. Parliament to assess culpability in the fiasco.

The governmental and legal investigation determined that the power plant designs were stolen from other conceptual power plants worldwide. However, the probe revealed that manufacturing shortcuts were the ultimate cause of the deaths. At that point, Forest finally began to stop defending himself and the geothermal power plant. He was no longer the innocent victim of the natural events of an earthquake and tsunami. He immediately went into hiding at Blackwood Castle while trusting his legal team to craft his defense in court.

The critics who enjoyed seeing the demise had the now-famous quote plastered everywhere. Forest knew he should have never said, "It would be evil not to give power to these people!" In the world of public opinion, he was officially renamed from Dr. Blackwood to Dr. Evil. Soon after his renaming, the infamous tagline with the picture of Forest flipping the power plant lever to the "on" position was changed to add the word "Dr." in front of "evil."

From this point forward, the tagline would read, "It would be Dr. Evil not to give power to these people!"

Forest's meteoric fall from grace to the devastation of personal and professional embarrassment sent him into a deep and dark depression. Even though he initially thought he had altruistic intentions, Forest knew in his heart that he was responsible. Forest set an unreasonable installation timeline and knew that Zag had stolen the designs. At the heart of the matter, Forrest acknowledged that he ignored the overwhelming risks.

The attacks from mainstream and social media continued relentlessly. Forest completely closed himself off from the world. Blackwood Castle became not just a home but a fortress to hide from society. He slowly but continually slipped into the embodiment of his newly earned media name, Dr. Evil.

Chapter 25

Chao Phraya River, Thailand
Present Day

Mac and the team finished the short debriefing from the Whispering Wind battery plant visit. The yacht cruised at maximum speed on the Chao Phraya River in Thailand. Mac asked Gunner, "Could you please escort our guest from the trunk to a spot where we can question him? Right now, he's our only source of a solid lead."

Gunner replied, "Of course, Mac. I will be gentle with him."

"It should still take another hour before the hand messenger awakens. I guess he's a little beaten up from bouncing around in the trunk while the guards were chasing us."

Gunner opened the trunk and did not like what he saw. He checked the hand messenger's pulse from his carotid artery in a vain attempt at finding good news. Gunner announced to everyone, "We have a problem."

The team members walked directly to the car's rear bumper. Gunner was right, and he added, "There must be a couple of dozen bullet holes in this guy. He will not have anything to share with anyone. At least the injection allowed him to be asleep, and he felt no pain."

For some unexplained reason, the team just stared at the hand messenger curled around the trunk's interior. It was not that they had never seen a dead body. Instead, the team members were each processing what to do for their next steps.

Mac broke the silence and said, "Dead men usually have something to say."

Ryker, who loved the yacht's open design and self-proclaimed skate park layout, was doing tricks on his skateboard when he zipped past the trunk. He suggested, "Give me an hour on my laptop, and I will identify this guy."

Mac said, "Do it. Also, can someone check this guy's pockets for anything we can use? Let's meet inside to look at his courier package together and regroup."

Brock rifled the hand messenger's pockets and found a couple of items. They all met in the main cabin and sat at a luxurious, spar-finished table. Brock started with his finds. "I found his French passport, which should help you give us intel, Ryker. I also found this receipt from a Paris restaurant."

Brock passed around both items.

Mac said, "We know this restaurant. Remember four years ago when I had dinner with the spy that wanted to kill me? This joint is the same restaurant."

Gunner responded, "Sure, we all remember the restaurant. I believe you had the duck with a lovely bottle of wine. My problem is trying to narrow down the list of spies that want to kill you. I am not sure if I can even remember his face."

Everyone snickered at the joke while recognizing the underlying basis of truth to it.

Mac replied to Gunner, "Okay, mister 'I will kill everyone who steps in the ring with me.' What do we know about that restaurant?"

Before anyone could respond, Ryker exclaimed, "Score!"

He was buried deep into his laptop screen, barely registering any of the team's discussion. Ryker continued, "I have been scanning every worldwide legal and illegal database. I finally found one small hit from the Department of Homeland Security. They have the owner of the restaurant on a watch list. It seems that the owner is a mercenary, and he uses the restaurant as a front to launder his money. Hold on. I may have some more data points."

Once Ryker had one piece of data, he was a miracle worker as he hacked into almost any database on the planet. He added additional color to what they already knew. "The owner's name is Abaddon, and this guy is a scary dude. He sells his services out to anyone willing to pay his price. He has 61 known kills to his name and potentially twice that number of unconfirmed kills. Hell, his name even means destruction or ruination!"

Mac wanted as many details as possible. He asked, "What else can you tell us about this master mercenary?"

"A lot now that I am piecing together all these databases. It's funny that everyone tracks the mercs, but no one has any jurisdiction to stop them. I think every Secret Service agency in the world is looking for him. Abaddon is a big guy with a distinguishing mark. He has a nasty, deep scar from his left eyebrow to his chin's right side because of a run-in with a Russian field agent. This picture is the best one I have found of him." Ryker passed around his laptop with a high-resolution image of Abaddon taken from across some street. Everyone saw that deep and disfiguring facial scar."

Ryker found more information and shared, "It says here that before becoming a paid-for-hire assassin, he was a street thug and brawler. He dislikes anyone in his way, especially young people because they do not give him the respect he deserves. This whack job has no moral compass. Interestingly, he went radio silent four years ago and became a ghost. I am not talking about him working as an agent for a spy ring. He simply disappeared."

Mac concludes, "Abaddon is our only solid lead. Let's hope there's a connection that can lead us to the secret investor. We need to get to Paris."

Valencia said, "I will ping the bird to fly us to the airport and have the pilot of the CIA jet file a flight plan to Paris. I already had the jet refueled, and it's ready to go."

Gunner teased her and said, "Of course you did. Is there anything you are not thinking ahead about?"

Valencia replied with a smile, "No. Not in your lifetime. We will be wheels up in approximately an hour."

Mac adds, "Perfect. Rick in *Casablanca* said it best if it doesn't work out, 'We'll always have Paris.'"

Chapter 26

Blackwood Castle, United Kingdom
Four Years Ago

Dr. Forest Blackwood was beyond low. At this point, no one on social media ever referred to him as Dr. Blackwood. Instead, his new nickname, Dr. Evil, was now prevalent when his name was used in the public domain. Even though it had been six years since the geothermal power plant disaster, his name still bubbled to the surface, associated with corporate greed and evil doing. Once a picture or article made it onto the internet, it never went away. Virtually everything published villainized Forest. At some point, Forest even started referring to himself as Dr. Evil.

Settling the lawsuits was financially painful for his inherited estate. However, he was still left with billions, and thanks to astute investing, his net worth more than quadrupled in size from six years ago.

Even with more money than he could hope to spend in ten lifetimes, he was still a Blackwood Castle prisoner. He had his network set up to ping him whenever his name or the power plant was mentioned in any public discussion. As a result, he continued with his self-flagellation and public humiliation.

The sanest and most confident person could not withstand the barrage of attacks. Forest spiraled further into the ugly depths of a dark soul. Society defined the place occupied by his dark soul with names such as a psychopath, possessed, serial killer, madman, deranged, and maybe most appropriately, sociopath. He was floundering in a dichotomy between depressive suicidal feelings of no worth and destructive feelings of revenge against society.

One more ping hit his computer with a particularly nasty reference to Dr. Evil. That social media posting by some coward who lived by the anonymity of the internet posting was the straw that broke the camel's back. Blackwood broke down, uncontrollably sobbing, and had to make a mad dash to the bathroom to purge what little food he could keep in his stomach. He stumbled back into his study and plopped down in his desk chair.

Blackwood gazed at his eclectic collection of antique contraptions with the underlying theme of movement created by inventors from centuries before. Before the power plant incident, he had a passion for his collection. The ingenuity fascinated him even though he could not necessarily discern the purpose of some items. His eyes settled upon an old, rudimentary fan. At least, he thought it was a fan. He walked over and picked it up. It was large and heavy and had some bizarre base containing what he assumed was a motor. He could not help but think about the fan's inventor.

He said out loud to himself, "I'll bet this inventor was ridiculed for creating a worthless piece of junk. Undoubtedly, he believed in it, but society rejected it and him." As Blackwood was known to do with his isolation, he carried on complete conversations by himself. He continued, "Why did you waste your life making something so useless?"

His alter ego replied in a slightly different voice, "Because it was going to change the world."

"Sure, and how did that work out for you?"

"They did not understand how important my invention was. It was not ready to be used by the public."

"So why did you push it onto the public?"

Blackwood paused at that question, and his alter ego replied, "Because I was too trusting. I trusted technology. I trusted everyone around me to appreciate the importance of the invention. I trusted society, and they turned on me."

It was unclear if his next question was being asked of himself or the fan inventor. From the dark place occupying his soul, he asked, "Now what?"

"Now, I will prove to society that I am truly God-like. I do not care whom I crush to get there. The means will justify the ends. Once I show them, they will understand." Blackwood ended his internal conversation and looked closely at the fan. He cursed himself for buying this piece of junk from the antique store in Greece at whatever price he absentmindedly paid.

As Blackwood held the fan in front of him and contemplated if he should toss the old relic, a small stack of papers fell out of the base onto the floor. They were ancient and coated in oil that must have come from the fan. That oil acted as a preservative for the papers, ensuring they did not crumble. He considered tossing them, but his curiosity got the best of him.

Blackwood opened the papers across his desk. They were the designs for a different machine rather than a fan. His biggest challenge in understanding the plans was that they looked to be written in German. As best as he could tell, this inventor used lightning to power something. They were very exacting and drafted based on numerous trials and errors. The inventor called the invention the Blitzpeicher.

While not a genius engineer, Blackwood did earn his Ph.D. in engineering and was quite bright. The plans included everything from designs to materials. The more he analyzed the drawings, the more he realized that these drawings could change the world. If nothing else, he confidently dated the fan back to the mid-1700s as the inventor acknowledged the Blitzpeicher was thanks to the recent work of Benjamin Franklin's kite flying in a thunderstorm. Surely, this fan and the plans were worth millions of euros to collectors at auction. Now, his curiosity was fully engaged.

He spent the rest of the day and the entire night analyzing the plans. By the following day, he had decided to forget selling the fan and plans at auction. He was uncertain if the Blitzpeicher would work, but this was a different way to make a battery. If it performed as claimed in the plans, this was the first working battery ever made.

There were some sophomoric notes in the margins that suggested the inventor had an assistant. The inventor used a completely different form and communication style with a much more professional and technical air. The assistant made several wild claims, like the Blitzpeicher could perpetually store the lightning, suggesting a battery that never ran out of juice.

This inventor was a genius well before his time. Blackwood felt there was a reason why he received these drawings and began to envision his new destiny. He needed Zag to weigh in on this. Zag was his only remaining employee from his power plant days, besides the few Blackwood Castle staff. Often, he considered terminating him, but his attorneys discouraged it in the event of additional power plant litigation. The attorneys said it was better to have the unethical engineer on his team because the other potential option was Zag as a hostile witness.

Blackwood partially blamed Zag for the power plant fiasco but inwardly knew Zag had stolen the geothermal technology and taken shortcuts to accomplish unreasonable timelines set by Blackwood. Blackwood knew they both were to blame for the geothermal power plant failure. Fortuitously, his engineer was still an available resource for this next stage. He called and told him to come to the study in an hour.

Arriving at the empty study, Zag sat in a guest chair in front of the desk.

Blackwood excitedly walked into the room with a zippy step that had not been seen for almost six years. He had taken a shower, shaved, and put on a designer shirt and a pair of slacks that befitted a multi-billionaire. He was running on pure adrenaline. Blackwood was a different man.

Zag barely recognized Blackwood. After confirming that this man walking toward him was his boss, he said, "Wow. Someone looks like they just got a new pony for their birthday."

Blackwood replied, "Call it what you like. Call it a gift. Call it divine intervention. Hell, call it a pony if you like. I don't care."

"Okay. I'll bite. Why am I here." Zag was ready for some good news.

"I'm back in the game. I have had enough of playing the loser. People are going to stop making me the butt of every joke. You and I are going to control all the power in the world."

"I think we were on that path once, and it didn't work out so well for us," Zag said.

"You're wrong. That was just a dry run. This plan is now the real deal. You have been tinkering with improving the geothermal designs, right?" Blackwood was setting the stage for the next iteration of his life.

"Yes. The designs are refined and perfect now if we utilize the specs from the other engineers. I must admit that I've seen this new Blackwood smoldering beneath the surface for a long time. It's exciting to see, but at the same time, I'm a little confused. You are making comments to me that make you sound more and more like me. It's like your nice side had historically held the dark side back, but now it's beginning to feel like the dark side is winning the fight."

"It doesn't matter which part of me wins the intellectual battle or how you feel about me. I need to know the status of my building blocks. Are these designs going to fail like your last feeble attempt?"

Zag was clearly taken aback by the direct and accusatory question. He defensively replied with a crack in his voice, "No. I have checked and rechecked the calculations."

"Are you bullshitting me this time?" asked Blackwood.

"No bullshit."

"Good. Zag, you have worked for me a very long time, and you probably know me better than anyone else in the world."

Zag nodded in agreement.

Blackwood continued, "If you screw it up this time around, you will not have a third chance. I do not mean I will fire you. I mean, you will no longer have a purpose in breathing air. Am I clear?"

"Clear. I thought we had a different, trusting relationship. I'm trying to understand this new man in front of me because that will help me implement our plans. I think your dark side has finally won out over anything good in you. I don't like that you are threatening me. I can tell from your tone that your threat is not idly given."

"I think you fully understand me. We still have a trusting relationship. Trust me when I say failure is unacceptable. It has only one permanent and painful solution for you. So that we don't go to that extreme, we need to get to work. I will lay out the plan for us to control all power generation in the world, but first, let's look at this design of a new battery invention called a Blitzpeicher."

They spent the next several hours discussing the Blitzpeicher, considering current technological advances. They concluded it was a brilliant design that utilized unique blends of materials.

Zag stated, "We could manufacture the Blitzpeicher in a much smaller format, such as a car battery with, hopefully, its same properties. However, I have a question. If it works, why don't we use it today? You said it must date back to the mid-1700s."

"I cannot answer that question. It could be a mystery the world may never be able to answer. I am not focused on the past. We need to focus on the future. Let me explain my plan to you. You are going to be busy. First, I need you to hire a business broker to quickly find and buy a battery manufacturer and convert it to manufacture the Blitzpeicher. No one can know about my battery plant investment because the foolish public would stop it before it got started." Blackwood stated.

"Okay. I will do that," Zag responded.

"Good. Keep me informed about the details. Concurrent with the first step, I need you to secretly build three geothermal power plants supporting North and South America. Somehow, we will knock out the power-generating abilities in North and South America, forcing them to use our geothermal plants. We will have a monopoly and control all AC and DC power while charging the countries for every kilowatt based upon their ability to pay. We are the drug dealer for the countries, except our drug will be energy. If they don't pay our demanded price, their country will experience life as it was in the 1700s with no power."

"I like how you are thinking! I don't know what happened, but I wish it would have happened sooner!" Zag exclaimed.

Blackwood proclaimed, "I am the antithesis of the man I was two years ago. I will prove it to you and the world. I will demonstrate my strengths as a great strategic thinker for all the jerks who called me Dr. Evil.

Zag said, "I love it. It's about time. We will look like a savior to the public by bringing clean energy to the world using geothermal technology and cutting-edge battery design."

"Just so we are clear if it's beneficial for me to have a positive public persona, I'll only do so as a front. I am no longer the savior type. We will capitalize on the world's weakness in their energy production." Blackwood said. The public persona of a savior belies his dark side, driven by his societal banishment.

Blackwood continued, "It was the public and those online fools that uncovered this new man. He was the man lying just below the surface all along, and this new man is my new and better self. We will make money this time, and a lot of it. How soon can we have the three geothermal power plants online?"

Zag replied after doing some calculations in his head, "Well, ordinarily, I would say ten years. However, with this new technology that I stole from a couple of universities and a major power company, I can have them fully operational in five years."

"What about the batteries?"

"I see what you were saying about the Blitzpeicher. It's ingenious. I am shocked that no one has developed this sooner. If it works, this is revolutionary and will make every vehicle battery on the planet obsolete. With the modern-day design and manufacturing at an existing battery facility to make the batteries, we can have them starting in production in three years."

Blackwood needed direct confirmation from Zag that they were in violent agreement on the objective of success at any cost. If Zag were soft on the new approach to achieve success, Blackwood would replace him immediately.

"Are you okay if, this time, we are ruthlessly to achieve success and make money? You should assume that we will break dozens of national and international laws. The world can go to hell as far as I care. I intend on being the first trillionaire, and I will share a generous portion of it with you," Blackwood stated.

"Absolutely. I have always felt that the world should pay us handsomely for allowing it to benefit from my inventions."

"We will control 100% of the world's AC and DC energy needs. I don't care whom we kill to get there. No one is going to be making fun of me anymore. I don't care if I must tear the world down to build it back up again."

Zag reflected on this refreshing approach and asked, "If we are going to play hardball, we will need some serious muscle. I heard about this mercenary who is supposed to be the most lethal person in the world. He owns a restaurant in France that he uses as his cover for his real profession as a merc. We could use someone who knows how to make things happen if we are going to push your plan through quickly."

"Great. Hire the mercenary and anyone else that is necessary. Also, ensure the power plants are operationally ready four years from today. This time, there will not be any failures. Failures will be dealt with permanently. Do we understand ourselves?

Zag replied, realizing he had just made a deal with the Devil himself, "Yes sir, four years it is, Dr. Blackwood."

Chapter 27

Blackwood Castle, United Kingdom
Two Years Ago

It had been two years since Blackwood had outlined his aggressive path to control the world's AC and DC power. With the overall direction defined, Zag attacked the implementation with enthusiasm. The first task completed by Zag was to engage a business broker. Zag sat across from the business broker in his office as they discussed the status of their various initiatives.

"What is the implementation status of the plan for the acquired vehicle battery manufacturer, Whispering Industries?" asked the business broker.

"I'm on schedule with executing the vision. We are close to reengineering the Blitzpeicher utilizing today's technology and in automotive sizes. I could not have gotten this far without your great work finding and closing on the Whispering

Wind acquisition. I must say that it is a pleasure working with you, and I'm glad we have become friends. You have achieved results in record time with your ability to skirt ridiculous rules and laws. I cannot believe it only took four months to identify the company, negotiate the transaction, and close the deal." Zag said with deep admiration.

"Thank you. I am glad to be a part of this global plan. Of course, I had to utilize some overtly aggressive negotiation techniques that paved the way for a smooth transition to close the investment. I know Blackwood doesn't care about my methods to complete transactions and only wants to ensure they conclude promptly. That's how I roll. I deliver on promises. How is your progress with the construction of the power plants?" asked the business broker.

Zag replied, "They are progressing on schedule as well. Dr. Blackwood and I work 18-hour days, seven days per week, to ensure we continue as planned. As Dr. Blackwood always says, 'A strategic plan is a living and breathing document that is subject to constant change.'"

"I like that flexibility. I constantly make changes and decisions on the fly. Since I have become an important part of the strategic plan, can you share it with me?"

"Of course. You are making things happen, and it's a pleasure working with someone else who's an implementer like me. You already know that we want to manufacture a new vehicle battery and need access to space satellites. What you don't know is that we intend to generate all the worldwide electrical power. One of our challenges with the continually evolving solution is forcing the countries to buy from our new power plants. We need to bring the countries in North and South America to their knees."

"I understand the overwhelming benefits of monopoly pricing to customers. However, I don't see how you can force a country to do anything it doesn't want to do."

"That is where my skills come into play again. I hacked into various databases and found designs for new technology to deliver the necessary lethal blow. The plans were on the secure network of a country that was a sworn enemy of the Western world. The technology requires firing the primary weapon from outer space. To test the weapon's effectiveness, we will use a smaller weapon released from a fixed-wing aircraft. To fully execute the experiment with the borrowed technology, we needed to acquire a company that could release its payload outside the Earth's atmosphere. As you can see, this acquisition is a critical aspect of the strategic plan's execution."

"Wow, this plan will make everyone multi-millionaires," said the business broker with a devious smile.

Zag asked, "What is the status of our next investment?"

The business broker was about to explain his challenges in winning approval from the target's Board of Directors, but Zag's phone rang. It was Blackwood demanding they both come up to his office.

* * *

The business broker and Zag arrived in the office with Blackwood and Abaddon.

Zag whispered to the business broker, "Abaddon is the one standing in the corner. He and his team were engaged as the "muscle" and security for the operation. While I recommended Abaddon to Blackwood, I must tell you that I get nervous just at the sight of the mercenary. Abaddon orchestrated the critical incentive in closing the battery manufacturer acquisition."

The business broker whispered back, "So that is the guy. He sounds like a great asset to have on our side."

"Abaddon's mercenaries appear to be able to overthrow a government with their military-like precision. What you don't know is that precision, along with four gruesome executions, convinced the European crime network to sell their battery manufacturer to us. Killing someone meant the same to these mercenaries as brushing their teeth to an average person. Abaddon and his team are perfect for implementing our strategic plan, assuming their loyalty doesn't change."

The business broker continued with a whisper, "You worry too much! I'll bet Abaddon already loves me."

Blackwood said, "If you are done whispering, please come in, gentlemen. I need to know the status of the tactics necessary to execute the strategic plan. Now that we are in the implementation phase of our business model, I need to make sure the chess pieces are played appropriately."

Zag was the first to respond, saying, "The vehicle battery plant is almost ready for conversion. As we had hoped, the Blitzpeicher is turning into a miracle battery. It's passed all our tests, and we have converted it to the size of the standard vehicle battery. We are still running tests, but we have no flaws in the conceptual construction and functioning of the battery."

Blackwood responded, "Excellent. Are we on schedule?"

"Yes. We should be making batteries within a year and stockpiling them for future sale," replied Zag.

"Fine. Now tell me about the status of the acquisition of the American company that conducts space missions."

"We are having resistance from two members of the Board of Directors who are stubbornly opposed to the transaction." The business broker replied and relished knowing the discussion was circling to him.

Blackwood asked, "Tell me what that means and your solution. I cannot function with vague generalities."

"It means we need both Board members to approve your acquisition, and they are refusing. I have met individually with them, and they are stubborn, old, and prejudiced-thinking guys. I am not sure why they are so opposed to the acquisition. Still, maybe they know they will be put out to pasture once you own their business," the business broker responded.

"What do you propose we do to tear down this brick wall?"

The business broker said, "Based on their staunch opposition to our logic, I believe we have five choices. The first option is to blackmail them, assuming there is something we can uncover. Another option is to kidnap one of their family members. Third, we could pay them off with obscene money. Fourth, we could give them something they want more than money, such as a lover. Of course, our final option is to kill them. If we kill them, it will take months to replace them on the Board, and the deal will stall, so I am taking that option off the table. I am working on a solution."

Blackwood responded, "Working on a solution is not included in your contractual tasks. I need a solution implemented. I will ask one last time. What do you propose to force them to our side?"

"I think blackmail. With blackmail, we can keep the dissenters in our back pockets and use them whenever we want."

"Go on."

"Both are powerful men running large companies and are supposedly family men. However, based on our research, they each have a history of multiple mistresses on the side. Using scandalous pictures and videos, we can insert our version of a mistress and convince them to proceed with the transaction. They will not want the public humiliation of a young mistress." The business broker sat back with a sly smile.

Blackwood said, "Perfect. How soon can we have their vote approving the transaction, or do we need some extra heroics?"

The business broker gleamed with a flashy smile and proclaimed, "You are looking at your hero! We will close within the next 24 hours."

"24 hours? That seems like an aggressive commitment, even coming from you."

The business broker said, "I assumed you would want me to move quickly, and therefore, I took the initiative and hired actors to play the role of mistresses. Both performed marvelously and sent me even better-than-expected juicy pictures and videos. The opposing members of the Board of Directors have already caved, saying they will vote to approve the transaction."

"Excellent. Well done. I like personal initiative, but why didn't you come to me with your predicament?" Blackwood replied.

"I am glad you asked, Dr. Blackwood. Partners trust each other to fulfill their commitments and do not bother one another with the minor details of the tasks at hand. That's why I work on my own and not with a firm. As you can see, I deliver. I am more than just a hired hand. I am a trusted partner for you. I would like to discuss how we can increase our partnership to benefit each other's gain. I'm sure it will have a killer return."

Blackwood replied, "Sir, are you angling for something larger for yourself? Are you renegotiating our arrangement?"

"I'm not renegotiating. I am simply stating facts regarding my value-added services."

"I suppose I am not surprised by this request. In most situations, I consider someone a weasel if they want to change a business arrangement after it starts. However, it appears you are close to delivering on your end of the bargain. I'm a little shocked that your request didn't directly ask for an equity stake in my estate or at least in this current power plant venture."

"Normally, I am much bolder with my requests, but I haven't done so because I respect you. I like where you are going with our partnership discussion and having me share in a portion of your estate. Then, you and I are assured of no conflicts and to operate in your best interest. As a starting point, I would like to suggest that I receive half of your estate. Based upon what I can do for you, your remaining share will be worth five times its current value!" replied the business broker with outstretched arms.

"If this request had come before the geothermal power plant disaster, I probably would have considered the proposal. Now, I see the world through a different lens. How can I trust you based on your tactics with the acquisition targets? Will you turn on me once you own half of my estate?" Blackwood inquired.

"I don't like where your questions are going. I have delivered everything asked of me. When I am in a deal, I deliver on my commitments. Maybe my opening salvo was slightly too high. How about I receive a quarter of your estate, and we move on from this discussion?"

Blackwood interlaced his fingers in front of his face with his index fingers pointing up across his mouth and smiled calmly at the business broker. Blackwood's calculated response was, "I think it's only fair we all receive what we have coming."

"Excellent. I will have the documents prepared once we work out the details in a private conversation. With our pending partnership, I would like to understand the overall strategic plan for the power plant. Can I ask why you are interested in acquiring a company that puts satellites in orbit around the Earth? What does that possibly have to do with power generation?" the business broker inquired.

Blackwood ignored the question and instead asked, "Will we be able to install whatever technology we want into the satellites?"

"Of course. Think about it. Does the public know what classified capabilities are installed in the private satellites circulating the earth? Naturally, we will need to dupe the government agencies, but that will not be any problem." the business broker replied.

"Do you have comfort that the Board members are now approving my acquisition of the company?" asked Blackwood.

"As I said before, I am someone who gets things done." The business broker smiled with his outsized mouth and confidently leaned back with his hands behind his head. He added, "Dr. Blackwood, I already have their signatures approving the transaction in documents sitting in my briefcase right next to me."

The business broker opened the file folder he was carrying and pulled out the executed documents.

Blackwood reviewed the documents, and he approvingly nodded at the business broker. He said, "It looks like you have resolved everything I have asked of you."

Again, the business broker flashed his smile as if they were life-long buddies. "Yes, you will have full control of the satellite company and can do whatever you want with it as of tomorrow when the documents in your hand are filed."

"Very good. Considering your desire to change our deal and become my partner, I think it's time you understood my terms. You and I can ensure we have killed any uncertainty when we communicate properly." Blackwood looked over at Abaddon as he stood behind the business broker. Abaddon had been silent the entire meeting with an emotionless expression. Blackwood gave Abaddon a slight head nod.

Abaddon walked up behind the business broker and, with his massively muscled arms, put the business broker in a chokehold. Abaddon's chokehold technique involved putting his right elbow around the front of the business broker's neck with his left arm applying forward pressure. This maneuver eliminated both the victim's ability to breathe and the blood flow to their head.

As Abaddon raised him out of his chair by the neck, the business broker could not stop the inevitable. He flailed his arms frantically as he tried to punch Abaddon's face behind him or pull the massive arms away from his neck. He kicked his straightened legs up and down, slamming his heels on the floor.

After the business broker stopped all his body movements, Abaddon continued holding for an extra minute to ensure there was no doubt about his death. He looked at Blackwood, who held up a dismissive hand and flipped it away as if he were sending an ill-prepared meal back to a chef. Abaddon pulled the business broker by the neck out of the room as if he were pulling a small bag of laundry.

Blackwood turned to Zag. Zag looked ghost-white. Blackwood said, "I hope you found that sleazeball's land-grab performance as distasteful of an act as I did. It was a relief to see Abaddon take the trash out before it smelled up my office any more than it already had."

"OMG! Did you see the way Abaddon crushed the life out of him? I find that very unsettling. I don't care that he is dead. He had been a critical part of executing the plan, but he got greedy. You know I will never get greedy on you, but once I have served my purpose, how do I know Abaddon won't take me out like garbage, too?"

"Stop this foolish talk. You have been my employee for several years, and I have no intention of breaking that bond with you. Do I make myself clear?"

Looking uneasy, Zag replied in an unconfident tone, "Sure. I have been loyal to you through thick and thin, and I will continue with my loyalty as an important part of the strategic plan. You have my word."

"I'd expect nothing less from you. It's time for us to move on to more productive matters. Is the EMP technology ready to install in the satellites?"

Zag confirmed, "Yes, we can reprogram the robotic arms to install the EMP guns into the satellites. However, it will take some time, and we will need to install them into future orbiting satellites. There's no way to retrofit existing orbiting satellites."

"Very well. Will the satellites' delivery system be able to deliver EMPs covering all of North and South America with a geomagnetic storm and take out all their electrical components and power grids?" Asked Blackwood.

Zag replied, "I believe so. It would be helpful to test it before we execute the full plan across North and South America. Plus, we need to ensure all our facilities are encased in Faraday cages."

Blackwood said, "You will have your test, but we will not use the satellites. If we don't hide their true purpose, they will be detected before fully executing the plan's critical aspects. Our enemies would just blast our satellites out of the sky. We will deliver an EMP in a much smaller way, but we can work out the delivery and location of the EMP test in more detail later."

"With no ability to generate power, the countries will have to crawl to you because you will have the only solution." Zag was trying to play to Blackwood's ego and, in turn, suggested that Zag was a loyal part of the team.

Blackwood said, "Agreed. The plan is coming together nicely with no loose ends."

Chapter 28

Abaddon's Restaurant in Paris, France
Current day

Paris was beautiful this time of year. The team was seated outside at a six-person metal table in the afternoon sun. Pedestrians were strolling by with the calmness of upper-class aristocrats who had nothing tugging at their time. Each person passing by was slender with the look of a fashion model. Lovers were walking past, held onto one another's arms, and filled with giggles suggesting secret jokes only they shared. The city was filled with beautiful people and romantics. After spending ten minutes here, it would be hard not to fall in love with it.

Most of the tables around them were filled with couples drinking red wine, nibbling on bread, and talking deep in thought. Their waiter, friendly, wearing a white apron and carrying a white napkin draped over his forearm, walked up. He asked, "Can I start the table with a bottle of wine?"

Valencia's sophistication shined through, and she responded in French, "Of course. We would like two bottles of good red and some bread for the table."

After the waiter walked away, Mac said to Valencia, "I like your style."

Gunner looked uncomfortable and was two sizes too big for his small metal chair. He said, "What I would like is for this place to have adult-sized chairs that do not sit on a stupid, uneven cobblestone sidewalk."

"But Gunner, this is part of the charm and ambiance," Mac said.

Valencia shrugged her shoulders, flipped her chic hair in a mocking display of elegance, and commented, "This is perfect. The sun, the atmosphere, the people, and the city are all perfect." She then blew a kiss to Gunner and gave him a bat of her eyes. Gunner shook his head and rolled his eyes in response.

The waiter returned with the wine and went through the obligatory cork popping and tasting. Once that ritual was completed, he poured wine for everyone at the table and then returned with the bread and appetizer menus. The team opened the menus with the requisite scouring to find the perfect combination with the wine.

The appetizer offering was spectacular. It was hard to remember that a world-renowned mercenary owned this restaurant. That mercenary had more kills than passengers you could count in a packed Paris subway metro system car during rush hour. The orders were placed with the waiter, and Mac asked to speak with the restaurant manager.

The waiter, concerned he had committed some atrocious faux pas, hurried off to find the manager from a back room. Mac could see a one-person podium manned by the maître de responsible for reservations and table assignments. A small man appeared from a back area and walked purposefully to Mac and the team's table. When he arrived at their table, he announced, "Monsieur, I am the manager of this restaurant. Do you have a complaint with our menu or service?"

Mac politely replied, "No. You are running an amazing restaurant, and we are all enjoying the experience. I asked to speak with you for a different reason."

The stiffness of the restaurant manager visibly eased, and he smiled at the compliment. The rest of the team nodded in agreement as he looked each of them in the eyes. He performed a slight head bow in acknowledging the compliment.

Brock jumped into the discussion by asking, "What we want to know is if you have seen the man in this photo." He pulled out the picture of Abaddon and gave it to the restaurant manager.

Given Gunner's foreign language fluency, he took over the conversation. Gunner added in French, "Abaddon is an associate of ours from certain non-restaurant matters."

Not waiting for the response, Ryker stood up and said, "If you all would please excuse me, I have to take a call. It might take some time, so please proceed with the wine and appetizers without me. If I don't make it back in time, you had better fill a doggy bag and a to-go carafe of that wine!" He then turned to the manager and said, "Please continue with your discussion, and I am sorry to have interrupted you."

Ryker was not entirely truthful with the manager. Yes, Ryker was going to get on a call. However, his call was to listen to the expected cell phone call that the manager would place to Abaddon. Mac anticipated the manager would deny knowing Abaddon but fully expected him to call Abaddon, describing his unknown customers.

Ryker had all his necessary cell phone tapping equipment set up and flawlessly running in the van. The recording equipment monitored fifteen separate calls, and Ryker needed to determine which cell phone the manager was using. He ascertained the appropriate line using the straightforward and time-tested approach of narrowing the list down based on when the call was placed. It was one of the many tools used in their spycraft.

The manager replied to Gunner with a slight quiver in his voice, "I have never seen this man before."

Gunner pushed the point further and reinserted the picture in front of the manager's face. He said, "We worked with him in his prior job responsibilities several years ago, and we have a mission-critical message for him. Can you please look more closely for us at his picture?"

The manager's neck turned a bright shade of red, his eyes were blinking way too quickly, and he looked up from the picture with obviously a very fake smile. Along with a dozen other tall-tell gestures, those reactions confirmed to the team that he was lying about knowing Abaddon. He also seemed terrified by just seeing Abaddon's picture and undoubtedly hated placing the call to him to inform him that someone was at the restaurant asking questions. Mac was sure Abaddon required some type of communication protocol to assess any potential danger.

The manager responded with another dead giveaway of lying by repeating Gunner's question and said, "Can I look more closely for you? Yes. Of course, I will."

After pretending to stare at the picture, the manager said, "I am sure. I have never met this man. Is he a customer?"

Gunner replied, "We're not sure. We were just hoping we could find him here. Thank you for looking. We are staying at the large hotel just around the corner if you think of anything else."

The waiter delivered the exquisite appetizers prepared to perfection. Mac kept an eye on the manager, who seemed to be just flittering about with no real purpose. He knew the manager was stalling until his required call to Abaddon. After everyone nibbled at the appetizers and drank the wine, Mac paid the bill and left an obnoxiously generous tip. They saw the manager frantically dial his cell phone in the restaurant's back area as they stood up to leave. The team was not close enough to overhear the discussion. However, the call quickly became much more agitated and animated as it progressed. Walking away, Mac was confident that Ryker was capturing every word.

Watching the tense interaction, Valencia said as they were leaving, "Some people are so predictable. It takes all the fun out of this job."

Mac added, "I could not tell if he was more terrified of Abaddon or us."

Brock joined in with, "My money is on Abaddon. Speaking of money, I think we need to get him into a high-stakes poker game with us. He sucks at lying."

Everyone laughed and climbed into the van where Ryker was wearing huge earmuff headsets with tape reels running.

When Ryker looked intense like this, you knew he had nailed something big.

Ryker pulled off the headsets and said, "Abaddon is in the UK, and he's pissed. First, he started screaming at the manager that the hand messenger had not shown up yet. It sounds like the hand messenger made regular trips. Their boss is so paranoid about cell phone tapping that he will only communicate via the messenger's hand-delivered packages. The boss is becoming unhinged because there's something big about to happen, and he needs information about the Thailand battery plant."

Mac responded, "Did Abaddon say anything about what happened to the hand messenger?"

"Absolutely. Abaddon described the abduction to the manager and said someone was digging into their organization. He told the manager to send another messenger or his restaurant managerial services, along with his life, would no longer be needed."

"Did the manager describe us to Abaddon?"

"No. The manager was terrified and not thinking clearly. He had no descriptions of us other than noting that the main person asking the questions spoke perfect French with a Paris accent. Abaddon was not happy about that either. We hit a nerve with him, and he does not like anyone asking questions at his restaurant. I think we should be careful because his only comment to the manager was that he would deal with the inquiring Frenchmen."

Mac asked, "I take it you understand that the inquiring Frenchmen must be us?"

"No doubt. The last thing Abaddon said before hanging up was a little weird and must be about the cleanliness of the restaurant. He said he was going to execute on Operation Busboy." Ryker replied.

No one had any good suggestions regarding Operation Busboy's meaning, so they decided to break for the evening and go to their five-star hotel about a block away.

Ryker reminded them, "Hey, did anyone bring me my doggie bag?"

Chapter 29

Paris, France Hotel

When Mac walked into their five-star hotel's main entrance, the hotel owner greeted him as he strode from behind the main desk. The hotel owner spread his arms wide and sincerely grinned, saying, "Mr. Declan Mac! Such a pleasure to see you. I am thrilled to see the rest of the team!"

Mac reached his hand out, and the owner took it with a long, healthy shake. Mac replied, "I am so sorry to barge in unannounced like this. Our travels took an unexpected change in plans, and of course, if we are in Paris, we are staying here. Could we reserve the rooms that we usually stay in?"

"Of course! How many nights will you and your team be staying this time?" The hotel owner asked.

Truly disappointed, Mac said, "Unfortunately, only one."

"That's fortunate for me. We are completely booked tomorrow night for an extended period."

"I guess it's fortunate for us too. We could not imagine staying at any other hotel. Nothing would compare. Could you arrange for a table for dinner in fifteen minutes?" Mac replied.

"Of course! I will ensure you have your usual table with a front view of the Eiffel Tower."

To ensure anonymity for the rest of the team, Mac always put all the rooms on his credit card. Mac suspected the hotel owner knew Mac was an operative for the CIA, but he never let on. Mac kept up his charade and always had a different business purpose for visiting Paris. The team went to their respective rooms to freshen up and then headed to the restaurant.

Not long after the team left the hotel lobby, a man wearing all black walked up to the hotel front desk. The hotel owner was nowhere to be seen, but a young clerk was behind the counter. The clerk was 18 years old and had just started working at the hotel. He enthusiastically greeted this first guest and asked how he could help.

The man said, "I seem to have lost my room key. Five of us just checked in a few minutes ago, and one of the other guys accidentally took my key. Could you please tell me our room numbers so I can find them?"

"Yes, I am happy to help. Let me just see who recently checked in. That's strange. I only found one new guest who checked in within the last hour. From the room assignments, it looks like your group has a total of five rooms, but I only have a name assigned to one of them. Are you Declan Mac?"

The man paused and concluded that this group of five must be the same group he was targeting. He replied, "No. I am not Declan Mac, but that is my group. Great job in finding us. That is impressive."

The young clerk was pleased to receive a compliment and smiled at the recognition. He replied, "I do not have the other room numbers, so I don't know your specific room. I can give you Mr. Mac's room if that is helpful."

The man smiled and said, "Yes, thank you. I can sort it out from there."

The young clerk provided Mac's room number to the man. After a terse nod and cursory thank you, the man quickly turned and walked away. The young clerk asked loudly, "Hey, I did not get your name."

The man didn't acknowledge the question and seemed focused on his cell phone as he walked away. He placed a call to his employer for this assignment. That employer was a merc who happened to own a restaurant around the corner.

The man said, "Target acquired. Operation Busboy a go at zero three hundred hours. Out."

Chapter 30

Paris, France Hotel Restaurant

Mac arrived first at the restaurant, and the head waiter welcomed him with a warmness similar to that of the hotel owner. The waiter showed Mac to his usual table with chairs already arranged for all five on the team.

The white tablecloth dinner was spectacular and lived up to any connoisseur's fine-dining expectation in Paris. The restaurant only used candles during dinner to help ensure each patron could enjoy the unobstructed view of the Eiffel Tower. Mac felt comfortable, given that there were limited lines of sight for a sniper. Plus, there was plenty of response time with the floor layout if a bad guy wanted to walk up to surprise him.

When Mac sat at this table, he always wondered if another set of eyes was staring down at him. He shut the CIA part of his brain down to simply enjoy the moment. He could relax, enjoy the evening, and become a CIA operative again tomorrow.

Tonight, there were no tails and no sniper scopes. It was just five coworkers, who were also best friends, having dinner together and enjoying the best that Paris had to offer. With the continual stress and confrontations endured by the team, Mac enjoyed watching each of them chatter about various topics and frequently burst into laughter. The Eiffel Tower, like every night, was lit like a shining symbol of French pride.

After dinner, they headed up to their hotel rooms. The team members exited the elevator on different floors as CIA operational safety protocol dictated. Given that all the rooms were to be charged to Mac's credit card, he wondered if he would see more of those ridiculous movie charges from Brock. Brock knew any expense unrelated to the mission made Mac crazy. Mac thought Brock didn't even watch the movies and was just trying to jerk his chain. When Brock stepped off the elevator, he looked back at Mac and winked.

Mac said to Brock, "Don't you even think about…." The elevator door closed, and Brock was gone. Mac thought he would need to find some appropriate payback for Brock. They all retreated to their rooms for needed shutdown time before tomorrow's trip to the U.K. to track down Abaddon.

Mac began his hotel room ritual that he used every time he had an overnight stay while on a mission. The first task was to add a Ryker-special, motion-activated video camera to the outside of his room. It worked very effectively because Mac always took a corner room, which generally resulted in no inadvertent false notifications from a guest walking past his door.

Having a camera posted in a corner was never even noticed by the typical person. Of course, they would probably feel more self-conscious if they knew someone was watching them. Mac arrived at his room door and looked at his cell phone to see himself standing with his room key in hand. Ryker's toys functioned amazingly well. Except, of course, for that damn Triple D downloading device that almost inadvertently killed Mac at the Whispering Wind office.

The next CIA-recommended task was to insert a rubber door stopper at the bottom of the door. While it was not a permanent deterrent for a bad guy breaking into the room, it would significantly slow his progress. That slowing could provide a precious few seconds for Mac to grab a weapon or take a defensive position.

All their rooms were one-bedroom suites. The rooms were adorned with modern straight lines of classic sophistication. The oversized floor and ceiling moldings were intentionally part of the guest rooms to remind the guests of the hotel's elegant history from the late 1800s when the hotel was built.

The room's best part was the personal balcony and the Eiffel Tower's unobstructed view. Most who walked onto the balcony had romantic thoughts of their loved ones, even if they were alone. Paris was the city for lovers. In times like these, the romantic ambiance embedded in the core of Paris made Mac miss Mary. As Mac stared at the Eiffel Tower, he wondered if the rest of the team was also thinking about their loved ones.

Mac adorned his typical gym shorts and tee shirt for bedtime and plopped down on the king-size bed. He closed his eyes and went through his pre-sleep mental checklist. First, Mac pictured his hotel traveling go-bag that included all his essentials to make a quick exit. He then mentally confirmed that his slip-on shoes were by his bed, his gun under his pillow, and his phone within reach. Upon confirming he was ready for a quick response, he pleasantly nodded off to sleep.

A few hours later, Mac was awakened by the sound of footsteps.

Chapter 31

Paris, France Hotel

The camera feed on his phone displayed a standard four-intruder team assembling and inserting a mechanical device that could undoubtedly open any hotel door. The four men were all big boys wearing black with matching black face masks. Mac's feet landed in his shoes as he hit the floor. He grabbed his handgun and phone with a quick assessment of his surroundings. The shooters had yet to breach the outside hallway room door.

Mac rushed to the door and grasped an eighteen-century chair to prop against it. Just before he reached the door, it opened about ten alarming inches. Mac used his shoulder to brace against the door, preventing it from gapping further. The first shooter inserted his gun inside the doorway. Mac used a handy decorative statue as a club to smash the shooter's wrist. The gun dropped to the floor, and the shooter screamed in pain.

Silenced bullets start to pepper around the door opening. Mac doubled down on his pressure against the door and managed to shut it. He forced the top of the chair back under the doorknob and jammed the chair's feet as a lever against the floor. Bullets continued to pop against the door around the knob. Thanks to its solid wood construction and the nifty rubber door stopper, the door was holding for now. Nothing would hold these shooters back for long.

Mac ran to the bedroom as the shooters started to slam their shoulders against the door. While the door was sturdy, it was not made for the onslaught of bullets and muscled shoulders, demonstrating their brute strength and awkwardness. As Mac flew into the bedroom, the shooters broke open the door. They assessed the inside of the room with weapons scanning in several directions. Seeing no immediate threats, they proceeded to the only other option, the bedroom.

Mac dashed for the balcony, knowing that staying in a firefight with these shooters was useless. Also, he knew there was not enough time for the cavalry to come to his rescue. The balcony was the only place left. Wild bullets were ringing out all around him, and he dove for the railing and grabbed it. Mac flipped over the balcony's edge as bullets ricocheted off the metal. Generally, the average person would not willingly drop from an eight-story balcony. However, Mac was not the average person. He had a plan. Maybe it was a foolhardy plan, but at least it was a plan.

The balcony railing off the seventh-floor room flashed past his face in a matter of seconds. He aggressively and frantically extended his arms forward. His forearms banged against and slid down the railing, allowing his hands to grab something before plummeting to his certain death. More than once, he was thankful for his rock-solid grip from years of forearm exercises, and this time, he knew his life depended upon it. While he managed to find a good grasp, his feet were awkwardly moving like a baby just learning to crawl. The problem was that this baby was hanging in mid-air seven stories off the ground. He finally found a foothold to take the pressure off his hands.

Unfortunately, there was no time to relax. The shooters dashed to Mac's balcony and opened fire on him. A barrage of lead was raining down from the four smoking gun barrels, anxious to find their target. Mac had no other choice. He dropped to the next floor's balcony with bullets whizzing around him. With his newly gained knowledge of the art of balcony leaping, Mac assumed the second time would go better than the first. He was wrong.

As his face plummeted past the sixth-floor balcony, he noticed something white and slightly moving in front of him. His mind could not register what it was until it was too late. The hotel had a strict rule not to hang pool towels on the balcony railings to avoid the wind inadvertently catching a towel and flying away. However, not every hotel guest follows the rules. The guest in this sixth-floor room was one of them.

The lead shooter demanded, "You three get down to the first floor! I doubt this wild man could survive his hair-brained balcony stunt, but we can't take any chances. After dealing with this guy, we will find and kill the woman and the three other men from Abaddon's restaurant. Go now!"

The three shooters followed orders and dashed out of the room, heading for the stairs.

Mac grabbed the railing with his left hand but only clutched a plush white pool towel with his right. The towel slipped as Mac desperately held on with his unencumbered hand. He looked down and saw the source of his aggravation flittering quickly in the wind to the ground below.

His first attempt failed at swinging his body to grasp something. He clenched his teeth, forcefully twisted his core toward the balcony, and thankfully grabbed the metal with his dangling right hand. His left hand's grasp was slipping, and he knew he needed to find a ledge for his feet before he fell. Using the momentum of his last twist, he swung his legs to the right and then to the left like a child on a swing set. He made one last valiant swing, and his right foot found the balcony floor.

Taking one short pause to rest his aching muscles, Mac caught his breath. Bullets started pinging off the metal around him. This spot was only a little better than the last balcony. He was going to have to change the shooter's angle. Just before executing his plan, he said out loud, "This is not a good idea." He leaped.

Mac nailed his aerial acrobatics as he grabbed the adjacent balcony. He looked inside the room and saw Valencia curled up on her bed. Trying to wake her, Mac found she was sleeping much too soundly. He pulled out his weapon and, in a valiant effort, tapped on the balcony metal.

Valencia did not move. If he startled her, he ran the risk of her shooting him in a reaction of self-defense from a balcony attack.

Mac was running out of options. He couldn't reach his cell phone, so he drew his weapon, aiming toward the balcony sliding door with the intent of firing a well-placed round into the glass. A shot rang out from above him. The errant shot did not hit Mac but hit his gun barrel. The forcefulness of the bullet striking his gun resulted in his release of the weapon. He helplessly watched as it clanged on balcony railings while snaking its way to the ground.

To create horizontal space from the shooter, Mac jumped to another adjacent balcony. The shooting stopped, and there was an eerie quietness. Mac dropped down to another guest floor, knowing that the shooters would likely try to beat him to the ground. If they were waiting for him once he landed, he was a dead man. As usual, Mac maintained a calm mind based on his years of training. He had never tried a controlled fall from balconies and realized it was not that hard once you got the hang of it.

His mind was diverted to one of his favorite Marvel Comic Book superheroes, Spiderman. As he continued to make his way down, he sang the old theme song, "Spider-Man, Spider-Man, does whatever a spider can. Spins a web, any size. Catches thieves just like flies!"

Mac stopped at the third and final guest floor, wishing he had Spiderman's web-making abilities. There were no more balconies for his descent.

The only available option was to drop on the first-floor awning over the front entrance. With no hesitation, Mac let go and dropped. As he fell butt-first, he expected the canopy to soften his landing like a circus safety net. Mac quickly realized this may be one of his worst plans ever. He also thought about how Ryker does his maddening free rock-climbing crap. Doing something like this must seem like fun to him. Crazy.

Mac's concern about the sturdiness of the awning was unfounded. He landed squarely on it, and the fabric held, acting as a softening ramp to the ground. Once he hit it, Mac slid to his feet and rolled to protect his bones like a highly trained stuntperson. As his forward rolling momentum slowed, Mac stood up as if nothing had happened, demonstrating that dropping from the eighth floor was as routine as taking an elevator. He brushed his hands together to wipe off dirt and finger-combed his hair.

Fortuitously, Mac's gun was at his feet, and he picked it up. He knew the shooters would be converging on his position in a matter of seconds. Mac looked at the hotel entrance and saw the doorman staring at him with wide eyes in disbelief. It would not end well for the doorman if the shooters showed up with him still standing there gawking. That doorman had worked at this hotel for years and was an exceptionally nice guy. He did not deserve to die that way. To protect the doorman, Mac strode up to him with a diversionary plan.

"Would you please go up to the eighth floor to bring down my luggage? It seems I have forgotten it in the hallway in front of my usual room." Mac asked.

Dumbfounded, the doorman mumbled, "Yes. Yes. Of course. But how did you get down here?" The doorman politely responded as he was beginning to recover from his shock.

"I am happy to explain later, but right now, I need that luggage. Please take the elevator because the stairs might be crowded, and the elevator will be quicker." Mac said.

"Yes, sir. I will leave right now."

"Thank you so much."

The doorman turned quickly to walk away. Unfortunately, there were still guests in the lobby and clearly in the lines of fire. Right now, Mac needed to focus on alerting the team.

Mac pulled out his phone and sent a group text saying, "Battle stations, gang. Either in the lobby or outside the hotel. Four shooters. I am at the front entrance and need immediate backup."

Each team member immediately saw the text and went into their version of "action," knowing how best to utilize their skill set.

Valencia awoke from her deep sleep, trained to listen for the unique sound of a team text. Without a second thought, she knew where she could add the most value. Valencia reached under her bed and felt for the case, knowing it would be there. She pulled it out and felt comforted that it measured the expected three feet by one foot with a five-inch depth. Flinging it on the bed, she snapped it open. Inside was one of her favorite weapons.

It was a Ruger Precision bolt action sniper rifle complete with a high-range scope and, if necessary, a silencer. Everything about it was highly customized, from the trigger pull to the adjustable skeleton-style buttstock. The rifle was broken down into pieces that were stored in their own cushioned compartment within the case. Valencia could have reassembled it with her eyes closed, but she did not. It went together quicker than most people take to send a text on their phone.

Valencia seated the magazine with a satisfying snap and dashed to the edge of the balcony. She looked down through the scope with the butt of the rifle on her right shoulder.

Valencia was ready to snipe anything that did not belong. The sniper rifle compliments the DGSE, France's version of the CIA, as standard protocol every time the team is in Paris. While in France, the DGSE took care of Valencia. This time, it could be the difference between life and death.

Brock slipped into his shoes, conveniently sitting beside his bed, and grabbed his gun and phone. He flew out his door in seconds and headed to the stairs, where he started bounding down three stairs at a time. At each landing, Brock did a quick check overhead and below him. The team knew most shooters would take the stairs.

Gunner was following the same routine. He blasted out his door, almost knocking it off its hinges. As he passed the elevator, it dinged its arrival, and Gunner stopped in his tracks. Gunner pointed his Glock at the opening elevator doors.

The doors fully opened, and fortuitously, no one was in the elevator. Gunner stepped in and took a calming breath as the elevator descended. The pleasant instrumental music in the background presented a strange dichotomy to the likely crisis on the first floor. Gunner concealed his weapon in his beefy hands while assuming a casual stance.

Ryker's routine was very different. He grabbed a can of Red Bull, his highly caffeinated drink of choice, and popped the top. He downed the first can and pulled out a second. With a fresh Red Bull in hand, Ryker's eyes focused with clarity. As he released a big inhalation, he said out loud to no one, "Caffeine should be considered a major food group. Anyone who disagrees should stop by their local Starbucks and see the long line of people desperate for their three to five-dollar Venti cup of rocket fuel."

He raced to his laptop and began tapping on the keys. His hands were so fast and efficient that they looked like a pianist's lightning-fast touch on the ebony and ivory. He hacked into the hotel's security cameras, and a dozen videos opened on his screen like a Zoom conference call.

The shooter, who was the last to leave Mac's room, had the unfortunate experience of inadvertently running into Brock. Catching his breath on the third-floor stairwell landing, the shooter momentarily paused. His only known quarry was somewhere around the hotel's entrance, likely flattened like a pancake from falling to his death. No one could have survived that, and he had his three men searching for the body. Gasping for air, he stopped for a few seconds for a break. Those cigarettes were going to kill him someday.

Brock wore specially designed rubber-soled shoes that made his steps impossible to hear. The shooter had a shocked expression when he looked in Brock's direction as he was bounding down the stairs. The shooter raised his weapon, but his fate was already determined.

The team members were all well-trained in close-quarters combat, and Brock landed just a few feet from the shooter.

Using his fingertips to jab deep into the shooter's throat below the Adam's Apple, Brock effectively crushed his windpipe, cutting off the oxygen supply to the shooter's lungs. Two quick punches to each side of the shooter's neck severely damaged the shooter's carotid arteries supplying blood to his brain. The shooter released his weapon and grabbed his throat in a vain attempt to stem the pain and oxygen loss. It was a useless gesture because his fate was already sealed. Brock kicked the fatally wounded shooter's gun down the stairs as the shooter stumbled backward, falling into a contorted death. Brock turned and continued down the stairs to help Mac.

Ryker used their comms to give everyone a sitrep. "Guys, we have three shooters already in the lobby. They are frantically looking around. Brock, I was impressed by how you took out that shooter on the third-floor stairwell landing. Take caution before you burst into the lobby because the other three will mow you down as soon as you open the first-floor door. Gunner, same with you as you exit the elevator. Mac, unfortunately, you're in the open with no cover and directly in the shooters' path."

Mac looked at the big picture and said, "How many noncombatants are in the lobby? From my position, I only count four."

"Negative. There must be at least a dozen hotel guests walking around. You cannot see them from your vantage point. I know you're concerned about collateral damage, but I think there are no other options except to take chances."

"Ryker, is there a position I can take to ensure no noncombatants are caught in the crossfire?"

"Negative, Mac. They are all scattered throughout the lobby."

"Since I cannot see most people in the lobby, can you tell the good guys and bad guys apart?" Mac asked.

"The three shooters are all in black and are carrying handguns. I guarantee you will know the shooters as soon as you see them." Ryker replied, trying to be as helpful as possible.

"Roger that," responded Mac.

Mac risked a quick look around the pillars at the entrance and saw two of the shooters. He concluded that Ryker was right. They were easy to spot unless you were lost doing something with your cell phone, like virtually every hotel guest. If the guests knew they were in danger, there would have been chaos in the lobby. The shooters would have likely mowed them all down to take control of the situation. This situation was one of the times it was a blessing that most of the worldwide population had no situational awareness.

"The guests have not yet noticed these guys." Ryker was now focusing on only six cameras. Four were recording from their perch in the lobby's corners, and two were focused on Gunner and Brock.

"Copy," said Mac. He knew it would not take long for one of the guests to identify the threat and scream out. It will be like yelling "fire" in a crowded theater, except that the shooters will have a different take on the concept of "fire." Noncombatants will run in every direction, which will not end well for them.

Timing his movements to minimize discovery by the shooters, Mac took another look around the pillars. The picture was burnt into his photographic memory, along with potential exits and the location of each hotel guest. He did not like what he saw. One shooter was led in front of the other two shooters. Mac concluded that he could not take them out with three shots. The two back shooters would return fire before he could pop them. These guys did not care who was killed because they swiftly walked through the lobby with guns, sweeping for potential targets.

Mac made a critical decision and stated in his comms, "I will draw the shooters away from the hotel guests. Look for me in the front around the hotel Amphitrite fountain." The center of the circular fountain shot up twenty feet and made quite a statement. It looked beautiful and a great place to flip a coin with a wish, but it would not stop many bullets. Still, Mac had to try.

In unison, the team all replied, "Negative Mac. You'll be a sitting duck."

Mac jokingly replied, "I loved playing with water guns as a kid." He stepped in the open and shouted, "Hey, fellas! Over here!" Then he turned around and bolted to the front of the fountain. He stood there with his handgun, ready for action but hidden behind his back.

Ryker gave his sitrep, saying, "The first shooter is at the hotel entrance. The next two shooters are trailing by ten feet."

When the first shooter reached the hotel entrance, he saw Mac. They stared at each other for a quick second. Mac could tell by the shooter's response that he was shocked at seeing Mac alive after basically falling from the eighth floor. Mac started running for cover, and the shooter gave chase. Mac turned backward and fired two quick shots at his pursuer.

Valencia acquired her first target and chambered a round. The shooter was in the open, between the hotel entrance and the fountain. Simultaneously with Mac firing over his shoulder, Valencia fingered her sniper rifle's trigger, and the skull of the shooter exploded apart. The momentum of the high-velocity round caused the shooter to land, where he took his last step. Mac looked back to see the shooter falling and considered that one of his crazy rounds hit the shooter for a split second. Then he pieced the scene together and said in his comms, "Nice shot, Valencia."

"Acknowledged," Valencia replied as she was already scanning for more shooters.

The last two shooters stopped and regrouped at the edge of the doorway. Gunner and Brock arrived at the entrance at about the same time. The scene immediately evolved into something that looked like a WWE tag-team grudge match. Brock took a running leap and landed with one foot on a chair while his other knee pumped up, extending his jumping distance as he flew off in the shooters' direction. The shooters were not looking backward and did not see this wild flying man grab them both by the shoulders and tackle them to the ground.

It was now Gunner's turn, and he deadlifted one shooter over his shoulders. The shooter was not a small man, but he was still no match for Gunner's sheer power. While performing this maneuver multiple times in the past, Gunner was accustomed to the roaring chants from adoring fans. In those ring situations, the movements were staged, but the fans did not care. In this situation, the necessary actions would not be planned, but Gunner did not care. In one fluid sweep, he dropped down on his right knee and threw the shooter headfirst down on the marble floor. The shooter's head cracked open, and multiple vertebrae were crushed. This shooter was down permanently.

The last shooter recovered at the same time as Brock. The shooter landed a strong punch, but Brock responded with a left jab and a right hook. The shooter countered with a stomach punch that would have doubled over anyone who did not have Brock's daily workout routine, including extensive abdominal training.

The shooter then attempted a knockout blow with an uppercut to Brock's chin. Brock blocked the punch and was getting pissed off. When the team must fight, the objective is never to duke it out with someone honorably. It was all about life and death. Just before Brock's leap, he slid his gun into the waistband of his shorts. He just needed enough spacing to pull out the gun and send two rounds into the shooter.

Brock delivered a sharp jab, and the shooter stumbled and fell to the floor. The shooter saw his gun on the floor next to him and reached for it. He whirled and pointed it at Brock before Brock could pull his weapon from behind him. It was certain death for Brock.

Gunner came to Brock's defense out of nowhere and jumped to the top of a radiator as if it were the ropes of a wrestling ring. He executed an aerial technique that he named the Falling Comet. Gunner leaped toward the prone shooter. He completed a backward spin and landed with his elbow, driving into the face of the shooter before a shot was fired. Unfortunately for the shooter, his head flattened upon impact, between the placement of Gunner's elbow and a hard marble floor rather than a bouncy wrestling ring.

Mac was running towards the front entrance, but Gunner and Brock did not need any assistance. Ryker announced the all-clear. He placed a call to the DGSE for their cleanup crew. The hotel would never know there was an altercation within an hour except for a few complaining guests.

Mac said in his comms, "I think we have solved the mystery of Operation Busboy. We were the dirty dishes for his shooters to clean up. This time, the dishes fought back."

Mac approached the hotel owner and said, "I am sorry for the disturbance. We have already called a local cleaning company to take care of any damage. They are quite good, but if you notice any additional damage, please put it on my bill."

The hotel owner was still just staring at him with his mouth agape.

Mac, trying to get the hotel owner to focus, said, "Undoubtedly, there will be a multitude of questions from hotel guests who observed this little dispute in your lobby. I suggest you tell them you were trying out some WWE entertainment for the hotel guests and that no one was hurt."

All the hotel owner could do was nod in agreement.

Mac replied, "Very well. We will be checking out earlier than planned."

Chapter 32

Blackwood Castle, United Kingdom

Blackwood, Abaddon, and Zag were strategizing their next steps. They were in Blackwood's office at Blackwood Castle in the UK. For having such wealth, the oversized room was surprisingly decorated with limited furniture. The main piece of furniture was a large and heavy desk. Its ornateness demonstrated its creation from eons long ago. There was a matching winged-back leather chair behind the desk and three modest guest chairs.

On the sides of the room were a few tables stacked with a variety of Blackwood's collectibles. Dozens of books adorned the built-in bookshelves on the walls.

"I couldn't care less about everything in the room except for two critical items. The first is this laptop that controls my burgeoning empire. The second is my life-changing fan," said Blackwood.

Blackwood gently caressed his fan and stroked it as if it were a purring cat. He said, "You know, this fan is just like me. It was somehow significant but tossed away like garbage by society. With some dusting and polishing, we will again be recognized for our inherent importance to the world. This fan belongs on a pedestal just like everyone will put me on a pedestal once I control all the planet's electrical power."

Stating confidently, Blackwood continued, "We know the EMP concept works based upon our success in Rio. Rio will be recovering for years, trying to rebuild its saltwater power plant. The payoff for insider information I bought regarding Rio's saltwater advancement was very valuable. I do not like competition from technology that could be used to replace us. Legally, they will be prohibited from rebuilding their power plant once they execute my exclusive power supply agreement."

"Hell, they will tear down the Christ the Redeemer statue and replace it with one of you," responded Zag.

Blackwood smiled and said, "Are we still on target for the simultaneous EMP attack in five days?"

"Yes, the satellites will be in position over North and South America. We tested the EMP delivery system before installing it on the satellites, and they work just as designed. They will release the broadly dispersed energy in the atmosphere without creating a nuclear explosion."

"Very well, Zag. Can we get away with releasing the EMP attack without the world tagging the blame on us?" asked Blackwood.

Zag nodded and added, "There's no way to detect the source of the EMP attacks that will cause the geomagnetic storm. Of course, there will be conspiracy theorists all over the internet suggesting a multitude of nefarious acts. However, there will be no proof of our involvement."

With the mention of the faceless cowards on the internet, Blackwood grimaced. He angrily slammed his fist on the table and screamed, "We cannot let our miscalculations cause criticism! We will focus on the positives and not the negatives!"

Zag calmed Blackwood by interrupting, "We will only be viewed as heroes. No, we will be viewed as visionary heroes with the insight to cover all our facilities in Faraday cages. The Faraday cages cover the power plants, the battery plant, and space rocket facilities. None of our operations will be damaged by the EMPs. The geothermal power plants are fully operational. The underwater cabling is laid, waiting to connect to the countries and bypass their EMP-fried power plants and relay stations."

Blackwood relaxed some in his seat. "Of course. You are right. We have laid the groundwork exactly as I have designed in our strategic plan."

Zag added, "The more I analyze the Blitzpeicher, the more I am convinced the guy who created it was a genius. Based on my calculations, I think the batteries could last a couple of years without replacement or recharging. There is no need to manufacture a vehicle. We will make a fortune just making all the car batteries. We will have a 500 percent gross profit built into our pricing. It's a gold mine."

"That's so true, Zag. Our return on capital will be dramatically higher by selling the batteries than the illusion of success by selling vehicles."

"The technology I borrowed from the Blitzpeicher was very straightforward to upgrade using today's standards. Plus, the technology borrowed for the geothermal processors is working better than we could have expected. Our power plants are prepared to function much more efficiently than our Congo facility. The countries will have no choice but to buy their power from us unless they want to live in the Dark Ages for several decades."

Blackwood was on the same page as Zag and shared, "After we have been running for two or three years, I think we can go public. The investors will bid the stock up to the atmosphere. The market will view us as a technology company with the payback from all my significant technology investments. I can confidently state that the valuation should be worth hundreds of billions of euros. First, I think we need to own the power delivery markets in Europe, Asia, and Russia to ensure those revenues are included in our IPO valuation. How are you coming with the delivery of non-perishable food?"

"We have more than adequate food supplies to carry us for several years at all our locations. Without fuel for agricultural equipment, the Americas' food industry will crumble, forcing localized, small-quantity growing and dependency upon European and Asian production," replied Zag.

Blackwood looked pleased with the news and shared, "Undoubtedly, millions of people will die from starvation, but that's the cost of those countries' arrogance and lack of foresight into the value I bring to the table. I hope this will force a worldwide depression. That will open the eyes of any naysayer who finds our high pricing unacceptable. At least I am giving them a solution that will eventually bring them back to today's standards. With the inevitable depression and deaths, there will be uncontrolled social unrest. What does our security situation look like at the plants and here at Blackwood Castle?"

Abaddon replied, "We could defend against an attack from a small army. Besides our main internal force, we will increase perimeter security at a couple of the plants. However, when you start talking about millions of people dying, you're naïve if you don't think we'll be attacked. Suppose we're assaulted as retaliation because of the staggering deaths. In that case, they will come after us with everything short of nuclear weapons, and then our security will be tenuous, at best. I don't know what you are talking about when discussing returns on investment or this technology nonsense. However, if we take on this high-risk level, my men and I need the appropriate payment for our services."

"You only need to worry about business security until we execute the EMP attack. We will need less security after the EMP. We will cripple the Americas, and they will desperately need our power generation ability. They would not even consider challenging us, and we will only have superficial security needs," replied Blackwood in a reassuring tone.

"I have the feeling you view my team's security as an afterthought. Let me state the obvious so you clearly understand the facts. My team and our objectives are mission-critical. You do not want my men coming after you if you decide to weasel out on paying us or me."

Blackwood cautiously responded, "Abaddon, I fully intend on honoring our agreement. We have growing security needs, and I am certainly willing to pay for that administrative cost."

"What do you mean when you call my security an administrative cost?" Abaddon's ire and voice were raised at the inference of not being an operational function.

Blackwood smiled and said, "Abaddon, do not take everything so literally. Security just rolls up into the administrative cost line. I am an administrative expense, too. I need you for our success. Let's just stay focused rather than worrying about each of our roles."

Abaddon glared and was not convinced. He managed to regain his composure and replied, "My men are battle-ready and all in."

"Okay. Good to hear. Now, back to more pressing matters. The more social unrest after the EMP, the quicker the countries will want to escape from their new normal, which means utilizing our energy. Of course, if we decide to sell power to the countries, we will add a generous premium to their pricing. Do we have instigators in place and ready for activation?"

"Affirmative. We have contracted with approximately 400 sleeper cells across North and South America to instigate riots and murders within the first week after the EMP. These instigators will keep raising the bar with violence until their country risks an overthrown government. If they do not develop plans quickly, there will be anarchy and disregard for social norms," Abaddon replied, visibly relaxing with the discussion of his role.

"Perfect. Most importantly, do we have communication access to the United States President, the Canadian prime minister, and the South American Heads? Once the EMP destroys all their electronics, including cell phones, we will not be able to offer our solution to their misfortune," commented Blackwood.

Abaddon responded with, "Most but not all. We understand that certain South American countries do not have

EMP protections for their governmental official's command and control. Not every country believes EMPs are a real threat or at least does not appreciate the devastating implications."

"Those fools will learn quickly about disregarding the importance of energy and the inherent risks to their power grids," responded Blackwood.

The three men laughed heartedly and shared vigorous head nods.

"We understand the more developed countries keep spare communication equipment in Faraday pouches. Those countries will be easy to contact. Irrespective of their level of preparedness, we have plans in place to approach each of the governments simultaneously after the EMP attacks," said Abaddon.

Blackwood became visibly more comfortable as the discussion proceeded. He said, "You told us about the CIA operatives' inquiries in Paris. You said you had it handled, but I do not believe we have heard back from your Paris mercenaries tasked to take out those pests. They do not seem to realize they must die."

"None of my shooters are responding to attempts to contact them on their burners. They are some of the best in the business, and I cannot fathom how simple-minded targets could stop those pros from killing them. My mercs are probably in the middle of their attack and are functioning in silent mode."

"Is there any way to track your mercenaries back to us? Of course, I am not saying they failed. Still, I am just curious in a worst-case scenario," asked Blackwood, barely hiding his concern about failure.

Abaddon confidently and definitively replied, "There's no possible way to tie my assassins in Paris to us. No way."

Blackwood took a full cleansing breath and said, "Gentlemen, you will be millionaires. We must now act as if it's business as usual and not draw any unnecessary attention. You have done well. At this juncture, there's nothing that can go wrong."

Chapter 33

CIA Jet

Aboard the CIA jet, it was time to let off a little steam. The powder keg in Paris caught the team off guard. They had all risen to the occasion, but the attack was a harsh reminder of the seemingly overly committed adversary in their path. They were dealing with people who would go to any length to ensure the success of their sinister plan.

Teasingly, Brock said, "Gunner, I cannot believe you did not keep at least one of the shooters alive. You could have at least kept one of them around for questioning."

Gunner countered by noting, "Brock, you killed one of the shooters in the stairwell. Plus, I am pretty sure the shooter Val put down with a gray matter splatter on the circle driveway pavement was not going to talk much after that."

"Whatever, dude. Hey, what was all that fake WWE bullshit you used in the lobby?"

Gunner stuck up his index finger, pulled it towards himself, and said, "Why don't you come over here, and I will show you a fake move or two."

Valencia jumped in the fun exchange. "Boys, boys, boys. We all just reacted to these shooters who were about to kill Mac. The way I think about it, I blame Mac for waking us up, forcing us out of bed, and ensuring we missed a tasty French breakfast! So, Mr. Mac, what do you have to say for yourself?"

Before Mac could deflect the attack, Ryker, working his keyboard, finished tracking down a lead and shared his findings. "I know the name of the Whispering Wind Industries' silent investor."

Everyone stopped ribbing each other and turned to Ryker with total interest.

Ryker said, "I had to triangulate into the answer from six different paths. Knowing that Abaddon was involved helped seal the deal for me. What led to the guy was this obscure file MI6 maintained in an offsite location from…."

Brock's impatience boiled over. "Ryker, stop! Tell us who it is!"

"Oh, sorry. Sometimes, I enjoy the chase so much that I cannot stop myself from sharing the detailed process! The silent investor in Whispering Wind Industries is a guy named Dr. Blackwood. Abaddon is most certainly involved, too. I found substantial funds transferred into Abaddon's restaurant from Dr. Blackwood's bank accounts," shared Ryker.

"The plot thickens. Now, if we just knew what Blackwood and Abaddon were up to." Mac added.

Ryker continued explaining more of his findings. "I also found some interesting details about Dr. Blackwood's business dealings. He has three power plants under construction just off the North and South American coasts. There have been continual pictures taken of them from satellites, but no one can get a good look because they are covered in a protective turtle shield. From the reports, the analysts conclude that the turtle shields are intended for secrecy. As a result, I cannot determine their level of completion."

Continuing his explanation, Ryker said, "Now the story takes a weird twist. A few years ago, Dr. Blackwood started building a conglomerate with a hostile takeover of a space rocket company. Under its new owner, the space rocket company has made several missions into outer space, including docking with the International Space Station and satellite launching. Before Dr. Blackwood bought it, it was a very successful company, and it seems to be even more successful now."

Gunner added, "Sure, we have heard about an independent space rocket company sending some astronauts to the International Space Station. That's been well-publicized in every media outlet. However, I don't recall the media talking about the company's ownership."

Ryker took his analyses one step further for the team and said, "They never once mentioned the company's ownership structure. That was likely because it was owned via a very intricate weave of shell companies worldwide. Now, let's take this analysis even more in-depth. We know there have been satellite missions. However, think about it. Besides some general innocuous verbiage about communication satellites, no one knows those satellites' real purpose. The public is always enthralled with just watching the television coverage of a rocket taking off with fire and smoke shooting out the rocket's main engines. Do we have any idea of the satellites' capabilities?"

Valencia was tracking with Ryker's train of thought and added, "Great point. We had much more comfort in satellite capabilities when they were controlled exclusively by NASA. Now that private companies place many satellites in orbit, the satellites' purposes could easily be manipulated."

Mac sat up straight in his chair and said, "Wait a minute. The mention of power plants reminds me of something. Is it possible that Blackwood is the guy who became the laughingstock of the power industry with his failed geothermal power plant for the Congo about a decade ago? Blackwood is not a very common name. It can't be a coincidence."

"Yes, I think you're right. That must be the same guy. He's been in seclusion after his public tar and feathering. Blackwood became the scapegoat of the fiasco from a huge earthquake and tsunami that caused a massive failure in his geothermal power plant. The power plant killed many people, and he was villainized."

Brock added, "That dude is screwed up."

Ryker added, "To tie a nice bow on it, remember the conversation using the cell phone listening device Mac planted at Whispering Wind Industries just before the explosion? Joe Whisp was talking to some guy named Forest. Whisp told him their attempt to eliminate us at our homes was unsuccessful. In response, Forest was furious. It must have been Dr. Forest Blackwood who was directing Whisp to have us killed!"

There was a moment of silence at Ryker's mention of them being under attack in their backyard. An assault of that nature had never happened before to a CIA covert operative team, and it was a shock to the system. They all worked on stifling their frustration and anger.

Mac broke the silence and commented, "Yes, I am sure we all remember that reference to Forest. You have done a fine job pulling disparate pieces of information together to give us a strong lead. Is there anything we can use to tie him to the EMP attack in Rio?"

"No." Ryker looked up with wide eyes as his mop of hair hung over his face. He froze with a thought. "Wait. I was not thinking about the Rio EMP attack. Let me double-check."

Mac cut him off and asked, "Could those protective turtle shields you described covering the plant be Faraday cages to protect them from a future EMP? Could Blackwood have orchestrated the attack on the Rio power plant? The two attacks have Abaddon's name written all over them."

"Of course! Let me start working on why he would target to destroy the new power plant," Ryker replied.

"I do not have a good feeling about this. My gut tells me Blackwood has a much larger and more sinister plan in the works. Ryker, please dig into all your sources and unearth everything about him. See if you can determine how he leaped frogged so quickly with his technology," Mac directed.

"One thing I know for sure is there was this guy named Zag who worked for him during the African power plant fiasco. From the resulting inquiries, it was found that he and Zag stole the technology from others. Maybe all the technology for their current operations was stolen as well. I am not sure I can find much else because the entire organization is hidden under a cloak of secrecy."

Looking at each of them with concern on his face, Mac said, "This is bigger than us and the attack on us. We were just a little piece in a much bigger set of events. One of the lessons I learned from consulting is what terrifies me now. I don't know what I don't know."

Mac was always sharing little snippets of insights they referred to as Mac-isms. Sometimes, they were more superficial and simplistic. Other times, they had a deeper meaning requiring some reflection. This Mac-ism required some contemplation to appreciate its far-reaching significance.

Now in full execution mode, Mac said, "We need to coordinate with MI6 once we secure some evidence against this cabal. I think we will potentially need more firepower for everyone's safety. Let's set a course for London. Brock, reach out to your MI6 buddy who saved my bacon a few weeks ago. What are everyone's thoughts on the plan for our next steps?" While Mac was very self-reliant, he knew there was always a higher likelihood of success when working together to develop and execute a plan.

Valencia said in a teasing and admiring way, "Since when did you start sticking to a plan?"

Mac replied, "Since our world as we know it and our very lives depend upon executing the right plan."

Chapter 34

MI6 Headquarters, London

The remaining part of the flight to London was filled with more questions than answers. After arriving at Heathrow Airport, the team took a car to their obligatory stop at the London Embassy. At the Embassy, the team checked in with their CIA counterparts and placed a quick call with Rainey. Fortunately, it was less than a mile from the building housing the British Secret Intelligence Service, MI6. It was about a ten-minute walk, but instead, they opted to take a car since every minute counted in this potentially world-changing, hideous plot masterminded by Blackwood.

Sitting in MI6's version of the Langley Situation Room, the team continued strategizing while waiting for their MI6 liaison. MI6's Situation Room was a conference room like every other Secret Service Situation Room.

MI6 Agent Rhys Cromwell strode confidently into the room. He wore a dark navy business suit, a white shirt with French cuffs, and a matching tie. Rhys had the appearance of anyone walking into the Langley Situation Room. He had a confident air about him that demonstrated his experience in field operations.

Everyone stopped talking in the room, and the faces turned towards Rhys. He nodded, smiled at Mac and Brock, and began the introductions. "I am Agent Rhys Cromwell. Welcome to MI6 headquarters."

Mac thought Rhys's elegant British accent made him sound more intelligent than the rest of the team. That concept was fostered by some long-ago ideal in American culture and perpetuated by movies romanticizing the debonair British Secret Service agent. Mac chuckled to himself and realized that Rhys was responsible for orchestrating Mac's helicopter rescue via the Vauxhall Pleasure Gardens.

"Hey Rhys, good to see you again, buddy. I didn't know you were behind my exfil at Vauxhall," Mac responded. They broke with formal tradition and heartily hugged each other, demonstrating a relationship stemming from being downrange together during their military days.

Brock followed Mac's lead and gave Rhys a welcoming, brief, and forceful man hug. It was clear that the three of them knew each other at a deep level.

Everyone else introduced themselves to Rhys, and they each shared a warm handshake.

Mac asked Rhys, "Were you behind my exfil from the Pleasure Gardens?"

"Well, officially, MI6 does not operate on British soil, and I haven't the foggiest idea of what you are talking about."

"And unofficially?"

"Yes, I pulled a few strings in the name of foreign country cooperation," said Rhys as he gave a modest smile and looked away.

Brock added, "Thank you. It was pretty dicey until your beautiful helicopter showed up." Brock knew Rhys needed to understand the depth of his appreciation.

Rhys responded, "From what I heard, you already had it well under control. Of course, except for the stack of dead shooters. The dead always seem to create a pile of headaches for some paper-pusher in the police department. All kidding aside, the memory stick will bring down a master network of bad guys located in the U.K. They were involved in everything from drugs to prostitution, to human trafficking, to illegal gambling, and finally, even murder. They had a worldwide reach, and we're shutting them down. They're the worst imaginable bad boys. We owe this whole team a huge debt of gratitude."

"Glad we could help. We are all on the same team fighting the same bad guys," said Mac.

There was a soft knock on the door. After Rhys replied affirmatively, an administrative assistant brought in complete tea service, a welcome sight for everyone. There was something very British about having tea. Some of them added sugar lumps, and some added milk. However, the ultimate pleasure was the aroma and taste of the pleasant treat. Mac noted that they did not offer coffee. It was just as well because the team had been in the U.K. enough to appreciate a cup of high-quality tea. They each held up their cup and took their first sips after a slight nod of their heads. There was a moment of silence as each appreciated the richness of their customized cup of heaven.

Gunner broke the silence and said to Rhys, "Mac and Brock will not tell us how you know each other. Before we get into the heart of the discussion, would you mind resolving our curiosity and determining who wins our side bet?"

Ryker added, "For the record, I think you and Brock both dated the same lady, but Brock warned you that the lady was no lady at all. She was part of a sleeper cell that was just activated to kill operatives all over the world."

"I must say, Ryker, you have a very vivid imagination. No, it was nothing so lurid as that." Rhys leaned back as if pondering a time from a different era.

"What! There goes my buck," said Ryker.

Rhys explained, "I was in the British military at the time on a routine patrol in Afghanistan. We were part of the NATO coalition, and the day seemed like any other long day in the sand. I kept getting irritated by a flash of light in my eyes coming from our ten o'clock. I assumed it was just some piece of garbage left on the top of the dune, and in another ten or twenty steps, I would be past the irritant."

Mac interrupted, "Careful using the word garbage!"

Ignoring the comment, Rhys continued, "We continued proceeding into the valley. About five minutes later, a wild American soldier began bounding down the dune, firing his M4 at some point not too far in front of us. It looked like he was confused, emptying magazines into mounds of sand at the bottom."

"Did you say American?" Gunner asked.

"Yes, this soldier was from your beloved country. Out of nowhere, a dozen insurgents popped up and began returning fire at him. It didn't take long for us to scatter and give those insurgents a healthy dose of hell as we filled their hiding spots with lead. One of the last insurgents stood for a better shooting angle and drilled a couple of rounds into the American. The soldier went tumbling down the dune head over heels. Of course, that was the last time that evil bastard ever fired on someone from NATO. I think we hit him a half dozen times with automatic fire."

Rhys took a breath and continued, "Between the several insurgents taken out by the American and the others eliminated by my team, the field of battle was clear. We ran over to the soldier, lying on his back with bullet holes in his legs. Fortunately, he was very much alive. As soon as he saw me, he said we were walking into an ambush, and he was trying to warn us with his mirror. Since we didn't respond, we left him no choice but to attack."

Stopping to collect his thoughts, Rhys was filled with flashback memories that he had not publicly shared since his military discharge.

Knowing this battle description had come to an end, Valencia politely said, "I still don't understand how you guys know each other. Sure, the guy was a war hero in jeopardizing his life to save you, but what does that have to do with Mac or Brock?"

It was Mac's turn to talk, and he said, "Rhys, you got most of it right. What you are missing in the story is that I had called in an airstrike on the insurgents. I had been watching them accumulate and knew we had to eliminate the threat tactically. You were less than seven minutes from a big bang. You were either going to be slaughtered by the insurgents or by our friendly fire. Fortunately, I was able to call off the airstrike after I knew we had won the firefight. The important thing you missed in the story is, rather than saying you were walking into an ambush, I said, 'Dumbass, you were walking into an ambush.' I did everything to try and warn you except sending you a singing telegram!"

Rhys said, "Details, details."

Everyone, including Rhys, broke out into a healthy belly laugh.

War experiences create a bond between soldiers that non-soldiers can never truly understand. There was something about the shared experience of the adrenaline-pumping events. It comes from knowing that the soldier beside you, or in this situation, the soldier running down a sand dune in front, has your back and would sacrifice their life for yours.

Rhys said, "My men and I will never forget or be able to repay your selfless courage under fire to save our lives."

"I don't think I will ever forget all those beers we had that night after the docs patched me up. I'm just glad Brock was there to help us keep up with you Brits." Mac said. He was hoping they would have time for some more beers once this mission was over.

Mac said to Rhys, "We need to read you in on our intel about a dastardly plot that could lead to the deaths of millions of people worldwide."

"Go ahead. You have my attention. Also, once you said worldwide, you were in my jurisdiction."

"Have you heard the name of Dr. Forest Blackwood?" Mac asked.

"Yes, of course. Blackwood is a very reclusive fellow. He was the mastermind behind a failed sham energy plot, resulting in countless deaths in the Congo. The chap has been hiding in his home, Blackwood Castle, for about the last decade. I believe if he steps foot in Africa again, he will be put in cuffs and escorted to the gallows for immediate execution."

"Blackwood is the mastermind and puppeteer in a new plot that will shake the very foundation of modern society. Let me start at the beginning and explain more." Mac shared the complete set of events with Rhys, including speculations to tie together the entire devious plot.

Rhys stared at Mac as the full breadth of devastation soaked in and said, "We need proof to take decisive action. Blackwood is still a British citizen, and we cannot barge into Blackwood Castle as we could in some other countries."

"Of course, we knew you would take that position. We would not put you in an awkward spot of siding with us or upholding the law. What we need is to have someone enter Blackwood Castle under false pretenses. If that person could wear a wire and pry a confession out of Blackwood, we could arrest him and quickly unravel the entire scheme," responded Mac.

Rhys stared at the ceiling and tapped his index finger on the side of his face. He said, "Now if we could only find someone willing to risk their life by going in alone to the Devil's Den at Blackwood Castle, place a concealed bug, and wear a wire."

Chapter 35

Blackwood Castle, United Kingdom

Mac pulled up in his car provided by MI6. No, it was not an Aston Martin DB5. He teasingly said in his comms, "Rhys, don't all MI6 agents drive an Aston Martin? I thought your special R&D department would have added a large array of gadgets to the car. I keep looking for the side and trunk machine guns, a passenger ejector seat, oil sprayers for the rear pursuers, and other goodies. I think MI6 is slipping."

"You Yanks watch way too many fanciful movies. By the way, for your safety and the safety of those around you, don't push any buttons or pull any levers, even if you think you know what they do," Rhys said with a sly smile and a wink at Brock.

That comment brought a smirk to Mac's face. He walked up to the guard at the entrance of Blackwood Castle and showed his fake credentials. Today, Mac was an attorney representing the relatively newly formed United States Space Force.

Although Blackwood Castle did not have a moat, it was just as well fortified with a front entrance double door six inches thick of solid wood stretching fifteen feet high. The large wood planks were held together with black iron slats secured by huge bolts drilled from the front to the back. When the castle was first built, it must have taken a small army to open and close the doors. Today, it is operated by pushing a button attached to hydraulic arms. Once a guest passed the computer screen checked by the guard, the doors opened, and the guest was permitted to enter the Great Hall.

Mac stepped into the Great Hall's massive stone hallway with its arched ceiling. Inlets along the hallway served as the resting place for knights' coats of armor, holding various menacing weapons.

The guard said in an Eastern European accent, "Please wait here momentarily. You will be assisted shortly."

Fortunately, the guard did not check Mac for his listening device. Even if he did, it was unlikely he would have found anything. Thanks to the CIA techno gurus, Mac's listening device was a basic-looking and functioning pen that could hear conversations from five miles away.

Abaddon walked down the hallway and greeted Mac. Mac recognized Abaddon immediately from his picture and hideous facial scar. However, Mac remained incognito, with his ruse still intact.

"I understand you are here hoping to meet with Dr. Blackwood even though this is an unannounced visit," said Abaddon.

"Yes, that's true. I just flew in from the United States and did not have time to call ahead. Please excuse my intrusion. I'm an attorney working for the United States Space Force and have a critical matter to discuss with Dr. Blackwood regarding his space operations."

"One moment, please," Abaddon said and made a call purportedly to Blackwood. Mac could not hear the discussion but saw Abaddon nod his head in confirmation.

Abaddon plainly stated, "Dr. Blackwood is exceptionally busy, but you are in luck. He has agreed to meet you for a short meeting."

"Excellent, that's very kind of him," Mac replied.

"Please follow me," Abaddon said, leading Mac down the long hallway.

Mac could not help but gawk at the display of the knight's shiny coat of arms while holding their vicious battle weapons from eons ago.

Noticing Mac's diverted attention to the coat of arms, Abaddon added, "Don't worry about the knight's weapons. If you don't touch them, you will not get hurt."

"Oh, I'm not worried about the weapons. I'm more concerned that some poor soul might be encased in one of those steel coffins. He would be trapped here with the misplaced hope of someday receiving great wealth," Mac replied, giving Abaddon a crafty smile.

Abaddon simply stared at Mac while trying to evaluate this attorney from an unknown United States space agency.

They walked up a wide stairwell and down another hallway to Blackwood's office. He was sitting at his desk.

"Your unexpected guest, sir." Abaddon stepped to the side, allowing Mac to walk into Blackwood's office.

"Mr. Blackwood, my name is Declan Mac. I'm an attorney from the United States Space Force." Mac stuck out his hand, and they shook hands in greeting.

"Sir, I have a doctorate. Please refer to me as Dr. Blackwood."

"Certainly. I meant no disrespect. We need to inspect your space facilities to confirm the capabilities of your most recently launched satellites."

Blackwood replied, "I have initiated multiple space missions since acquiring the company. We have flown to the International Space Station to deliver badly needed food and supplies and launched several communication satellites that successfully orbit the Earth. I find it thrilling to watch the space rockets take off. The flights require engineering and brainpower from scientists with decades of experience. My employees and outside attorneys are exceptional at their jobs."

"Have you had any involvement once the spaceship left the launchpad?" Mac asked.

"Yes, we most certainly do. We have total control over the missions from beginning to end. My Vice President of Operations and Technology, Zag, and I monitor from my laptop on my desk," added Blackwood as he gestured to Zag, sitting quietly in the corner. Zag was obviously not allowed to talk during the meeting.

Mac looked at Zag, squiggling in his seat, and suspected that Zag had no title in the organization. Blackwood must throw around lofty business titles to impress the uninformed. He didn't appreciate that the only effect of using this grand title was to make Zag uncomfortable.

Mac's questions began to bounce around topics to throw Blackwood off his game. He said, "Our laptops are certainly impressive compared to the Apollo-era computers that had only a fraction of our cell phones' processing capacity. Not to change subjects, but I see you have quite an eclectic collection of items on those tables. What people collect is always fascinating to me. I fancy myself as a collector, too. Do you mind telling me the story behind the items?"

Blackwood boasted, "My collection is like no other you will find. During my worldwide travels, I have sought out mechanical inventions from yesteryear. Most people look at these treasures and incorrectly conclude they are better placed in a garbage heap. However, they are quite naïve. Each of my items has paved the way for bigger and better inventions that have positively impacted today's society."

Mac reached for the old fan on Blackwood's desk and said, "As an example, what's the history of this old fan?"

Blackwood jumped out of his chair and screamed, "Stop!"

Mac pulled his hand back quickly as if touching a hot handle from a pot with boiling water. However, before releasing it, he inserted a palmed MI6 listening device into the fan's base. "Sorry. I didn't realize it was fragile."

Blackwood grabbed the fan, protectively holding it like a baby. "It's not that it is fragile. In fact, it's amazingly sturdy. This particular item has great personal significance to me, and I do not let anyone else touch it."

"I certainly meant no disrespect, sir," Mac wrote off Blackwood's strange behavior to his eccentricity. He was pleased that Blackwood did not see the placement of the bug.

Mac then focused on his second objective of tricking Blackwood into admitting some wrongdoing and asked, "What's the strategic significance of the divergent blend of businesses? From what I know, you have a spaceship company, a battery manufacturer called Whispering Wind Industries, and power plants."

"Correct. Those are each of our subsidiaries. Each subsidiary is significant. The combination of the subsidiaries is about cash flow and not about strategy. Strategic consultants are not very fond of conglomerates that combine seemingly unrelated businesses. It's just not very popular anymore. What they are missing in the vision comes down to cash flow. I manage each business separately from one another. My goal is to generate cash flow," Blackwood stated.

"Interesting. I hope you are generating the cash flow you are targeting from your business units. Some of your industries are ripe for payoffs to get things done quickly. Many people in this world move like wintertime molasses until you dangle some incentive in front of them." Mac leaned forward as if a buddy was going to whisper a confidential secret to his other buddy. "You are a guy who gets things done. Have you had to grease some palms to move your businesses so quickly?"

Blackwood replied with an air of superiority, "Sir, I only have legal businesses. I would never consider involvement in illegal activities you haphazardly describe as greasing some palms."

"I'm impressed. Most business owners I know use whatever means necessary for success. I'm glad you're above board. From everything I understand from your past, it seems like you have recreated yourself into a different person."

"I am not a different person! I am an improved person," Blackwood responded and started getting agitated.

Mac was covertly trying to push all of Blackwood's buttons by using a consulting interview technique of bouncing around disparate topics to confuse the interviewee. "If your conglomerate is about cash flow, how do you intend to generate cash from power plants centered around countries rich in natural resources?"

"Mr. Mac, patience is critical in the game of life. I know the world will eventually realize the benefit of clean thermal energy, especially with the growing greenhouse effect. Just think if we could harness the power of the earth without damaging the planet?"

"But what about damaging the space around the Earth with satellites?" asked Mac.

"They provide critical strategic support for the network that binds the world together with resources and provides a consistent way of life," Blackwood replied with a canned answer.

"Like communication satellites?"

"Yes, but with much more long-term importance than you can possibly understand."

Mac once again changed the discussion topic and asked, "Speaking of understanding, the United States Space Force would like to inspect your spaceship launching facilities. While at the facilities, we would like to review the paperwork on your existing satellites' capabilities. When can that be scheduled?"

"Mr. Mac, my satellites have several purposes, but they generally are focused on communication. Most people do not realize the importance of satellites. For example, satellites provide many television services, GPS navigation, rural cell phone services, business transactions, weather monitoring, and many other uses. Each of these revolves around communication, and what I do is critical to maintaining the quality of life that you enjoy." Blackwood thrust his chin up in the air as if he were forced to endure an unpleasant smell in front of him.

With Blackwood's misplaced arrogance and uppity attitude, Mac reflected on the enjoyment he would have in bringing this ass down several notches.

Blackwood looked frustrated and confused by the continual questioning and abruptly said, "I am sorry, but my work is too important to spend more time with you. I am sure you are doing what you think is your definition of important work. Quite frankly, I have had a lifetime of attorneys asking me questions. I suggest contacting my attorney if the United States Space Force has concerns with my communication satellites. You might also quite possibly consider contacting the British government. I assume you know I am a British citizen. This meeting is over."

Mac felt an oversized hand on his shoulder. It caught him off guard because he did not hear Abaddon walk up behind him. Mac's awareness of any situation was always at a heightened state, and he was rarely surprised. He concluded Abaddon must have stealthy skills and training after slipping silently behind him. Mac knew Abaddon was someone who was dangerous and must be closely watched.

"Time for you to leave, Attorney-Man," Abaddon said in a deep and authoritative voice, grabbing Mac's shoulder while forcefully assisting him to stand up.

Mac reached out to shake Blackwood's hand in saying goodbye and said, "Dr. Blackwood, it was a pleasure to meet you."

"I am sure it was. Goodbye." Blackwood turned away from Mac without a handshake or as much as a head nod.

It was clear that he was dismissing Mac from his presence. Mac did not hear any incriminating comments from Blackwood. Blackwood was too careful to slip up in front of a stranger. They were going to have to rely on the bug implant. Mac could not help but think that his team would be visiting this arrogant psychopath soon. Very soon.

Chapter 36

MI6 Communication Monitoring Vehicle

Two miles away in a nondescript countryside barn, the rest of the team was in the MI6 Communication Monitoring Vehicle, the CMV. The CMV was more like a fancy condo, including the convenient accessory of hot water for a nice cup of tea during a stakeout's long and monotonous hours.

Ryker had been listening to Mac's interaction with Blackwood on a headset alongside his MI6 counterpart. The bug also clearly picked up the discussion and was being broadcast on the CMV's speakers for everyone to hear. Mac had just left Blackwood Castle, and Blackwood was talking with Abaddon.

"That Space Force attorney was incredibly irritating. He kept pushing me with his stupid questions." Blackwood was very flustered and had a burning need to gloat during the debrief.

"Whatever. The attorney is gone now. You did a fine job with him," Abaddon replied.

Starting on a roll, Blackwood pronounced, "I did much more than a fine job. Those idiots will be thrown back into the Stone Age once my satellites release the EMPs over North and South America. I hope that someday I get to see that attorney's face once he realizes the United States must buy all their power needs from me."

"The guy is worthless and has no bearing on our future. Let it go," Abaddon said.

"That attorney will not have any more threatening questions once he understands the situation. It won't be just the United States begging for my mercy. Every country will be scrambling to determine what happened and to reestablish power. They will have to buy billions of euros of electrical equipment from Asia and Europe. Then they will be forced to buy billions of euros of power from my power plants to run their new equipment. Their power plants will not be back online for years."

Blackwood was venting, and his thoughts kept circling back to his broader strategic plan. He continued, "Once the countries agree to pay my demanded price, I will sweeten my deal by forcing them to buy all their vehicle batteries from me. North and South America will be wholly dependent upon me for all their power needs. That's just Phase 1. Phase 2 will be the rest of the world. The attorney is going to regret the day he met me."

Abaddon responded, "I will repeat it. Forget that attorney clown. What is much more important is that I'm still trying to identify who kidnapped my messenger in Paris. I'm upset that my men did not kill the kidnappers when we had the chance. Fortunately, the Whispering Wind battery plant will have some more time to get up to speed if they need it. Look, we fried the Rio power plant, so that competition is gone."

"I agree. Everything is falling into place. We are virtually ready to go," added Zag.

Countering the dismissive comments, Blackwood replied, "My frustration is not about our success implementing the strategic plan. What pisses me off is the attorney. It's the principle of it. He was incredibly disrespectful to me, and I will not accept impertinent behavior. You can believe me. I fully intend to see him again."

* * *

In the MI6 CMV, Rhys was the first to acknowledge the conversation. "By God, we have them. Also, Blackwood's devious empire is clearly within MI6's jurisdiction, given that his plans are to be executed outside British soil and are a threat to our sovereignty."

Valencia asked, "Can you provide the court order necessary to arrest him and search Blackwood Castle? I'm ready to make a game-changing move."

"Absolutely. I'll need a few hours. However, based on the reprehensible planned acts, I'm confident we will have all the legal cover we need." Rhys replied.

"We need to move before they have a chance to execute any of their tactics. I'm sure we all agree on that," Brock stated.

"What do you suggest, Brock? Even with Abaddon, I cannot imagine we will receive any resistance when serving our search warrant. We will take the lot of them into custody," Rhys responded, trusting Brock's judgment.

Brock said, "According to Mac, both the Whispering Wind Industries offices and its battery manufacturing facility had several heavily armed guards. Their initial and subsequent attacks on the Rio power plant had a limited number of shooters. Based on everything we've observed, I think we can assume there'll be roaming guards, but they will not be in overwhelming numbers. I'm more concerned that Blackwood Castle has secret passageways for them to sneak out before we can place them in cuffs."

"What do you suggest we do to shut down all the egress areas?" Gunner asked.

"I think we should have a small team on each side of the castle, with the primary group entering through the front entrance. It may be overkill, but we cannot afford to let them escape," replied Brock.

"That sounds like a good plan to me. However, you should know that I am unaccustomed to a mission requiring such a display of force and am much more comfortable in the espionage game rather than police or military actions," Rhys replied,

The rest of the team confirmed their agreement with Brock's plan. An overwhelming force with flanking on all sides was generally always a good strategy.

Mac walked into the CMV and said with a teasing grin, "It sounds like this brain trust decided on a plan concocted by Brock. What did I miss? On a matter of principle, anything coming from Brock scares me, and I'm tempted to vote no."

Everyone chuckled at Brock's expense and the good-natured teasing. The team described the plan resulting from the intel on Blackwood's discussion with Abaddon.

Mac added, "While I was at the castle, I did not see any guards other than Abaddon and an entrance guard. However, we should not underestimate Abaddon. That guy is sly, and we need to cuff him immediately when we see him. He has not stayed alive in the mercenary business for this long without knowing how to take precautions. I like that it will be a joint operation with MI6, the police, and our CIA team."

"Are we confirmed?" asked Brock.

"Given the necessity to shut Blackwood down immediately and having no better intel on their military strength and castle layout, I concur with the plan. I don't think we have other options that will meet the timeline. I'll let Rainey know," Mac concluded with concern in his eyes.

Gunner said, "Come on, Mac. Don't worry. We'll overwhelm them with our sheer numbers on each side of the castle."

"We may or may not have them beat in numbers, but I think we need to address one more of the castle's sides."

Chapter 37

Blackwood Castle, United Kingdom

The operation was supposed to be a simple nighttime insertion and extraction exercise. Unfortunately, in the spy game, nothing was simple.

As the team converged on Blackwood Castle, they felt like they were covering every possible side. Mac's intuition told him something different. The side that was not being covered was the roof. Even though a helicopter escape was a remote possibility, Mac took no chances and executed his solution.

Mac was skydiving to the castle roof after jumping out of a fixed-wing aircraft. He dropped spread-eagle and dressed in full black camouflage with a black parachute. He pulled his ripcord and began his slow descent to the castle.

Mac saw unexpected movement on the walkways at the top of the walls. He was wearing clear skydiving goggles with a night vision attachment. A small army guarded the wall walkways, and Mac was even more concerned by what was sticking out of the corner towers' windows. As best he could tell, the corner towers were fortified with M60 machine guns. Fortunately, the shooters had not yet noticed the good guys converging on the castle. If the guards saw a small force attacking every side, the tactical advantage could disastrously shift to the guards. From the sky, he could see the alarm could sound at any moment.

Mac yelled a warning on his comms, "Abort. Abort. Wall tops and towers filled with shooters. I say again, abort!"

"Negative. We are all in the open field surrounding the castle. Our best bet is to get close enough to the castle and find protective cover before they notice us. Ground team, you need to double-time it," said Brock, directing from his comms. He did not like this turn of events, but they were too committed to reverse direction.

The ground team was close to converging on the castle. The ground forces consisted of a full contingent of police, MI6, and CIA representatives. The police officers entailed SCO19 members, the highly trained version of the U.S. SWAT. They were dressed in black military camos and helmets to blend into the night, and those assigned to the three side walls were equipped with night vision goggles. If necessary, the primary insertion group was to breach the front gatehouse entrance with overpowering force. The rest of the group coordinated backup from the other three walls.

Brock said in their comms, "This is Ground 1. Ninety seconds out. Report."

"Ground 2. Sixty seconds out," replied Gunner.

"Ground 4. The SCO19 and I are still two minutes to the side of the castle. Our boots are sinking in some bog and peat shit. It's like running in bloody quicksand." Rhys complained.

"I hope you tied your shoes, or you will be barefoot once your boots are permanently stuck in the mud," quipped Gunner.

Valencia teased, "Remember that time when we were all in flip-flops and Hawaiian shirts in Fiji, drinking at a local bar? Gunner decided to deck a cop, and the other 5-0s chased us down the shore at the water's edge. I had blowouts on both flip-flops and left them stuck in the sand. Thanks to Gunner, they are probably still stuck there."

"Hold on, now. That cop was drunk, in plain clothes, and took the first swing because he thought I was stealing his girlfriend," Gunner replied.

"This is Ground 3. We're about 45 seconds from the castle's front entrance and will slow our approach for you slow asses to get into position. For the record, Gunner, you were, in fact, stealing his girlfriend. Out," Valencia calmly stated.

* * *

Inside Blackwood Castle, Abaddon could not sleep. The encounter with the attorney from the U.S. Space Force was clearly bothering him. Lying on his bed, Abaddon asked the ceiling, "What the hell am I missing? Why are there so many unusual outside interactions at this critical stage? Damn it! These events cannot be coincidences! First, there was the explosion at Whispering Wind Industries headquarters. That was followed by the kidnapping of the messenger and a car chase at the Whispering Wind battery manufacturing facility. Then, there was a visit by some unknown French team inquiring about me at my restaurant. Now, we had a visit from the attorney with the U.S. Space Force. Think, mate!"

Abaddon froze and popped open his eyes with an idea. He called his restaurant manager and asked, "Are our hidden security cameras still operating?"

The restaurant manager answered immediately and responded, "Yes. I would have told you if there was a problem with them."

Abaddon ordered, "Send me the recording of the five Frenchmen who were looking for me. I want to see their faces."

"Give me a second to find it."

"Your second is up. Send it now."

"Okay. I just sent it. You should have it in your inbox."

"Received. Do you expect me to watch your entire night? You're an idiot. When did those shits show up?"

The restaurant manager provided an approximate time, and Abaddon fast-forwarded the video to when Mac's team arrived and said, "You were within a minute of the French group showing. At least you can use a clock." Seeing the correct number of guests seated at the outside metal table, he asked, "Were they the ones asking about me?"

The restaurant manager replied affirmatively, "The big guy with all the muscles was the one leading the questioning."

"Hold on. I want to look at all the faces." In a matter of seconds, Abaddon's eyes bulged, and he said, "Son-of-a...." He abruptly disconnected the call before finishing his sentence.

POWERLESS

Abaddon had a frame frozen on the picture of one of the Frenchmen. That guy was the same visitor claiming to be an attorney representing the U.S. Space Force. This was not a coincidence. He called Zag.

After answering, Zag asked, "Why are you calling me so late? Can't this wait until tomorrow morning?"

"No, it can't. We have a big problem, and I damn well hope you can help with the answer."

"You guys need me for everything. What can I solve for you?"

"Do you have any facial recognition software? I need someone identified."

"Sure. I thought you were asking for something difficult. I borrowed software from a Chicago airport named after some Irish WW2 aviator. I have never needed to use it before, but this should be fun trying it out."

Abaddon sent the freeze-frame picture to Zag, and Zag loaded it into his software.

Zag said, "Hey, isn't that the Space Force attorney? Why are we identifying this guy if we already know his name?"

"Just do it and stop asking stupid questions."

"That's fine. There's no need to get testy with me. The software is processing and almost done now." Zag waited a few more seconds, and the results were spat out. "Just like he said to us, his name is Declan Mac. However, he is a bit of an enigma because he doesn't work for the Space Force."

Abaddon commented, "That guy must have huge balls to use his own name brazenly. Keep digging because there's more to him than meets the eye."

"Okay. I'll use the login credentials of that dumbass Joe Whisp. With the help of his tech team identifying a secret backdoor into the U.S. governmental agencies' databases, maybe I can learn more about Mr. Mac."

"Trust me. You'll find something. I just hope what you uncover is not too devastating to us.

Zag's computer completed the research. He stared at the screen in front of him and said, "Oh boy. We have a problem."

"No shit. Stop crapping your boxers and tell me what you know."

"Declan Mac is not an attorney from the U.S. Space Force. It says here that he is not even an attorney. There's a 99.7% likelihood that Mr. Mac is a CIA Senior Field Operative. Most of his stuff is so classified that even I cannot break into his mission records."

Abaddon yelled, "I knew it! I'm going to find a way to squish that little prick. He's playing games and spitting right in my face. Keep looking for more information on Mac. I'll call my men, and we'll start devising a plan to stop this bullshit. I'm going to kill him myself."

Abaddon hung up on Zag and dialed the security office. When his first lieutenant answered, Abaddon didn't wait for a hello. He screamed into the phone, "The CIA is on to us! An operative was here in the castle earlier today. I had my hands on him and could have snapped his neck, but he slipped through my fingers."

The shooter said, "How do you know? Are you sure?"

"Stop asking questions. This changes everything. We need to find out everything they know about us, so let's create our mission plan in the morning. No wonder I couldn't sleep!" Abaddon ended the call and rubbed his face with his hands. He needed time to think and casually walked to his corner window to gaze at the stars. He froze as he strained his stare at the ground. An unknown number of intruders converged from at least two sides that he could see from his window.

Abaddon grabbed his handheld radio from his nightstand and raised it to his mouth. He started screaming at everyone who was listening, "Alert. Alert. We have an unknown number of assailants descending on our position. We are being breached. Fire at will."

Out of nowhere, the castle came alive. Tracer rounds started firing from each of the turrets. The good guys were sitting ducks, and it would not have mattered if their foes were using bows and arrows or modern-day armament. The M60s laid a blanket of lead on the ground team. Body armor was no match for the M60's armor-piercing rounds. The turrets also were equipped with several single-use RPGs and grenades for extra explosive power. The wall guards used scoped rifles to systematically drop targets as quickly as they could shoot, reacquire, and shoot. The shooters in the towers and walls all had night vision goggles that effectively eliminated the stealthy nighttime raid's surprise.

There was nowhere to hide. The good guys tried to charge ahead at the castle, but there was no hope of surviving the onslaught. Those not killed or wounded were forced to withdraw and carry their wounded to safety. Brock was hit with a round in his leg, causing substantial bleeding. A nearby MI6 agent dove to the ground beside Brock's position and began working to slow the blood loss.

Rhys was running at a sprint when an abdominal shot took him down. A long barrage of fire popped a half dozen SCO19 team members. Gunner was hit next with a penetrating round in his upper chest that went through his body armor like a paper target. While his anger was screaming at him more than his pain, it still stopped him in his tracks.

Valencia almost reached the front gatehouse by zigging and zagging between the protective cover. Unfortunately, a shooter dropped a grenade on her position and, just like a good horseshoe throw, was close enough to score points. Shrapnel peppered her lower body. An MI6 operative took most of the grenade shrapnel above the waist.

Mac watched in horror as the slaughter below unfolded. It was a massacre. The fundamental mistake in their battle plan tactics was underestimating their opponent. Mac's fear of losing team members blocked his ability to process a covert counterattack. His damn Overactive Protective Gene dictated his following thoughts. He reacted without any concern for his safety or possible mission success.

Mac began emptying magazines from his shoulder-slung machine gun at the shooters who were delivering the carnage to the ground team. He took out four shooters who mistakenly thought they had the advantage of their protected positions. The shooters were confused about the source of the blanketing machine gun fire leveling them from one of their flanks. Eventually, they saw the muzzle flashes coming from the sky and returned fire.

Mac was circling his descent to avoid the unwelcoming bullets. Once he landed on the main castle's roof, he pulled off the shoulder straps on his chute and ran to the edge of a wall. It gave him a firing position at the now exposed shooters. He ran from one wall to the next. Suddenly, blinding lights came on from a small penthouse shed that likely provided roof access via a stairwell. The lights were so bright that Mac could not hope to look in their direction. Mac heard a door swing open and fired a couple of wild shots toward the sound.

The shooter, who was opening the door, anticipated Mac's move and dove sideways to safety. Mac heard a booming laugh coming from the edge of the building and fired in that direction. Abaddon recognized the person before him and bellowed, "I wondered when I would see you again. U.S. Space Force attorney Declan Mac, or should I say CIA Operative Declan Mac, welcome again to Blackwood Castle."

Mac replied, "Go to hell, Abaddon."

Another healthy laugh came from the same place. Abaddon called out, "Mac, you might as well give up. You are standing with no coverage for your position, with searchlights pointed directly at you. I have you scoped by two snipers on both of your sides with an order to shoot if you take one step in this direction."

Recovered from his blinding focus on protecting the ground troops, Mac mockingly replied, "So that I understand, what if I step in another direction? I don't want to be shot. Why don't you better define the direction for me."

"What direction? You are such an irritating prick with your wise-ass comments. You are a fool. You should not have started shooting at my men from above. Once you did, we knew someone was attacking us from the sky, and you had no place else to land except the castle roof."

Mac's intention of firing at the shooters while parachuting was twofold. First, he wanted to force the shooters to take cover and focus their fire on him, allowing the wounded on the ground to be pulled to safety. Second, he was taking revenge and killing as many of those bastards as possible. Both goals were accomplished. Now that he had given a reprieve to the ground troops, he thought it would be best to see if he could do some damage wherever they took him into the castle. He looked right and then left, pulled the sling of his automatic weapon off his head, dropped it on the ground, and raised both arms in surrender.

Abaddon did not rush to his new prize. He cautiously padded over and walked behind Mac. He grabbed Mac's left hand from behind and pulled it aggressively down. He then twisted his right hand down and forcefully held both wrists together until he fished out a zip tie from his pocket. Mac's hands were then zip-tied together behind him with unnecessary snugness.

In defiance, Mac said to Abaddon, "You're an asshole."

Abaddon raised the butt of his AK-47 assault rifle and crashed it down on the base of Mac's skull. Mac dropped to his knees and then to his side as Blackwood Castle faded to black.

Chapter 38

Blackwood Castle Dungeon

The first thing Mac registered was the pain in his shoulders. There are numerous types of pain, and Mac was experiencing all of them at once. He tried to raise his head, and a splitting headache forced his chin to crash down on his chest. Mac had experienced pain and torture several times previously in his career, but it never seemed to get any easier. Some people try to ignore pain. Mac dealt with it by focusing on it. He assessed each inch of his body and knew he had already taken some punishment. Mac's best way to beat pain was to stare it down like the town sheriff in an old western showdown whose eyes are burning holes in the ugly face of a lawless criminal.

Mac was starting to come around more and more. He realized he must be in the Blackwood Castle dungeon. The word dungeon conjured up pictures of medieval torture machines stretching spines and extracting pain from those who would never escape. The room was cold and damp with a putrid odor, suggesting this was not the first time it had been used. There was no electricity, and torches lit the chamber.

Mac's wrists were bound by metal brackets that were chained to the ceiling. The chains were just long enough to allow him to stand once he was awake. However, his heels did not touch the ground, and his calves were beginning to cramp. His commando gear was gone, leaving only his pants and a tee shirt.

Abaddon saw Mac start to come around and, stepping from a shadowy corner, said, "Welcome back to Blackwood Castle. I hope you are enjoying your stay. We are going to enjoy torturing you. We will kill you more quickly if you tell us everything you know about why we were attacked. If you decide not to share your knowledge, we will still torture you but will do so until you beg us to kill you. Between you and me, I hope you decide not to tell us anything."

Mac replied, "How about you let me go, and I'll answer you in seventy or so years?"

"You don't have seventy minutes, smartass. As you can see, almost all the fun dungeon toys once kept in this room are disappointingly gone. However, have no fear. We have hundreds of methods to maximize your pain.

"I love what you have done with the place. Is this part of the scheduled tour?" Mac said, wanting to delay for as long as possible to provide for his hopeful rescue. The ground team knew he had dropped from the air and must have seen the muzzle flashes from his machine gun.

"Your special tour is going to include just this room. I am sure we will have fun." Abaddon stared at him with a devious smile. Two other rough-looking mercs showed themselves and stopped next to Abaddon.

Mac said, "Well, do you as you wish. I'm just hanging around."

They all laughed, and a muscle-bound shooter punched Mac in the abdomen.

After catching his breath from the vicious blow, Mac asked, "Why do it? You know you are on the losing side. The British military has probably already called in an airstrike to level this place."

"You think that scares me?" Abaddon laughed with a loud burst and said, "If you thought we were ready for a land assault, you should see all the toys we have for an air assault."

"Maybe the British government will be lenient on you if you say you were just following orders from that whack-job, Blackwood," Mac responded.

"That's funny. You know it doesn't work that way. We are either dead men or rich men. We are prepared to defend against the second wave, but I don't think that will happen. Dr. Blackwood has backup plans in place if something unfortunate like this occurs." Abaddon confidently smiled with the power of the upper hand.

"I'm sure it's already started. Your French restaurant is shut down along with all your bank accounts. The British government officially owns you."

That comment earned Mac a particularly vicious punch in the face by Abaddon. Mac saw stars, and blood started flowing freely in his mouth.

Abaddon angrily spat back at Mac, "No one owns me. Do you think I give a shit about that restaurant?"

Mac insightfully replied, "If you have nowhere to spend your money, I am not sure the money will do you any good."

"We are way ahead of you. At this moment, Dr. Blackwood is talking to the heads of all the countries in North and South America, telling them his offer."

Mac pushed his point and asked, "What could he possibly have to offer? I don't think you will receive a plethora of offers to stay at this Bed and Breakfast. I suggest you put some paint on the walls. By the way, what are we having for breakfast? I hope something very British."

Smiling at the shooters through bloody teeth, Mac said, "You might as well tell me what Blackwood is discussing with the heads of state. I'm sure you are assuming that I will never check out from this pleasure palace."

"That is above your pay grade, Mr. CIA Man," replied Abaddon.

"Once Blackwood gets his big payday, do you think he's going to share any of it with you and your guys? What possible value could you offer him once he has his money?"

Abaddon glared at Mac and stated, "He needs me for protection.

"Protection from what? Some bloggers on the internet?"

"Shut up!" screamed Abaddon as he punched Mac in the stomach like he was a hanging punching bag.

Once Mac caught his breath, he took a calculated risk and said, "I would not be surprised if Blackwood and Zag were up in his office right now making plans. Do you wonder why they put you down here with me instead of taking part in the end-game payday discussion?

"Shut up!" Abaddon stared ahead as he evaluated his predicament and said, "I know the singular mission we share in common is greed with the love of money."

"Come on. Wake up and smell the dungeon. You know that ass is ruthless and not trustworthy. I'm sure Blackwood has figured out that he could save himself millions of euros if he provided the means for the death of you and your men."

Abaddon focused his eyes, and he commandingly gave a slight nod. He then looked at his two mercs and said, "Those two little weasels had better not be alone in Blackwood's office planning without me. We are too close to the final execution to take any chances."

Looking at one of the shooters, Abaddon said, "You come with me." He said to the remaining muscle-bound merc, "You stay here and have as much of a workout as you want."

"As much as I want?" the merc asked excitedly.

"As much as you want. Goodbye Mac. I would like to say it has been nice knowing you, but I prefer to be honest with dying men," said Abaddon as he turned and walked out of the dungeon with one of the shooters in tow.

"We are going to have some fun. I have not been able to work out with a punching bag for a long time," the merc stated as he began shadowboxing to warm up.

"I don't suppose you have the key and would be willing to unshackle my hands for a free fight?" asked Mac.

"Yes, I have the key, but no, we will not be freeing your hands. This game is played with me punching you for as long as I want. At some point, you die. Eventually, after you die and I finish my workout, I will leave you hanging there for the next few hundred years until someone finds you. You will provide me with a great workout. Thank you."

The merc placed a couple of thunderous body blows that sent pain searing through Mac's body. This game was not going to be fun for Mac. Mac questioned, "Do you have the old key for the wrist bracelets?"

The merc smiled and reached into his pocket to show him the prize possession that kept Mac a victim. It was a black skeleton key. The merc was so close that Mac could smell his garlic-tinged breath. Mac had one shot at freedom before his body finally crumbled under the punishing body blows.

Without hesitation, Mac brought his knees up to his chest. In the spirit of most guys' reactions, the merc used his hands to cover his nuts. Mac's knees flew past the merc's cringe-worthy vulnerable spot. He anticipated the merc's response and needed more distance between them if there was any hope of recovering the key. Mac thrust his feet forward, heels first. They landed on the merc's chest with a solid thud.

The merc was a man with a considerable upper body, demonstrating his dedicated upper body weightlifting years. However, he ignored his lower body during his weight room visits. The merc's legs appeared like they would have snapped under the weight of his massive shoulders and arms. His weak legs caused him to stumble backward and lose his balance. While doing so, the skeleton key flew out of his grasp, hitting Mac in the chest on its journey to drop directly down at Mac's feet.

The merc took four or five stumbling steps and was abruptly stopped by the wall behind him. Protruding from the wall were sharp metal hooks that could have been coat hooks if fashioned in another era. One of the coat hooks became the final resting place for the merc as it impaled him through his heart and extended through the front of his shirt. He looked at Mac in shock for his final few seconds of life until his head dropped to his chest.

Mac wasted no time lengthening his body and squeezing the skeleton key between his toes and the ball of his foot. The next move was critical, and he likely had only one shot at it. Thanks to years of stretching and core strengthening, Mac raised his feet to his chained hands. He carefully exchanged the key from his foot to his hand. After lowering his feet and standing for a second to give his body a short rest, he inserted the key into one of the locks, constraining his hands. The lock mechanism gave an incredibly satisfying click and popped open. He then performed the same Houdini trick on his other hand and was freed.

Dashing past the merc towards the stairs leading to the rest of the castle, Mac grabbed the door latch, but nothing happened. The door was locked from the outside. One hard shoulder slam confirmed that these centuries-old doors would never budge without the key or some major explosion. He ran back down the stairs, desperate to find a way to pry the door open. It was a fruitless attempt, but he did stumble across something interesting. There was a heavy iron plate on the wall, and a slight breeze blew through a crack at the edge of it. Mac saw the plate was attached to a five-foot lever on the wall. When he pulled the lever down, the plate rose after protesting from eons of non-use.

The hole was only large enough to climb through on his hands and knees. It was pitched downward, making the trip slightly less taxing. The tunnel was several hundred yards long and smelled like an old sewer. Mac was hoping it was an escape tunnel. Still, it suddenly dawned on him — this was likely the sewer tunnel dating back to when the castle was constructed. As nasty as that sounded, it was a most welcomed potential escape route. Mac began to see the nighttime sky in front of him, and when he reached the sewer tunnel end, he was fortunate not to find a gate blocking the entrance. He crawled out and fell on his back, taking in the fresh air and appreciating that no one was punching him.

Chapter 39

Blackwood Castle, United Kingdom

Blackwood and Zag were talking through final preparations. The thwarted intrusion was forcing up the timeline.

Abaddon and his associate walked into Blackwood's office, suspicious of what they would find. Abaddon said, "What is going on in here? You are not planning the next steps without us, are you?"

"Don't be ridiculous," Blackwood said as he barely looked up from his computer. "Well done in repelling the attackers." He and Zag looked as if they were focused on their discussion rather than as if they were caught with their hands in the cookie jar.

Their innocent reaction and Blackwood's compliment caused Abaddon to stop in his tracks, and he replied, "My men performed well. We had a few KIAs, but I consider us still at full strength."

"Do you know who they were?" asked Blackwood.

"They were generally wearing the black-clad uniforms of SCO19. They also executed their plan as you would expect from highly experienced operatives who train together. Unfortunately, they took away their dead and wounded. However, we have an interesting outcome to discuss."

This comment received Blackwood's undivided attention, and he asked, "Yes?"

"Do you remember the supposed attorney from the U.S. Space Agency?"

"Supposed? Of course. How could I forget that jerk?" asked Blackwood.

"This evening, I realized that jerk named Declan Mac is not from the U.S. Space Force. I pieced it together and identified him from some old photographs. Yes, his name is Declan Mac, but he doesn't work for some space agency. He's a highly successful operative from the CIA," said Abaddon.

"The CIA!" Blackwood exclaimed. "If the CIA is involved, there is no doubt the implementation schedule just moved up."

Abaddon proudly added, "Oh, there's a happy ending to the story. During the raid, the fool parachuted onto the castle's roof. He took out several of my guys, but we easily captured him."

"What are you doing to take care of our problematic guest? We had a problem with the CIA at Whispering Wind Industries, and the last thing we need is another CIA operative knocking on our door here." Blackwood decided not to tell

Abaddon about his failure to kill the first CIA team. It was not the time to show any weakness to his subordinates.

"It's in process. Declan Mac is currently hanging from ceiling chains in the dungeon, with one of my strongest guys using him as a punching bag. He will have fun until he pulverizes him to death," Abaddon proudly stated

"Perfect. The CIA will think he was killed during their raid," replied Blackwood.

Abaddon, asking his actual question, said, "Let's be clear, gentlemen, we are a team, right? Can I trust you guys?"

Blackwood paused and then said, "Of course. Why would you ask such a question at this time? We are about to enter the seminal part of the implementation phase."

Abaddon glanced over at his associate by the door. His associate shrugged his shoulders. Abaddon said, "Talk in straight English. I have no idea what you mean."

The discussion was interrupted by a loud, dinging bell. Blackwood said, "It will be easier if you hear it for yourself, Abaddon. It's time for an international conference call with the governmental leaders from all the countries in North and South America as well as the U.K. Prime Minister."

Blackwood was standing in front of the projection screen. He pushed a button, and all the world leaders appeared, each in small boxes on the side of the screen, with his calm face commanding most of the screen. The world leader's facial expressions ranged the gamut from curiosity to anger.

The U.K. Prime Minister jumped in first and shouted, "Sir, I demand to know what is going on."

Several other leaders immediately followed the Prime Minister's question. With all the leaders talking simultaneously, none could make out what the others were saying.

Blackwood said in a progressively louder voice, "Gentlemen and ladies! Please be quiet to ensure we have a productive discussion. Given that I politely asked for this call, please give me the courtesy to explain myself."

The world leaders quieted as instructed.

In his authoritative Board Room voice, Blackwood stated, "Let me start by apologizing to you for this call's short notice. This call's purpose was made under the pretense that I would soon attack your countries. I will not attack your countries in the traditional sense. I have a business transaction to propose to you, and you may experience some collateral damage because of the arrangement. In response to my proposal, I will give you a choice of either Option A or B. This call aims to determine the outcome for your countries when they have no electrical power or functioning electrical components."

There was a murmur across the talking heads as the call's gravity sank into their deepest fears. No one directly interrupted Blackwood. While all were still in denial, he had their undivided attention and complete control of the discussion.

"All of the Americas will very shortly receive EMPs that will fry all electrical components. Your countries will become wastelands with no power and jettisoned back in time to the 1700s. I hope you have several candles." Blackwood smiled at his joke, but no one else found it funny.

Blackwood stated, "By now, I am sure you have all heard about the unfortunate EMP incident at the new Rio power plant. At this juncture, I think it is essential that you know the EMP was not an accident. I released a low-level EMP to test our capabilities. As you know, it was incredibly successful from my perspective. I assure you that I have the technology to release much stronger EMPs that will drape over all of the Americas."

Blackwood continued, "Even if you can buy replacement electrical components from Europe and Asia, your power plants will take years to come back online. I am offering you a solution. Option A is for you to immediately execute a power supply contract with my fully operational and strategically placed geothermal power plants located off your coastlines. You will pay a substantial amount upfront and significantly higher power rates than you currently pay. Your cost is non-negotiable. The power supply contract is exclusive for all your countries' power generation needs for the next one hundred years."

Pausing to let Option A sink in and to give the dramatic effect for Option B, Blackwood said, "Option B is to reject my generous offer. Your countries will be without power for years and possibly decades. Your societies will crumble and likely be taken over by other countries that chose Option A. You will forever be frozen out of any of my power plants, and I will not consider providing you with power in the future. If you do not choose Option A, you are dead to me, and I will not even take your phone calls."

The world leaders looked shocked and sat with dumbfounded expressions.

Blackwood raised his index finger and said with a smile, "Oh yes, there's a sweetener I am offering you in Option A. I have a revolutionary vehicle battery design created by my research and development team, and it's ready for distribution. As part of Option A, every vehicle operating in your country will utilize my battery. I realize you will not have operating vehicles in your country for quite some time, but that will eventually change if you do your jobs. Unfortunately, the electrical components necessary to pump the gas will be rendered useless for several months. The beauty of this sweetener is that my battery is better than anything the world has ever seen. It's revolutionary. It may not need a recharge for a year and possibly years. This battery will be a piece of welcomed good news, and I will be the hero in all your public communications."

There was still no response from the world leaders, so Blackwood concluded, "I do not expect an answer immediately. I will give you three generous hours to respond to me. Now, you may ask questions if you have any."

The world leaders began blurting out questions. They sounded like reporters hoping to have their specific questions answered to spin their story to their news outlets.

"Quiet!" Blackwood screamed. "I will not accept this rude behavior. I will take two or three questions. Mr. President of the United States, please ask your question."

The U.S. President asked, "If we agree to this outlandish extorsion attempt, how can we be assured you will keep your end of the deal?"

"Excellent question. You can't be, except that you have my word. Yes, Mr. Canadian Prime Minister?"

The Canadian Prime Minister inquired, "If you can fry all our electrical components with an EMP attack, how do you expect us to restore power?"

"Another excellent question. The answer is for you to figure it out. We are just here to provide a high-quality service. If you choose to delay reestablishing electricity in your country, I suspect you will not get reelected by your constituents. Presidente de México, you may ask the last question."

The President of Mexico asked, "Sir, how are you going to release an EMP strong enough to do what you say? Will you detonate nuclear explosions on our soil?"

Now, Blackwood was enjoying himself. "Well done. That's the best question of the bunch. You need to ask yourselves if I'm bluffing and if I can execute that part of my plan. I assure you that I have developed the technology to execute the plan. No, we will not drop nuclear warheads on your countries. That is barbaric. The EMP is not part of your choice in Options A or B. The EMP will happen. I suggest you print out all those lovely family pictures stored on your phones. You have three hours before all those pictures are fried forever. Oh yes, more importantly, did I say you have three hours to tell me if you are choosing Option A or B? If I do not hear back from you by then, I will assume you are choosing B. Your country will permanently enjoy the 1700s. It is a pleasure doing business with you."

Blackwood abruptly pushed the end-call button, and the screen went black.

Chapter 40

Blackwood Castle, United Kingdom

Blackwood turned to the others in the room and confidently smiled as he basked in the glow of his successful sales presentation. He was very pleased with himself and loved negotiating with people when they had no choice but to accept all his terms. Today was a glorious day.

Zag said, "They will all pay our price."

Seeing this as nothing more than a business transaction, Blackwood said, "Agreed. Let's have their power supply contracts ready for execution."

"Done. I sent the contracts via email to each government leader during the video call. What's the plan now?"

"Because of the simple-minded spies and police who prematurely attacked us a few days before we were fully ready for execution, we need to push up the timing of the strategic plan. Zag, are you sure we are ready with the satellites' EMP technology?" Blackwood asked.

"Yes, I am sure. We are good to go and awaiting your orders to fire," Zag responded with a giddy tone, suggesting his joy at the thought of seeing his technology released onto the world.

"Before we fire, are you completely sure the Faraday cages will protect my power plants? Also, are the satellite control center and the battery plant safe from the EMPs because of their geographic location?" Blackwood asked.

"Confirmed. The Faraday cages will do their job to protect our plants, and the other two facilities are not even close to the EMPs' strike radius. Most importantly, the EMPs are not even in the zip code of the satellites' central operations control facility at the English Channel," replied Zag.

"Okay. I will trust you. I still do not like going to the English Channel for the satellite control room. You cannot tap a few keystrokes and move all operational control to here at Blackwood Castle?"

Zag was a little irritated by being forced to answer a question that Blackwood already knew the answer to, and he responded, "We have discussed this several times before. You can control the EMPs' intensity and intended attack coordinates from the laptop that's on your desk. It's a dual safety backup system from Blackwood Castle and the English Channel's satellite control room. The only function we have not had time to transfer is the actual hard-wired firing button. If we had another week, we could have programmed that function to be here as well. Still, the trip is less than an hour via the helicopter."

"Fine. We did not control the timing of this one. You and I need to leave immediately." Blackwood said and then stood up.

Abaddon said, "Thanks for letting me listen to the video call with all the bigwigs. With you two leaving, what are my men and I supposed to do?"

Blackwood replied, "Continue to guard Blackwood Castle. We will be back to pick you up before we all leave for a long beach vacation."

"It seems my guys are taking all the risk by staying here. You'll get rich, and we'll get killed."

"Of course, you are taking on the risk, but that's what you are trained and paid for," Blackwood plainly stated.

"We are not trained to take foolhardy risks. If you are deserting Blackwood Castle, why do we need to defend it?" Abaddon incredulously asked as he pushed for an answer that he believed was honest.

Blackwood replied, "Don't be a twit. Blackwood Castle is our main base of operation until we finally decide to leave it."

"Sure, but you said you could control each of the power plants from your laptop, and you will just take your laptop with you."

Blackwood asked dismissively, "Abaddon, what is the source of these questions about loyalty? You are reading into this way too much. If you are concerned about being left behind, I will leave my laptop here in my office. Zag and I will go to the satellite control facility in the English Channel and release the EMPs as soon as the three hours are up. I hope at least some countries choose Option B. It will be fun to see them beg and set an example for expanding into Europe and Asia. Once the EMPs are released, we will return for you in the helicopter and decide how to fortify or leave Blackwood Castle. We have plenty of time for those decisions."

Abaddon looked at his Second-in-Command with a head nod. His first lieutenant turned and walked purposefully away to deliver a previously determined insurance policy. Blackwood naively thought they had an agreement with Abaddon.

Chapter 41

Outside Blackwood Castle

Mac laid next to the opening of the old castle sewer pipe. He was uniquely positioned to see Blackwood and Zag board their helo and head south in a frantic hurry. He had no idea why they would be leaving Blackwood Castle but would tuck that piece of information away to address it later.

The ornate gardens provided a valuable cover for his escape. He would have to remember to thank the lawn keeper if he ever met him. Mac pushed his comms mike in his jaw and said, "This is Mac. Anyone copy?"

There was no answer.

Mac did not know if any of the team survived the attack, and his guilt was on high alert thanks to his Overactive Protective Gene. He said into his comms again, "Repeat. This is Mac. Anyone out there?"

A faint but familiar female voice replied, "Mac, this is Valencia. Over."

"What's your sitrep?"

"Not good. Everyone was hit except Ryker. He was in the communications van with that other tech guy from MI6. Everyone else is still in surgery."

"What about Rhys?" Mac asked as he felt equally responsible for their MI6 counterpart.

"He was hit, too. Also, a lot of the police were taken out. Blackwood and Abaddon's crew were ready for a war, but we only expected a little skirmish. We were sitting ducks. We have pulled back to regroup and determine a battle plan with our new intel on the castle's defensive capabilities. Everyone is working together, and many people are anxious for payback," said Valencia.

"Have you heard anything about how the surgeries are going? Any KIAs?" asked Mac, desperate for information.

Valencia said, "Not certain. The rest of our team is still in surgery. The docs performed battlefield triage and staged me for the next round. The Brits saved our asses with some courageous field medic actions that showed gallantry under fire."

"I wish I could pin a medal on each of their chests," Mac said sincerely.

"Mac, what's your sitrep? I never even saw you land."

"I landed and took out a few of the shooters," Mac replied.

"Oh. Now I understand why the mercs stopped attacking us. That pause gave everyone the necessary time to rescue the wounded, including me. You saved lives today."

"Good to know." Mac rarely accepted compliments because he felt like what he did was part of the job. This situation was even worse because he thought he had failed the team by not arriving on the roof quicker and thwarting some of the carnage.

Mac continued, "Abaddon and a couple of his Choir Boys captured me and decided to play a little game of *Rock-em Sock-em Robots*, but my robot had his hands tied. I escaped but otherwise have been out of the fight because I could not break back into the castle."

"Mac, two nurses just showed up to take me into surgery."

The first nurse said, "Ma'am, a surgical room just opened up, and we need to get you in immediately. You have serious wounds, but we'll take good care of you."

The second nurse noticed Valencia whispering to seemingly no one. The nurse did not appreciate Valencia's critical conversation with Mac on the concealed comms device embedded in her jaw. Her concerned nurse said to the other nurse, "I think she's delirious with pain because she's prepped for surgery, talking to an imaginary friend. We need to immediately get her into the room before the pain completely overwhelms her."

The nurse then turned to Valencia and stated in her confident medical voice, "Ma'am, I am giving you a sedative to take the edge off."

"Wait!" Valencia shouted because she wanted to provide more of a debrief and discuss the next steps with Mac.

"Sorry, ma'am, but I already gave it to you. We'll make that pain go away."

"Mac. Call Ryker on the backup channel. Some of our comms were damaged, and Ryker switched us to the back...." Valencia was out, and the comm went dead.

Chapter 42

Outside Blackwood Castle

Mac switched his comms to their backup channel and called Ryker. "Ryker, this is Mac. Do you copy?"

"Mac! Dude, we thought we lost you!" Ryker screamed in Mac's ear.

"Negative on losing me, but I need some help."

Recapturing his composure, Ryker said, "Copy that. Tell me what you need."

"I need to get back into Blackwood Castle to figure this out. I saw Blackwood and Zag take off in a helicopter heading south. That bastard Abaddon must still be controlling the defenses of Blackwood Castle from the inside."

"I am sitting next to the guy who can pull that off." Ryker relayed Mac's request to the MI6 tech guru and Operation Support Analyst, who had become tied to Ryker's hip since the op started. "We will have a platoon and full assault team there within two hours. Once you give us the go, we will rain holy hell down on that castle to level it."

"Negative. Abaddon let slip that they have significant antiaircraft capabilities, and we know they are more than ready for a ground attack. It would be insanity to try the same battle strategy a second time."

"Then what's the plan?"

"I need a new set of fatigues, my tactical weapons, and thermite. I will sneak back into Blackwood Castle the way I escaped and jam the thermite down Abaddon's throat if that's what is necessary to stop their plan. Also, I need to talk with Rainey to get her up to speed."

Ryker looked over at his new best friend from MI6. Without a pause, the Analyst gave him the thumbs-up and relayed how quickly Mac would have the supplies. Ryker said, "Affirmative. You will have a pack within thirty minutes at your current location. Copy that?"

"That's a good copy."

Ryker sent a short text to Rainey identifying the unknown U.K. phone number as coming from the team and that it was cleared on a secured comms line for her to answer.

"Standby while I relay your call to Rainey," Ryker told Mac and transferred the call before hanging up.

Rainey picked up the call from an unknown U.K. phone number.

Before she could say anything, Mac said, "Rainey, this is Mac."

"Mac, I heard you didn't make it out from Blackwood Castle," Rainey said in a relieved tone.

"I was captured and roughed up, but I escaped. Look, I need to give you a sitrep and ask about some intel I need."

"No need to tell me about the failed attempt at Blackwood Castle. I already know. I am also being kept up to speed on the status of everyone's surgery. I will tell you that the team and Rhys are all in critical condition from their wounds. Unfortunately, there were some KIAs, but as of now, none from your team. We took a pounding." Rainey had an omniscient way of knowing everything happening in the field with her operatives.

"Understood. I heard there was over-the-top courage under fire as the wounded were treated and evac-ed. I have no idea what Blackwood is up to next, but I saw him and Zag board a helo and head south."

"I have to read you into a Priority One situation." Rainey's voice turned from concern to deadly serious.

"Go ahead."

Rainey explained, "Blackwood had a short-notice video call with all the North and South American heads of state. He intends to release EMPs strong enough to fry all electrical components in the Americas. That event will send us all back to the Dark Ages until we replace all our electrical components. Blackwood then demanded that each country purchase all their power needs from his conveniently placed geothermal power plants that are in locations just off our shores. As a sweetener for himself, he's also demanding that we agree to buy all our vehicle batteries from him. I don't think it can get any worse except that he says he needs a response in 2.5 hours from now."

Mac looked at his watch and made a mental note of the exact time of the threatened attack. He said, "I need to get into Blackwood Castle for more intel. Ryker's MI6 buddy is setting me up with what I need. I will report back to you as soon as I can."

"Do you have a plan to stop this madman?"

"I have a few thoughts on how they might release the EMPs, but it will be a game-time decision on how to stop them. There's a secondary location that I need to find and shut down before they push that button."

"Mac, things don't look good from where I sit at Langley. We do not have enough time to implement countermeasures if there's a secondary location with operational readiness. You are our only hope."

"Great. No pressure. Rainey, I'm on it. I'm not going to let this madman steal electric power from the people."

Chapter 43

Blackwood Castle, United Kingdom

Mac heard the recognizable sound of a helicopter's rotary blades within twenty-five minutes as it approached him. The bird was jet black with no markings or numbers, suggesting it was from MI6. Its altitude was very low as it buzzed treetops, keeping its signature below detection from the Blackwood Castle's expected radar capabilities. The helo hovered and descended quickly to an open field. Standing just outside the landing zone, Mac was doing his best to shield his eyes from the wind and dust generated by the rotor blades.

Once landed in the LZ, Mac sprinted in a crouched position to the helo. The side door slid open, and Mac was handed a large duffel bag. The soldier screamed in his loudest voice, "Ryker said he threw in a couple of extra toys for fun in the bag. Good hunting, sir."

Before he turned away, he looked at the pilot. Even though the pilot wore a helmet and visor, Mac thought he recognized him. He could have sworn the pilot was the spitting image of one of the Royal Family members who served in the RAF, the U.K.'s Royal Air Force. The pilot nodded at him and gave him a smart salute. Mac snapped a salute and did his reverse crouching run away from the LZ.

Mac changed his clothes first. He was thankful for his lightweight and quiet tactical combat boots. Mac found his favorite weapons, including an M4 rifle with its collapsible stock and shortened barrel, a 9MM Glock, a spring-assisted foldable knife, and extra ammo magazines for the guns. Most importantly, he found the thermite that would allow him to breach the dungeon door and enter the rest of the castle. He stuck his hand around the edges of the bag and said, "Ryker, you just gave me your version of the perfect skateboard." He pulled out four grenades and a fiber-optic viewing system. Mac also found four flash-bangs whose blinding light and loud explosion could be handy in disorienting targets.

T-minus 2 hours and 6 minutes. Time was ticking. Mac covered the two-mile run back to Blackwood Castle at a six-minute-per-mile pace. He re-entered the sewer tunnel that was previously his escape route and crawled into the dungeon opening. He passed the merc, who was still hanging lifelessly from the wall hook where Mac had left him.

He ascended the stairs three at a time and placed the thermite on the door's lock. Mac had never been fearful of any weapon at his disposal. However, he was respectful of firepower and knew this was not like the movies where explosions always needed to be bigger and brighter than the last scene.

Keeping that concept in mind, he inserted the sticky thermite into the lock to melt it without waking up the neighborhood. Mac knew that thermite was an incendiary weapon that did not explode like plastic explosives. Instead, it burned at an excessively high temperature, melting everything it contacted and hissing with a snake-like sound.

The lock popped open with the thermite ignition, and no one came running with their guns blazing. Mac pulled the door open and slipped into a hallway. He ran in the direction of where he believed Blackwood's office should be located. Thank God for his quiet tactical boots.

Approaching a T-intersection in the hallway, Mac slowed. From experience, he knew this type of junction was incredibly dangerous because it was impossible to see both directions while peeking around the corner. Mac glanced to his left side and froze inches away from a merc. Noticing Mac out of the corner of his eye, the merc reacted immediately.

Mac could not allow the merc to alert his cohorts. If Mac found himself staring at a dozen mercs and survived the encounter, he would likely end up again in the dungeon with no hope of escape. It was at times like these that an offense was the best defense. Mac drove hard around the corner with his hand on the merc's mouth. The merc responded with rapid punches into Mac's torso, which was still tender from the previous onslaught when he was the human punching bag. Mac felt his aggressiveness lessen from the body blows.

The merc raised his machine pistol that was hanging from a shoulder strap. Mac had no choice but to grab the weapon's barrel to ensure it was not pointed at him, and the two stumbled to the opposite wall. Mac used the leverage of the weapon's barrel that was held upright thanks to the shoulder strap.

Defying gravity, Mac forcefully ran up the wall as if he had sticky shoes or the orientation of the world had just turned 90 degrees. When his feet were higher than the merc's head, he flipped one leg over the merc to his shoulder and thrust his other leg to the merc's vulnerable neck. Mac crossed his ankles together and locked his legs while letting momentum carry them both to the floor. Mac intended to cut off the blood flow to the merc's brain until he passed out. However, the cement floor did the work for him.

The merc clumsily fell head-first, knocking himself unconscious. Mac knew this guy would not be waking up for several hours with severe head trauma like that. Mac dragged him into the nearest doorway, gagged him so he could not cry out in alarm, and securely zip-tied his hands and feet to a metal pipe running from the floor to the ceiling.

The next merc was much easier to address. He was walking down the hallway, and Mac slipped quickly into an adjoining room. As the merc walked past the doorway, Mac swung the butt of his 9MM into the merc's temple. The merc dropped in a heap, and Mac dragged him into the room. Mac gagged and zip-tied him to a bedpost that was too heavy to ever budge without industrial-grade mechanical tools.

Mac kept proceeding down the hallway, but it felt like he still had a long distance to traverse. Plus, every nook and cranny seemed to have another merc. He heard voices in a side room and pulled out his optical scope device. The device's primary part was a pencil-thin tube with a camera on one end. The other end was connected to a base with a joystick that allowed the operator to snake it around corners and other obstacles. No one would ever notice this silent tube slipping about three inches into their room. Mac could see the snake's field of view via a wireless pair of goggles.

The scope did its job, but it did not mean Mac had to like what he saw. Two mercs were facing the door, and there was no way Mac was going to slip past undetected. Mac was getting frustrated with these delays as he was fighting a countdown clock. He said to himself, "Where the fuck did that asshole find all these mercenaries? Is Abaddon buying these guys in bulk from a member-only wholesale club?" Mac was losing valuable time.

Mac withdrew the scope and returned it to his bag. He stood up and stopped in front of the doorway with a shoulder-wide stance and gun pointed at the mercs. "I don't suppose you two bad guys would like to surrender and tie yourselves up so I can leave and save the world?"

The two mercs looked at each other with curiosity as if they were considering the offer. The mercs squinted their eyes and swiftly raised their guns in unison. Mac was forced to shoot them with his silenced weapon before they could pull their triggers. He said, "I guess your answer is no."

Mac continued sprinting to the end of the corridor. Surprisingly, he did not encounter any more mercs on his exceptionally long trek to Blackwood's office.

Chapter 44

Dr. Blackwood's Office, Blackwood Castle

Mac recognized the hallway leading to his destination. When he arrived, he heard Abaddon and apparently his Second-in-Command discussing some military extraction. Mac snuck a peek around the corner of the office entrance and saw Abaddon sitting at Blackwood's desk chair with his Second-in-Command across from him. Abaddon was holding the antique fan that Blackwood obsessively protected from others touching. Sitting in his chair and holding the fan was Abaddon's act of defiance to reassure himself that he still had some level of control over his life.

Mac overheard Abaddon saying, "I do not think they will come back for us. We are on our own."

The subordinate replied, "I disagree. It's difficult to believe that those wankers will not handsomely reward us for such an effective job protecting this castle. No client has ever stiffed us for our fee."

"Those two idiots don't care about us. Did you see Blackwood's pause before he responded to my direct question about trusting him? The only way we would have gotten paid was if I had demanded our money while we were under attack. Now they think they don't need us. I told Zag to call me before they took off in the helicopter to pick us up on the return trip. If they don't call first confirming that they are coming back for us, we know we are not part of their plans and will not see a dime from those thieves. Did you leave the package in their helo?"

The Second-in-Command responded, "Confirmed. The package is well hidden under a seat. It will become armed once they are airborne on the first flight. If Blackwood or Zag contacts us saying they are returning to Blackwood Castle to pick us up, we can unarm the package by texting it. If they decide to leave us here, there will be an execution sequence based upon a preprogrammed altitude during their second flight."

"Outstanding. I gave clear instructions to Zag to call before they left the control center. Part of me does not want them to call. I must say I hate those two bastards," Abaddon commented with a grimace.

Mac could not help but think that planting that simple thought in Abaddon's head had its intended effect of tearing the cabal apart from the inside out. He looked at his watch. There was only one hour and 36 minutes until Blackwood initiated the EMP attack. Mac needed more intel on

Blackwood's plans and disarming the EMPs, and he needed it fast.

Abaddon asked, "Do we have our exfil birds ready to pick all of us up?"

The merc replied, "Yes, they are at a small airport about ten miles from here, fueled and ready to fly in once they are cleared to land."

"Very well. I think Blackwood was full of shit when he made his grandiose statement that he would leave his laptop that controls the satellite firing directions. That was just to get us to stay. I'll bet he has another way to aim the stupid things. I wonder if we should fuck with them. Maybe I cannot fire the EMPs from this laptop, but if we are not getting paid, I could point them to fire at each other, rendering them useless. I saw Blackwood play with these a dozen times, pointing at different targets. All I need to do is enter the longitude and latitude coordinates on this screen, and it's easy to send them firing in any direction."

Mac didn't have the time to wait for Blackwood's plan to implode on its own greed. He needed answers now, and the only information source was in the room in front of him. Mac needed Abaddon alive to question him. Shit. Killing this bastard would be incredibly satisfying, but using lethal force was not an option. He pulled out a flash-bang and tossed it into the room as he closed his eyes and covered his ears while slipping back around the corner.

Abaddon and the other merc didn't respond quickly enough once they processed that it was a flash-bang. The flash-bang did its job, and both Abaddon and Zag grabbed their ears and squeezed their eyes shut. They were temporarily helpless to the onslaught of pain in their senses of sight and hearing.

Mac ran into the room and delivered a single punch to the Second-in-Command. The man simply flopped sideways from the blow. It was a blessing because it relieved him from his painful flash-bang disorientation.

Mac jumped and completed his perfect Major League Baseball slide across the desk, planning to pin Abaddon's arms with zip ties. He grabbed one of Abaddon's wrists and twisted it behind him.

Abaddon was still disorientated by the flash-bang but recovered quickly based on his training and sheer determination. He immediately went into an aggressive attack mode with his superior size and strength. Mac utilized his quickness to counteract Abaddon's moves.

They both had decades of hand-to-hand combat training. It was a fight of equals. Mac made the tactical mistake of focusing too long on subduing Abaddon by the wrists. Abaddon managed to pry his wrist away and turned while standing to face Mac. He tossed the chair to the side like he was sweeping pieces of paper off a table. Then he swung a left hook towards Mac's head, and Mac skillfully ducked below the blow. Mac's counterpunch was a jab to Abaddon's left armpit, partially paralyzing Abaddon's arm temporarily.

That move was a costly one for Mac. Abaddon pivoted around with a stiff right jab to Mac's jaw, making him see stars. It was clear to Mac that Abaddon was having trouble raising his left arm, and Mac thought of a couple of quick-kill moves to make use of his advantage. However, he needed Abaddon alive to learn about Blackwood and Zag's plans.

While the punching and Judo match was going on, the Second-in-Command awakened from Mac's blow. The merc looked over his shoulder and spied a Medieval spear with deadly blades on the top and bottom. Dashing over to the spear, he picked it up and turned with a wicked smile. He grabbed the spear with both hands slightly wider than shoulder-width apart. Swinging it in a figure-eight movement, the Second-in-Command appreciated the balance of this centuries-old weapon.

Abaddon threw a hard punch at Mac, but Mac ducked and countered with a stunning blow to Abaddon's chin. Abaddon was rendered out of the fight for a short period, allowing Mac to focus on the menacing spear coming his way.

The merc first tried a midsection jab with the spear, but Mac pulled back enough to avoid the spear's tip. The merc spun 360 degrees with the spear's sharp edge, slicing the air directly at Mac's neck. Mac ducked just in time. The merc was working the spear just like a skilled baton twirler.

Mac found himself standing next to a shield from the same period as the spear and grabbed it. He skillfully blocked two attacks using the newly acquired piece.

The merc was perfecting his technique of manipulating the spear as an effective weapon. His attacks up to this point were just practice. He faked as if he was swinging wide for Mac's head. As he did so, Mac raised the shield to block the attack. Mac's response left his mid-section open, and the merc dropped the spear to slice across Mac's stomach.

At first, it only slightly hurt. Then Mac looked down, saw the blood already pooling on his shirt, and noticed it was painful to move his abdomen. It was lucky that Mac had a six-pack instead of a potbelly because a protruding extra ten inches of fat would have been sliced wide open.

The merc said, "I like this weapon. It feels good in my hands." He looked at the blood on one end of the spear, showing his growing confidence. The merc then attempted an angular slicing stroke that hit the shield. The blow forced Mac to use his core to brace himself. Mac's hold on the armor weakened with agony radiating from his wound, and it fell to the floor.

Mac's back was to the desk, and he looked around for any possible weapon. The only object within reach was an old mechanical clock, and he grabbed it. The merc went for the final killing jab now that Mac was defenseless without the shield. Mac stuck the ancient clock in front of his chest as his only possible defensive move. The spear pierced the makeshift shield while splintering through the clock's face and poking two feet out the other side. Mac glanced down and saw the blade stop within an inch of his chest.

From the hopeful kill move, the merc was off balance by extending himself too far forward. The spear was embedded solidly into the clock, and Mac used the leverage afforded by his grasp on the clock to twist. The merc fought the twisting action, but the spear slipped in his hands and further threw him off balance. Mac utilized this advantage of the merc's awkward positioning and exploded forward while grabbing the spear pole past the clock.

The merc stumbled backward and fell into the leather chair where he first sat. The spear impaled the merc, hitting the lower half of his heart and continuing through the back of the chair. The merc's arms jerked a little, and his eyes bulged as his body completely shut down.

Thanks to Mac's distraction in dealing with the Second-in-Command, Abaddon had a chance to recover from Mac's last strike. He rushed around the desk aggressively and attacked Mac. The two begin to share blows. Abaddon was mentally and physically strong. He quite possibly was the most challenging opponent Mac had ever faced. Mac used his quickness and agility rather than going in close Judo or wrestling style against this beast of a man.

Abaddon tried using a few of the convenient mallet-like Warhammer and battle-ax medieval weapons. Fortunately, the swings were thwarted by Mac using his wits and modern-day training. Mac had to be careful when using the war toys against Abaddon. He knew that a poorly placed blow from one of the relic war weapons could prove deadly for Abaddon, and he needed Abaddon alive. Both men were beginning to tire from the exertion of the fight. Abaddon picked up his next weapon, a bottle of wine, sitting on the table. Abaddon broke the bottle to use the sharp edges as a makeshift knife.

Mac looked at Abaddon and shook his head. "That's a shame. That was a lovely bottle of Château Lafite Rothschild 2016. You didn't need to do that."

Abaddon attacked with wild swings of the broken bottle and backed Mac into the desk where he had no more room to retreat. Mac put both hands on the desk for stability as he tried to find a way to avoid the slicing glass. He saw the spear with one sword-like end still sticking out of the merc and its other end pointing chest height directly at Mac. Unfortunately, it was five feet away, and Mac would never reach it in time.

Attempting his final attack, Abaddon swung for Mac's jugular with the bottle. Out of reflex, Mac executed a jumping front snap kick toward the onrushing Abaddon. Mac's foot landed on Abaddon's extended chin, and Abaddon started falling backward from the blow. He didn't make it to the floor. He fell on the extended spear like a shish kabob on a stick that was also skewering his dead Second-in-Command sitting in the chair.

Mac saw the event in horror and cried out, "No!"

Abaddon looked down at the spear protruding from the front of his shirt. He looked up at Mac in shock, and blood started trickling out the side of his mouth.

Mac yelled desperately, "Where are Blackwood and Zag?"

"Those bastards? I hope they rot in hell."

Seeing the life drip out of Abaddon, Mac knew there was no loyalty to the two double-crossers who left him behind.

"Help me stop them," Mac pleaded.

"Fuck them. Blackwood and Zag went to the satellite control facility south of here just off the coast in the English Channel." Abaddon said, seething with anger.

"Where in the English Channel?"

"It's on the map over…." Abaddon's head dropped, and he never finished his sentence. He died as he hung from the spear that impaled him.

Mac started frantically flipping through papers on the desk and in drawers, but he did not find a map. He needed a location that was closer than somewhere just off the coast in the English Channel.

Turning to the computer screen, Mac saw a global picture of the satellites' location compared to the Earth. He rifled through files on the laptop with fast fingers on the keyboard. He found a file with all of Blackwood's sites, including the satellite control facility. "I've got you!"

Mac checked his watch. T-minus one hour and 18 minutes. He tried his comms, but they were down, likely due to the facial beating and punishment on his jaw that he just took. He picked up Abaddon's phone and called Ryker. "Ryker, this is Mac."

"Great to hear from you. Did you disarm the satellites?" Ryker asked.

"Negative. Still in process. I need an Uber lift ASAP from the same location as the earlier drop-off. I have a map and coordinates of where Blackwood will fire their EMP weapons," replied Mac. He told Ryker the coordinates for the satellite control facility and hit print from the laptop. A detailed picture with coordinates of the satellite control facility's location was dropped in the laser printer's tray.

Ryker replied, "Pick-up is on its way. It'll be there ASAP."

"Make it quicker than ASAP." Mac used a famous quote from the movie star John Wayne and said with a deep, commanding voice, "We're burning daylight."

Before leaving Blackwood's office, he returned to Abaddon's original laptop screen displaying all the satellites. Mac had an idea.

Chapter 45

Satellite Control Facility, The English Channel

The simple design and efficient layout of the sparsely furnished satellite control facility bore no resemblance to Blackwood Castle. Blackwood's facial expressions betrayed his inherent dislike of his surroundings. An engineer's paradise, the room was only equipped with a few metal chairs and an array of control panels. It sat on what was once a functioning oil rig, complete with a massive steel center tower and a helipad outlined in green. It had been in service for so long that rust ran down the white paint on its four legs. It was a functioning oil rig at one time, but its working days had long since passed. Scheduled for demolition in about a year, Blackwood secretly acquired it and converted it to use for his purposes.

Blackwood was perched uncomfortably in a metal chair and said, "The leaders of the Americas have around an hour and a quarter before their two continents go dark. I'm not sure I can sit on this metal contraption you call a chair for that long. Why didn't we buy more civilized furniture for this room?"

Zag, sitting relaxed, was in his comfort zone in the satellite control facility. He responded, "Every scientific engineer knows that a room like this with chairs like this is where important things happen. In a place like this, everyone who is anyone wears a white lab coat. The rest are just administrators living off hyper-intelligent engineers' hard work."

"I will accept that I'm now in your playhouse. Just remember who bought this playhouse for you. I hope your team of geeks has planned for the contingencies."

"There is nothing that can go wrong now. After so many years, we have finally pulled it off," Zag replied.

The two were drinking scotch, and they clinked their glasses together in a celebratory gesture. The champagne could come once the EMPs were released.

Blackwood said, "I don't like that they attacked Blackwood Castle and forced us to play our hand before we wanted."

"Don't worry about it. It still turned out fine. Abaddon and his thugs repelled the attack. You are about to hit that trillionaire status you wanted."

"I will feel better when the money is wired to me instead of just signatures on energy services contracts. However, you're right. I am becoming a trillionaire. Much more importantly, I will finally have the respect I deserve. Oh, if you're worried about your payout, don't be. I have not forgotten your role in all of this. I've not decided how much to pay you, but your payout will be in the tens of millions of euros."

Zag took a big gulp to finish his scotch and said, "We will have never-ending, perpetual contracts to supply the Americas with all their power."

"Don't forget about the requirement to buy all their vehicle batteries from us. We will make billions from that portion of the contract alone." Even in the uncomfortable metal chair, Blackwood happily smiled and proclaimed, "I am a King!"

Blackwood closed his eyes and fantasized about his riches. He wished his parents could see him now. He was the most powerful man in the world. "I sure would like to know who invented the Blitzpeicher. The guy was a genius."

"Agreed. I doubt we will ever know the story. The inventor probably got greedy, and no one wanted to pay him for it," replied Zag.

"If that's the case, he didn't understand strategic positioning. We positioned ourselves such that no one had an option for other alternatives. We then flawlessly implemented our tactical integration of technological advances and the business monetization of the advancements. We deserve what we get. So many inventors do not know how to make money off their inventions. Of course, my present company is excluded!"

That comment earned a hearty belly laugh from both schemers.

"The problem is genius engineers like me are necessary to invent things but do not understand the business aspects of the invention. The worst of the engineers have this naïve concept. They will just give it away to make the world a better place and never get rewarded for their work. Technology belongs to the individual, and we deserve to get paid for our work." Zag pontificated his ego-centric accomplishment.

"I wish we had another video call with the heads of state when I hit that button firing the EMPs."

"Well, wait! All those heads of state will immediately have all their communication equipment fried, and they will drop from the video call!"

They both had another good laugh.

Blackwood asked, "Do you think they will all accept our terms?"

"Most have already. There are a few holdouts like the Canadians. What are they thinking? Do they expect to send the Canadian Mounted Police to Blackwood Castle to stop us?"

"Since they will not have any other options for transportation, they might need the Mounties on their horses!" quipped Blackwood.

Again, there was a loud laugh. Blackwood and Zag downed their scotches, and Zag refilled the tumblers. There was nothing left to do but wait and drink. Of course, not too much. The two needed clear enough heads to enjoy the EMP moment.

Zag noted, "Speaking of Blackwood Castle, it's a shame if it gets blown up by the RAF. I have no doubt they mistakenly think it's the center of the operations. The buffoons are probably planning to blow it off the face of the earth."

"Who gives a toss? It has been my prison for the last ten years. With my money, I can buy every castle in the world," Blackwood proclaimed.

"Okay, but what about Abaddon and his men?" retorted Zag.

Blackwood responded, "They are professionals and know the risk. I do not suspect any of them will make it through the RAF attack. I can find hundreds of mercenaries, the likes of Abaddon, and they're easy to hire. They all have a price. That makes all of them expendable once their usefulness is outlived. However, if Abaddon happens to survive the counterattack on Blackwood Castle, we will need a loophole not to pay him. If he doesn't survive, it will be all the better because then I will have saved the cost of his payout."

Blackwood looked lovingly at the red button programmed to fire the EMPs from the satellites. He asked, "What happens if we lose power on this old rusty rig before I get the satisfaction of pushing the fire button?"

Zag replied with a coy smile, "I thought you would never ask. I know you want the satisfaction of pushing the button. I even set up the large monitors over the control panel to replicate the EMP releases utilizing a computer-generated view of the Americas' EMP paths. To ensure you are not robbed of firing the EMPs yourself, I installed a backup system that will kick on like a backup generator if the power goes out. I oversaw the completion and installation of a Blitzpeicher under the control panel behind you."

Blackwood was not convinced. He said, "What if something bizarre happens, and we are hit with an EMP just like we are releasing over the Americas? Then we lose the Blitzpeicher also."

"I have the Blitzpeicher encased in a Faraday cage."

"Okay. I will accept that I don't have to worry about that. Still, how do you know the little Blitzpeicher vehicle battery will have enough voltage to run all necessary equipment in this room?"

"Surely, you don't think I would take any chances like that, do you? My uniquely designed Blitzpeicher is about the size of two coffins stacked on each other. There is enough stored voltage in this massive Blitzpeicher to run a city for a year. Don't worry. I guarantee it will turn on during any power outage." Zag sat back and took a sip of his drink.

Blackwood relaxed and took a deep breath, saying, "You're right. There is nothing I need to worry about." He extended his glass, and Zag responded with another tapping of the two drinks together.

Zag asked, "Not that I care about the deaths, but have you run any scenarios regarding how many people will die in North and South America after the debilitating EMPs? With fewer people in our service areas, we will have lower revenues and make less money."

"No one knows, but by my calculations, millions will likely die from starvation and the loss of basic life necessities. They are collateral damage to the implementation of the bigger picture. We cannot distract ourselves with details that are out of our control. I have no patience for anything except for my success."

"You mean our success, right?"

Blackwood froze and said with a guilty tone, "Of course, whatever you say."

"Thank you for acknowledging that. Our success is from thousands of hours of hard work from both of us," Zag stated.

Jerking his head up in a gut-wrenching realization, Blackwood said, "Where is my fan? I forgot it when we hurriedly left Blackwood Castle. It set us on this journey. It turned around my life and inspired me for our current path. I need my fan, and it's sitting on my desk. Leave immediately in the helicopter and bring it to me."

Zag replied, "Can't Abaddon bring it? I am too critical not to be here." He stared desperately with anticipation at the EMP button.

"No. I would prefer that you retrieved it."

"How about sending one of my junior staff people?"

Feeding Zag's ego, Blackwood said, "No! You are the only person I trust with it. You said the only remaining task is to push the button. That fan was the turning point of this entire strategic plan."

Zag smiled with pride and said, "Certainly, Dr. Blackwood. I will pick up the fan for you. Then I will come back so we can drink fine champagne to celebrate our success."

Blackwood replied, "Yes. We deserve everything we get!"

Chapter 46

Blackwood Castle Helicopter

Zag boarded the Blackwood Castle helicopter to pick up the beloved fan as ordered. He had a drink in his hand before the wheels left the ground.

Zag began rambling into the helicopter's intercom to the pilot. He said, "There had better be plenty of booze on this booze cruise. Frankly, I can't remember if this is my third, fourth, or fifth drink. I guess I don't care. I am going to pick up that stupid fan, so it's going to be a painful trip."

The pilot correctly assessed the situation and replied, "Sir, I am not sure you're feeling any pain in your condition. However, I will get you there as quickly as possible."

"I'm not sure, but do you know if there was something I was supposed to do for Abaddon before I left the satellite control room in the English Channel?"

"Negative. You and Mr. Blackwood did not share anything with me on the flight plan."

"How the hell am I supposed to remember those meaningless details when I am the real technological mastermind behind this entire plan? Do you know that Abaddon's feelings were hurt when he thought he was being left out of the final planning? What a childish insecurity from such a large and dangerous man!"

"I'm not sure how to respond to those questions. My responsibility is to fly this helicopter.

Zag slurred while yelling, "I hate the idea of flying back to Blackwood Castle while thinking the RAF could be planning a bombing run! Abaddon said he could repel any attack, and I am forced to trust my life to that gun-hungry freak. Abaddon knows he is physically intimidating and can bully me whenever we are together. I simply despise that imbecile!"

The pilot, clearly irritated at the rambling drunk in the back of his helicopter, rolled his eyes and replied, "Sir, I have no comment. Also, I need to focus on my flying. I am going to turn off the cabin comms. I suggest you sleep it off while we are on the flight." With that comment, the pilot flipped off the cabin comms toggle.

Zag didn't hear a word from the pilot. He continued his one-sided rant and said, "Whether Blackwood only trusts me or not, retrieving an old antique fan is a stupid little errand boy task. Blackwood does not appreciate how the entire operation comes together because of me. After all, who created the geothermal power plants and installed the EMP weapon into the satellites? Who modernized the Blitzpeicher designs and began its manufacturing with that idiot Joe Whisp? Who did all this? I did it!"

Not realizing he was speaking to a dead mic, Zag continued, "Maybe I will quit once I receive my tens of millions of euros. That's plenty of 'F-You' money. I love the concept of having enough money to say 'F-You' to anyone I want. That's even more money than I originally dreamed. Do you know that I was worried Blackwood was going to kill me at one time? What a joke! Blackwood will always need me. I'm critical in running the plants and satellites. And yet, here I am, sitting alone in the back of your helicopter fetching a rusty, old toy."

Zag had another gulp of whisky. Given the alcohol's negative impact on his ability to function, his one-sided discussion was better characterized as a one-sided slur. The helicopter softly took off from the helipad and quickly shifted to forward movement across the English Channel.

Continuing with his drunken self-admiration, Zag said, "You have no idea what it is like being treated as inferior by Blackwood and Abaddon. They will come crawling back to me as soon as there is a technical need, but they will have difficulty tracking me down. I will buy a beach house on an island and sip drinks with little umbrellas. I will have an all-female staff to attend to my every need. No, wait. Hell, I am going to buy the entire island. Of course, I will still have an all-female staff. What do you think about the staff's uniforms being red swimsuits like that old TV show?"

When there was no response to his question, he asked, "Hey, pilot? Pilot? Are you there? I should have guessed that you'd ignore me too!"

Zag's fanciful daydreaming was cut short when his drink slipped from his fingers. He exclaimed, "Damn," and reached down for the glass that rolled under the seat. Instead of the glass, he found a green duffle bag. He unbuckled his seatbelt and pulled the duffle bag to his lap. When he unzipped the bag, his intoxicated mind was having trouble processing the contents.

The bag contained bricks of some beige material that were connected via wires to a metal box. Embedded into the top of the box was a digital readout of numbers. He progressively saw the numbers decline from 30. The 30 quickly became 25 and then became 20. Suddenly, Zag's eyes popped open with a sobering startle.

Zag screamed, "Shit, I think we might have bricks of C4 plastic explosive back here with me!"

The readout number hit 15 as it continued to countdown. Zag saw that as the helicopter increased its altitude, the numbers on the box decreased. By now, they must be a couple of miles away from the satellite control facility. Still, that damn pilot was increasing his altitude too.

There was no time to take chances, and Zag screamed in the cabin to the helicopter pilot, "Descend! Descend!" The pilot did not respond. He wore a helmet that blocked all the noise that wasn't communicated via the radio, and the radio to the cabin was still turned off. The readout on the box reached eight.

"The countdown is heading quickly to zero! Please tell me that you are listening to me! Descend!" The readout read five, and the helicopter kept steadily ascending.

There wasn't enough time to throw the bomb out the door. Zag plopped back in his seat and shouted, "Maybe I'm wrong. Maybe it's not a bomb. Ha! If it's a bomb, at least I can say I will be remembered in textbooks as a genius engineer who changed the world with my inventions."

The last thing Zag saw was the box reading zero. The immense power of the C4 explosion caused the Blackwood Castle helicopter to vaporize. Nothing was left except small pieces of the burning helicopter shooting out in every direction like fireworks.

Chapter 47

MI6 Helicopter

Mac had just boarded the MI6 helicopter, and it took off in a hurry. The single crewmember in the cabin looked like the same fellow he had seen with the first drop-off. Mac slid headphones over his ears so that he could communicate with the others. "Thanks for the lift, guys."

The crewmember nodded, and the pilot replied with a refined English accent, "All in a day's work, sir. Anything for Queen and Country. What's our destination?"

"Fly south. Our destination is a facility in the English Channel. I have a map with its exact coordinates." Mac passed the map and coordinates to the co-pilot.

Once Mac assured himself they were heading in the correct direction, he said, "I need to re-gear up. Do you have any toys for me?"

The crewmember in the back replied, "Your guy, Ryker, must think you are going up against an army. I am surprised that chap didn't give you a tank, too."

"What? No tank? I need to have a conversation with that young lad." Mac reached into his bag and began to pull out gear. Ryker thought of everything, and MI6 must have opened the doors to the toy box. Mac gunned up.

"Looks like you are all set for a playdate with the killer toys you're carrying," the crewmember said.

"These toys are perfect. It's about time for me to have some fun," Mac said with conviction.

"You look a little banged up. Let me patch up that abdominal wound. I don't think you have lost much blood, but I need to make sure you are battle-ready."

"I'm fine. There's no need."

"Negative, sir. I am under strict orders to fix you up. They warned me that you would refuse treatment."

"Who's they?" Mac asked.

"Let's just say you have friends in really high places. Now it will just take me a minute," the medic said, lifting Mac's shirt without asking for more permission.

Mac let the medic do his job because there was nothing else to do. The patch-up went well beyond providing a few pain medication tablets. The medic's skills helped ensure Mac was equipped and good to go. Besides bandages, he provided Mac with a Kevlar chest and stomach shield that gave him some critical body armor.

The pilot came on over Mac's headset. "Are you sure you want to be dropped at the waypoint? I radioed my brass about our destination, and they told me to drop and go. We are going to rain fiery coals and brimstone on that target just before the three-hour deadline hits."

Mac replied to the pilot, "I assumed that would be your orders. I need to talk with my boss at Langley. Can you patch me through?"

"Roger that."

After giving the number and being connected with Rainey at Langley, Mac said, "Rainey, this is Mac. I am heading to the satellite control room. I can still take out Blackwood and Zag before they release the weapon. Don't attack yet."

"Mac, this is out of my hands now. We have several countries demanding the Brits eliminate every possible site where the EMPs could be controlled."

"Look, I understand why they want to eliminate all potential targets, but I think it's a huge and deadly mistake."

"What does everyone have to lose?" Rainey was pressing with the logic she heard bantered about while on conference calls with world leaders as she sat in the Oval Office with POTUS and his top advisors.

"How about over two hundred years of progress? How do we know Zag didn't install a failsafe function in the satellites that will cause them to fire unless the firing sequence is turned off?"

"We don't. As I said, it's out of my hands, but let me talk with POTUS."

"Copy. I also might have a backup plan, but I am unsure if it will work."

"Mac, I need you to understand that I don't think POTUS will change his mind. He was pushing for the airstrikes once you sent us the coordinates. There's almost no hope of changing the airstrike. You have exactly 30 minutes to avert a worldwide catastrophe."

"Copy that. Mac out."

The helo did not fully land on the helipad. Mac jumped from the open side door while it was hovering a few feet off the deck. He knew helicopters were exceptionally loud, and he had just announced his arrival.

As the helo began to lift for its departure, Mac turned around and glanced at the cockpit. He saw the same pilot who was flying in his last encounter with the MI6 helicopter. This fly jockey was as brave as they come and must have flown Combat Air Rescue in the RAF. Now Mac was almost sure there was a Royal behind the stick.

Chapter 48

Satellite Control Center, The English Channel

The trek to find Blackwood felt practically insurmountable. There were workers and guards everywhere. Mac had no choice but to take them out with terse efficiency. Everyone at the facility must have been alerted by his arrival via the helo – time to move.

Mac sprinted on a gangway leading from the helipad. A few hostile shots banged off the metal around him. The first two encounters were with shooters who were too slow to respond. Mac fired double taps into each without breaking his stride. His silenced weapon gave him the hope of keeping others from being alerted. Still, he knew there was virtually no likelihood of that bit of luck.

The subsequent two encounters were with workers with white lab coats carrying clipboards. The more reactionary of the lab coats stepped forward and yelled something Mac could not hear. As the lab coat charged, he put his clipboard in front of him like a police anti-riot tactical shield. His overtly obvious plan was to ram Mac over the railing. Before he reached his prey, he stumbled on the gangway's metal flooring and rolled over the edge to his death. Mac was not waiting for the second lab coat to decide what to do. He delivered a flying punch and followed up by slamming the lab coat's head into the metal railing. That lab coat was not getting up for several hours.

A shooter on the ground was almost hit by the first lab coat guy falling off the gangway. He skirted backward and saw Mac head-slam a second white lab coat guy into the railing. The shooter did not need any additional input to know the gangway's black-clad guy did not belong there. He fired a rainbow of automatic weapon bullets in Mac's direction. Mac hit the far side of the gangway flooring. The shooter hid behind a metal condensing unit that gave him the perfect firing vantage point. All he had to do was wait until Mac stood, and then he would have a clean shot.

Mac didn't have time to wait. Mac popped up and fired three consecutive shots that ricocheted off the metal condenser to entice the shooter to focus strictly on the top of the gangway. The shooter returned fire but remained standing with his rifle concentrated on the top railing. It would be an easy kill shot as soon as Mac popped up again.

Mac slipped through the gap between the gangway flooring and the siding, grasping the bottom of the far side railing opposite the shooter. The shooter didn't even notice he was there as he held onto the flooring's edge, dangling below the gangway. Mac's bullets hit home, penetrating the shooter's chest, who went flying backward.

Three more shooters blasted through the door at the end of the gangway with their weapons at the ready. They paused with shock and confusion when they didn't see any unknown intruders in front of them. Charging ahead, their boots clanged on the metal floor of the gangway. Mac began swinging himself from side to side. He managed to lock his feet on a railing post. The shooters were no more than ten feet away, and Mac inserted his head and gun arm under the railing. The first two shooters were dropped with three salvos from Mac's Beretta 9M pistol. The third shooter got off a few rounds before Mac landed his shots, sending him to the deck with his cohorts.

Mac tried to reach with his right hand to climb up, but excruciating pain riddled his body. Seeing a bullet had pierced his right shoulder, he used his body to roll onto the gangway floor. Mac performed a quick field assessment of the gunshot wound and saw he was not bleeding too badly, suggesting no major artery was hit. It was a through-and-through shot, and the pain was already starting to ebb. He knew it was time to keep his ass going before it was too late.

Once in the building, the hallway only led in one direction. Mac sprinted in desperation to find Blackwood. He came across a room that had windows across the entire hallway side. Inside, the room was filled with a cadre of panels and lit lights.

Mac was not interested in anything in the room except the man standing with his back to him. Blackwood had his eyes glued to a series of large computer screens. T-minus six minutes.

Mac flung himself into the room with his gun drawn. "Blackwood, stop!"

Blackwood froze and slowly turned to the doorway. "Why if it isn't the CIA's best man, Declan Mac."

Mac said, "Cut the crap. Step away from the computer unless you want a bullet in your forehead."

Retrieving his MI6-provided cell phone from his pocket, Mac raised the phone while holding his Beretta steadily at Blackwood. Mac hit the send button that placed a preprogrammed direct-dial call to Rainey. She answered almost before it rang. He needed Rainey to hear a compelling reason to call off the airstrike.

"Rainey, Mac here. I have a gun pointed directly at Blackwood, and I would like you to hear our enlightening conversation."

Rainey replied, "I'm listening."

Mac asked Blackwood, "Why? Why do you want to destroy the world with a scorched earth approach to become a King of nothing?"

"So those discourteous and faceless little online twits and the talking news heads will treat me respectfully. All they want to do is cast the blame on someone. I have listened to them for far too long and will show them I control everything. You said it right. I'm a King, and there is nothing anyone can do to stop me."

"It seems I have a gun pointed at you, and you are helpless. Exactly how does that correlate to me not stopping you from releasing the EMPs?" Mac asked in a last-ditch attempt to determine if Blackwood would divulge any backup plans.

"Mr. Mac, you underestimate me. Do you think I would make such a huge strategic blunder by not installing a failsafe in my satellites? If I don't abort the EMPs in the next five minutes, it will fire whether I push the red button or not. I'm just here to experience the joy of hitting the EMP fire button myself. If you kill me, no one will know how to operate my power plants that are necessary to save the world."

"Rainey, abort the airstrike. I don't believe this madman is bluffing about a failsafe. Do you copy?" Mac loudly announced into the speakerphone while glaring at Blackwood.

After a short pause, Rainey said, "Confirmed. Aborting the airstrike on the satellite control facility."

At hearing what he perceived as his success, Blackwood said, "Good choice. You are right to surrender in this negotiation. I was not bluffing about a failsafe."

"If I kill you now, you will not be able to enjoy the fruits of your labor," Mac said.

"If I die, the world will still remember me as the best strategist ever."

Mac thought he would make one more attempt at Blackwood's sense of righteousness that may still be buried deep in the psychological catacombs of his brain. "What changed you, Blackwood? From what I understand, your parents were good people. You used to be a good person from everything I have read."

"My fan changed everything."

"That rusty old relic in your office?" Mac could not understand the point.

"It was divine intervention. I was low. No, I could not go lower. Then I found my fan, and it inspired me. After the plans for the Blitzpeicher inadvertently fell out of the fan's base, I knew I was on to something. The truth is, I have been the person I am today since I was a little boy. I used to be afraid of social rejection, so I worked to play the good-guy role for the world to see. No one knew me until now. Today's version is me, and I couldn't care less about anyone else. My fan gave me the Blitzpeicher. What are the odds? I knew at that point that I would eventually be the most powerful man in the world."

Mac finally accepted that this egomaniac was clearly beyond logical thinking.

Blackwood said, "You know, it has been two hours and fifty-six minutes since the countdown started. In four minutes, the world as you know it will come crashing down. All the countries, including yours and the final holdout, Canada, have caved to my demands. This simple business transaction is a microcosm of the flawless execution of the perfect strategic initiative."

"Simple business transaction? Are you mad? Millions will die. It's ridiculous that you refer to this as a business transaction. It's extortion. No more. No less."

"Mr. Mac, you are missing the beauty of this. The loss of life is just meaningless collateral damage and a distraction from my accomplishment. The negative part of the transaction creates immense motivation for each country. Why do you think any contract is executed? One of the sides wins while the other loses. That's the foundation of any business. I am a master strategist and have created a successful business. There are always those critics who do not appreciate what it takes to be successful."

"No. That's not the definition of a successful business. That's taking advantage of people for your financial gain."

Blackwood leaned on one of the control panels and sneakily pushed an intercom talk button. Before Mac could react, he said, "This is Dr. Blackwood. I have an intruder in the satellite control room."

Jerking his head towards the window, Mac saw two guards sprinting down the hallway toward the room. He hit the floor on the hinged side of the door. Blackwood was waving his arms like a maniac, serving to do nothing but confuse the guards. Mac stepped out and dropped the first guard with an iron fist blow to the jaw. Mac then landed a knee on the floor and spun his body in a full circle, using his other leg outstretched to catch the second guard at the ankle. Upon impact, the guard toppled over in pain. Mac responded with a forceful hand chop to the guard's windpipe. The guard grabbed his throat in pain and gasped for air.

Mac sprung over the control panel to Blackwood. In desperation, Mac screamed in a menacing tone, "If you are not going to stop the EMPs voluntarily, I will force you in a very unpleasant way."

Blackwood was reasonably skilled in the art of defense because of lessons his parents required him to take when he was a teenager. He lashed out with attacks and counterattacks to keep this CIA operative away from him. However, his moves were ineffective outside the safe environment of a dojo. Mac picked up a pen and jabbed it through Blackwood's hand as he squealed in pain.

Mac yelled, "Tell me how to turn this off! We have run out of time!"

Blackwood looked over at his computer screen to check the clock. There was slightly less than a minute left. Mac had been counting the time down in his mind and did not need to look at any countdown clock. His photographic memory was much more helpful at this juncture. Glancing at the computer screen in front of him, he recalled the coordinates he entered on the satellites' directional vectors from Blackwood Castle's laptop. With satisfaction, he confirmed that the revised coordinates were still locked into the satellites.

While Mac was a much superior fighter, Blackwood landed a blow on Mac's wounded arm that momentarily sent shockwaves through his body. As he began to reach for Blackwood, one of the guards from the doorway crawled over and tightly grabbed Mac's leg. That split second gave Blackwood the opportunity he needed to take a step so that his hand could hover over the red button.

Mac said to Blackwood in a menacing voice, "Don't do it!"

"I must do it. It's part of my strategic plan. I am a savior. I am a god who is giving power back to the people."

The voice in Mac's head was screaming a Mac-ism at him. It said, "You only need to be as tough as the situation requires." Mac turned and kicked the ankle-holding guard in the chin, rendering him unconscious. Rather than attacking Blackwood, Mac listened to his internal voice and froze. He didn't need to stop Blackwood physically. That decision likely saved Mac's life.

T-minus ten seconds.

"Mr. Mac, I win. You lose."

Mac smiled at Blackwood and said, "I think you'll be shocked when you realize mankind wins."

Blackwood squinted his eyes at Mac's smile, not realizing that Mac knew something he didn't. He abruptly turned to face the control panel. The moment had come. Blackwood giggled to himself and proclaimed, "Time for me to cleanse the world of meaningless peasants and pave the way for my trillionaire status!"

He paused for a second as he stared at the red button controlling the satellites' release of the EMPs. Without another thought, he triumphantly smashed his hand down on the red button while gazing expectantly at the computer-generated satellites on the big screen. Confused, he watched the satellites fire their EMPs to a single point on Earth.

Blackwood screamed, "No! Someone has changed the EMPs' target coordinates!"

There was a pause in the stream as the EMPs from the satellites collected into a single point directly above the oil rig and released their hideous strength on the coordinates entered by Mac at Blackwood Castle. Mac's pause before his last departure from the castle was world-saving. Once the coordinates were entered, the satellites simply followed orders. It was Mac's version of a "Hail Mary."

Blackwood was frozen in horror. Immediately, everything on the oil rig went dark, including the satellite control center. The room was bathed in a blanket of eerie blackness. However, the surreal scene didn't last long.

True to his word, Zag had installed a massive Blitzpeicher under the control panel. The Blitzpeicher was saved from the ravages of the EMPs by a Faraday cage. As designed, the Blitzpeicher came to life approximately five seconds after everything went dark. While operating as if it were a backup generator, the Blitzpeicher was 10,000 times more powerful.

Zag's habit of taking shortcuts found its way into the installation of the satellite control facility's Blitzpeicher. In his haste, he didn't limit the release of colossal amounts of stored electricity. Still, the catastrophic implication of this careless installation could have been averted if he had bothered to ground the release of excess electrical current. He did not.

The Blitzpeicher's transient surge of electricity sent millions of volts directly to the control panel. Electricity does not have a mind or a soul. However, its power and properties have rewarding predictability, especially in the case of Blackwood. Poetic and ironic justice prevailed as Blackwood found himself leaning on the control panel with both hands. The electrical surge danced across the control panel in frolicking sparks. Fortunately, the current did not jump to the surrounding metal, thanks to the oil rig's construction. Blackwood's body acted as a conduction agent with the current surging through him. His body convulsed and shuddered as he was electrocuted and cooked like a moth in a bug zapper.

Mac's hair shot outward like he was touching a static ball, but he was spared from electrocution. He fortuitously was not in contact with the control panel and found himself standing on a thick rubber pad. Zag installed the mat to cushion the stress on his legs if he was forced to stand on the hard floor for hours. Mac watched for a few brief moments as the bright, blue-colored electricity spirited across the metal control panel and illuminated the room. He thought he could feel the hum of the electricity and resisted the natural urge to jump away from it.

After five excruciating seconds of the Blitzpeicher fully releasing its guts of lightning-like stored power, everything went dark again. Mac did not doubt that Blackwood's plans were thwarted, and he was likely the only one left alive at the satellite control facility. However, there was no time for celebration. He shifted his focus to his new mission – his team. Mac had to get to the hospital and retraced his steps to the outside platform as he slowly emerged from the darkness.

Chapter 49

London Hospital

While the London hospital was white and sterile, it was the happiest place on earth. The entire team and Rhys sat around a large Visitor Room, laughing at their wounds.

"Brock, I thought you were tough. Why are you lying around here whining about the food?" Mac started the team's teasing ritual.

"Who's whining? I love the food. Hell, even the afternoon tea is fabulous. Instead of me, we should all be talking about Rhys. Since we have been here, all I've heard from him is barking orders to the nursing staff like a little boy complaining to his mommy." Brock replied with a smile.

"Chaps, I am more concerned with my health now after being in a hospital room next to Valencia. She was talking in her sleep about the fate of the next shooter in her path. It's terrifying to any male who cherishes all the parts God gave him." Rhys countered in a calculated attempt to deflect the teasing to someone else.

Everyone broke out in laughter, and Valencia rolled her eyes. She said, "You're right that I have gruesome plans for the next shooter, but I also have some gruesome plans for any jerks that are coworkers. Why don't you come over here, and I'll deliver some attitude adjustment?"

That comment earned even louder laughter with some oohs. A couple of the guys gave a slight push on Rhys' back in the direction of Valencia. Rhys had officially been accepted as an honorary member of the team.

Mac sealed the membership with the reminder, "Rhys, don't forget you still owe us those two bottles of Dom Perignon."

The team cheered with the reminder while folding their arms across their chests in a mock show of seriousness. They only held their pose for a few seconds until someone snickered, and they all cracked up. It was not just Mac feeling a life-long comrade-in-arms relationship with Rhys. Until just now, Rhys had forgotten the deep bond between military brothers and sisters.

Rhys's cell phone rang, and he answered, "Good morning, sir. Yes, sir. We are just talking about that now, sir. Of course, sir. I will tell them now, sir. Thank you, sir. You have a splendid day as well, sir." Rhys hung up.

"Rhys, I have to admit that I have never heard someone use the word sir so many times in one call. Who the hell was that?" Mac asked.

"That was one of the Royals. We briefed the U.K. Prime Minister and other top officials as the situation unfolded. An unnamed Royal wanted to help win the fight. He used to fly helicopters for the RAF and demanded that he pilot Mac's missions. He asked me to tell all of you to have a speedy recovery, and you have the full gratitude of the United Kingdom," Rhys shared.

Ryker replied, "That's very nice of him to call. I don't know about the rest of you, but I am ready for knighthood." It was clear to everyone, especially Rhys, that it was a monumental moment in one's life to be sincerely thanked by a Royal with overflowing accolades.

Trying to avoid the compliment, Brock said, "Speaking of knights, I think every one of those nurses is waiting for a romantic dinner offer from Gunner tonight. For someone who likes to spend his free time tossing other big men out of a ring, he always ends up with the ladies."

"Hey!" Valencia exclaimed.

"Okay. Fair point. Not all ladies. Present company excluded," clarified Brock.

"Thank you."

Mac cut the friendly banter off and said, "I am getting Rainey on the speakerphone." He hit the speed dial, and Rainey picked up on the first ring.

"Mac! I am happy to see your number on my phone," Rainey replied enthusiastically.

"Rainey, you have the whole team plus Rhys on the speakerphone," Mac announced.

Rainey said, "Everyone, let me debrief you on what I know. First, I want to say thank you to all of you. The six of you saved the Americas from certain devastation, the likes of which humankind has never experienced. POTUS also sends a sincere message of a job well done. Of course, there will be no fancy medals, but you have the leader of the free world who will answer any of your phone calls."

"That sounds a lot like a get-out-of-jail-free card to me. I think Gunner and Brock could use that if they keep breaking hotel furniture," Mac teasingly said with a turn of his head and raised his eyebrows.

Gunner and Brook looked at each other with their best innocent faces and mouthed, "Who me?"

Rainey asked, "Mac, POTUS would like to know what the hell prompted you to redirect the EMPs the last time you were in Blackwood's office. We would all have been thrown back into the 1700s if you hadn't aimed the EMPs towards the satellite control center in the English Channel."

"I just thought it was time for us to out-strategize Blackwood for once. We needed a backup plan, and that was my best idea on short notice," Mac replied.

"With Blackwood's plot averted, we have been able to unwind his empire. All the mercenaries at Blackwood Castle surrendered without a fight once they knew they had no payday. They threw Abaddon under the bus as the mastermind of the dastardly deeds. They also claimed the raid on Blackwood Castle was from someone trying to steal their technology. It's a nice try, but those mercs are going to jail for the rest of their lives," Rainey stated.

Rainey continued, "It'll take years to test the geothermal power plants before anyone is comfortable using them. No one wants another Congo event. However, many power engineers are hopeful the technology could be the first true environmentally safe energy source. World leaders have agreed that every country will have equal ownership of facilities and technology if the plants pass rigorous inspections. The energy production will be for the benefit of everyone."

Rainey continued explaining as if she were briefing POTUS, which she had just completed before Mac's call. Shifting to the satellites, Rainey had a different message. "As far as the satellites go, no one should have that kind of power. We have directed top-secret outer space technology to eliminate all of Blackwood's satellites. No one should have the ability or power to create EMPs of that nature. The good news is that this attempted attack has focused most countries on developing contingency plans against EMPs. While it will take years and several billions of dollars, our energy infrastructure and the power grid will be protected from EMPs, cyber-attacks, and terrorist attacks. It was a helpful wake-up call for everyone in the U.S. government to prioritize the Department of Energy."

"The Whispering Wind battery plant is a complete game-changer for vehicle batteries. No one is ready to convert all the vehicle batteries in the world to these, but preliminary testing is very positive. We have been able to trace Zag's efforts to create the battery from the drawings of the Blitzpeicher. The Blitzpeicher invention was quite ingenious. Who would have thought that this was invented in the mid-1700s? We have a team researching archives to try and identify who invented this battery. It appears there may have been a primary inventor and one assistant. Whoever invented the Blitzpeicher, schoolchildren should have to memorize his, her, or their names, just like they know Benjamin Franklin and Thomas Edison. I am confident our team will get to the bottom of it." Rainey said with admiration for the inventor.

Mac commented, "While we are on the topic of those to thank, I want to make sure all the U.S.'s senior leadership, including POTUS, knows the critical role of MI6 in this operation. The mission would have failed without their vital assistance."

"I say, old Chap, we were happy to play our part in the operation. I am sure we will work together again in the future," Rhys responded in a very refined and authentic British accent.

Brock smiled and jumped in with, "When we work together in the future, let's make sure no one is injured like this time!"

"Confirmed." Rhys knew Brock was kidding him but acknowledged the comment for the sake of everyone in the room to silently make the point that they would all have better planning for the next mission.

Mac added a perspective for everyone, especially himself, "We have been through a war together and survived. This hell makes us a stronger unit. Rhys, you are now part of the deep team bond. If you ever need anything or want to jump the pond to another agency, all you have to do is call any of us."

Talking about this new bond with Rhys was a cathartic release for everyone because hiding emotions is usually a way of life in the espionage game.

Rainey said, "Blackwood had us in a heightened state of emergency. Keep in mind that it was the strength and commitment of this team that thwarted his evil plan. Thanks to each of you, we will have a safer world as we rethink the vulnerabilities of our power and grid network."

Mac commented in a definitive tone, "As long as I am alive, no one is ever going to leave the world powerless."

Epilogue

Mac and Mary's New Home

Declan was roughhousing with the kids as they rolled around on the floor and the sofa. As usual, roughhousing ended with the three kids piling on top of each other and Mac falling on them with a pretend crush. For effect, he slowly added some of his body weight to the pile. The kids screamed in joyful and giggly dismay as they teasingly exclaimed that their dad was crushing them to death.

Mary entered the family room and broke up the fun by reminding the kids that it was time for school. Everyone scampered out the door. Walking down the sidewalk as a happy family, Declan and Mary listened to the kids carry on about their critical life events of the day. After dropping the kids off at school, Declan and Mary walked back alone to their house.

Declan and Mary stood in the front yard of their new house. It was a lovely two-story with a contemporary mixture of stone and painted siding. One of the two chimneys was visible from the front, with the porch displaying five inviting rocking chairs for late evening chats. The yard was a carpet of lush green grass. Of course, the CIA had already added the necessary extras to the house that Declan kept to himself.

Declan said, "I won't be happy with this house until there's a white picket fence in front."

Mary looked at him and said, "Okay, Declan Mac, you have some explaining to do for me."

"Explain what? Oh, you mean how much I love you." He grabbed her by the waist. Declan knew that sometimes evasion worked in a hostile questioning situation.

Mary replied, "We are not going anywhere near where your mind is taking you until I know what's going on. The people you left us with answered all my questions with emotionless eyes. All I was told was that you had a client who was a nasty guy, and he was upset about your project's outcome. Their answers felt rehearsed and devoid of any tie to our reality. Everything fits together too neatly. I need answers. No, I deserve answers. Are you in trouble? Did a project go bad at work? Are we still at risk, or is this over?"

"Yes, of course, you deserve answers," Declan replied and knew that living a secretive life was by far the worst part of the job as a CIA operative. "Let's go inside where we can have a complete discussion. I want to answer your questions, but not while standing in our front yard where anyone can hear us."

They walked inside, and Declan headed to their family room. He turned around and saw that Mary had stopped just past the front door with her arms folded across her chest.

Declan knew Mary could be tenacious when she wanted. He also knew he was facing a full-frontal attack. This was serious, and Mary was pissed. Declan walked up to her and gazed into those beautiful eyes. He reached up with one hand and gently squeezed her shoulder. His other arm was still in a sling from the bullet wound, and he knew he physically looked pathetic, so he needed to be on his game to escape this pending crisis.

Declan said in a conciliatory manner, "I know my work results in some strange clients and difficult travel commitments. I'm sorry about that. I indeed had a bad guy as a client. We terminated that problem situation. There are bad guys everywhere, and I have always tried to keep them away from our family. This time, I was not successful."

"I'll buy that, but how did you know how to use the gun? Also, what the heck was that tunnel in the basement?" Mary asked.

Declan ignored the gun question and said, "Oh, that tunnel. I found it and was going to tell you about it. The best I can determine is that it must have been some sort of decades-old bomb shelter that dead-ended at our house. You know how crazy everyone was in the late 1950s as they tried to protect themselves from nuclear fallout if Russia attacked the U.S. Our house must have been part of a bomb shelter group in the neighborhood. I was going to do some research into it but had not gotten around to it. Maybe the neighbors have the same bomb shelter access."

"That could make sense, but how did we get this lovely house we live in now? By the way, I like this house and neighborhood even better than our last one. You were gone while we were in temporary housing. I then received your text with this address and a picture of our new house. How did you find it if you were out of the country? Did you just buy this house without talking with me first?" Mary asked as she still wanted more answers.

"Yes, our last house was perfect. It was perfect for me because of all the fun memories we shared there as a family. However, the physical structure was meaningless to me. Our home is where the five of us live. My company bought us this house in partial compensation for the work I just finished. I am going to take a few weeks off so we can add all your touches and make it your home just like you want it."

"Okay. Just make sure you don't have any more clients that are bad guys. I don't think we can take any more disruptions in our lives. And Declan, I don't want anything happening to you."

Mary put her hands on his cheeks and drew his lips to hers. The romantic kiss was soft, warm, and extended. Do you want to see if we need any improvements in the bedroom?"

Declan raised his eyebrows and said, smiling, "Anything you want, babe. I do great bodywork."

She turned and led him by the hand to their bedroom. "You are going to enjoy your two weeks off." She licked her lips in a seductive gesture.

Declan's CIA-issued phone chirped as he received a text from Rainey. All it said was, "Crisis. Come now."

Mary stared at him sternly and said, "What does work want now? I thought you had two weeks off."

Declan replied, "I'm not sure, but you know they wouldn't ask unless it was crucial. I need to leave now and will text you when I know my schedule. I'm sure a client is dealing with a hostile situation that needs an expert. Earlier, you asked me who I was. Mary, you know I'm the same guy you married."

"Okay, mister. I know who you are here, but who are you at work?"

Smiling with a boyish grin, he looked over his shoulder while dashing out the door and said, "I'm Declan Mac."

* * *

Author Bio

Jeff Hyland has spent his career focusing on business. He has been a Partner in management consulting firms, providing interim CEO management and consulting advice to domestic and international clients. Jeff has also been the CEO and Director of a public, global consumer products company. He has an MBA from the Kellogg School of Management at Northwestern University.

Made in United States
North Haven, CT
10 May 2025